WORDS *of* VENOM

HANNAH POLANCO

authorHOUSE®

AuthorHouse™
1663 Liberty Drive
Bloomington, IN 47403
www.authorhouse.com
Phone: 1 (800) 839-8640

Published by AuthorHouse 04/13/2018

ISBN: 978-1-5462-1874-6 (sc)
ISBN: 978-1-5462-1872-2 (hc)
ISBN: 978-1-5462-1873-9 (e)

Library of Congress Control Number: 2017918283

Print information available on the last page.

This book is printed on acid-free paper.

SABLE: THREE AND A HALF YEARS AGO

I heard the singing before I saw my sister, her gentle voice almost enchanting as it rose from within the grove of trees. Her sweet lullaby—one of the few songs she knew—filled the chilly air, traveling the cool wind alongside dried leaves and snow flurries. Our mother used to sing it to us, but it had been so long since I heard it, I couldn't seem to recall the words. Mama's voice hadn't been used for anything but ordering me around in . . . a while.

"Pennah?" I called. The ethereal music didn't stop, so she probably didn't hear. Suppressing a groan, I rolled my eyes as I walked toward her voice. I hated when she came this far into the forest by herself, but sometimes it couldn't be helped. I only wished she was more attentive instead of daydreaming and singing, enticing danger of both the magical *and* mortal variety to sneak up on her.

Pennah's song continued, and soon I heard the squeak of the wheel and the strain in her voice as she hauled up the bucket of wintry water from the well. "Pennah." I finally caught her attention. When she stopped singing, the tune seemed to continue on as the first songs of the forest birds picked up where she left off, filling the trees with life.

"Sable!" Her emerald eyes lit up. "Oh, good. Could you help me carry the buckets back to the house?" With a grunt, she set the second bucket on the ground beside the first. Water splashed into the dirt, forming a small puddle before it seeped into soil. Knowing Pennah's twelve-year old arms wouldn't be able to carry much, I nodded.

"I brought you some bread." I offered her the stale morsel I had been carrying in my pocket. A forced smile appeared on my face, but guilt gnawed at my stomach, agitating the burning hunger that had already taken up residence there. This was half the bread I could buy with the meager money we had left. Winter was just about over, but I honestly wasn't sure we were going to make it through spring and into harvest season. Hopefully the traps I set up yesterday would catch some game.

Pennah took the bread with her free hand, biting into the stiff chunk and chewing it with a sour face she tried to hide. It wasn't exactly a feast, but it would fill her belly. I had brought the other half to Mama in our lonely house in the woods, quite a walk away from the main village. She told me where I could find my sister.

"Finally," Pennah sighed, exasperated as she wiped the sweat from her flushed brow with the back of her bony hand, pushing the damp golden hair from her face. "I was wondering where the rest of our bread was. I couldn't find any in the cupboard." I smiled again, but it felt false. There was no bread in the cupboard, stale or otherwise; there hadn't been in days. Not even a few crumbs to scrounge up. This was it. I had even given my portion to my little sister, as I often did. I knew she'd feel guilty, so I never told her when I did so. At fifteen, I was already caring for two people. It didn't help that Mama hadn't left her bed for anything more than her chamber pot in several weeks.

Steeling myself, I lifted the larger of the two buckets. "Are you ready?" Pennah took a small bite of the stale bread before nodding and grabbing her bucket, sloshing a little bit of water as she picked it up, her thin arms straining to carry the weight. We only took two steps before a weak voice called behind us.

"Could you spare a little? I need some food and drink, but I don't have the strength to lift a bucket." An old lady smiled at us from her place at the well, her hunched form hidden by frosty rags. I couldn't help grimacing at her rotting teeth and the dirty, gray hair that sat atop her head in thick mats. She didn't look very nimble, but I hadn't heard her approach. Many things in the Black Forest were off, though. People said it was full of magic. Those who wandered in didn't often come back out, but I always wondered why—if there were magical creatures in the forest—they never came too far out of it. After all, it wasn't as if dragons attacking villages was a problem.

Pennah grinned, practically glowing, happy to help any poor soul. "Of course!" She took the woman's worn cup and filled it with water from our bucket. "You look parched." Perhaps we should draw up another bucket simply to dump on the woman and get that top layer of filth off. Pennah pulled her portion of bread from her pocket. Anger wrenched at my heart as Pennah tore off a large chunk from her portion. She had less than half of it left now. She offered it to the woman with a pretty smile, but before the woman wrapped her parasitic fingers around it, I lunged forward to stop the transaction. "No!"

"What's wrong, Sable?" Pennah, in all her glorious naivety, tilted her head in confusion, her trusting, green eyes seeming to shine at me.

"That is *your* bread," I reminded her firmly, standing between Pennah and the old woman. "We cannot go without it. This *hag* can take care of herself." I glared at the old woman, who stared grimly back, her wrinkled face devoid of emotion.

"Sable, this woman needs our help. Besides, it's my share. I can do what I want with it!" Pennah snapped back at me like the child she was. I knew what would happen though. We would get home and her stomach would begin to growl. And she'd ask if she could share my portion. But that *was* my portion that she was wasting on a useless lump of life that couldn't even take care of herself.

Pennah reached around me and dropped the bread in the hag's waiting hand, but I snatched it back, unwilling to let my sister starve herself. Pennah's eyebrows pushed down and the songbirds quieted suddenly.

"Sable!" she shouted at me, but I would not give in. Not this time. There would be no more indulging in Pennah's childish whims.

"No!"

"ENOUGH!" A blinding light flashed all around us. My knees buckled and Pennah and I stumbled back. When my vision came back, the hag was gone. In her place stood a mesmerizing woman with hair even paler than her fair skin. A silvery blue dress that looked as soft as rose petals draped around her and onto the ground, mingling with the dark, damp leaves. Her dark gray eyes enveloped both me and my sister in their bewitching gaze. They were both beautiful and deadly. I knew what she was. This was a creature I had hoped never to meet, but living in this forest made that nearly impossible. This was a fairy.

She first turned to Pennah who trembled, from fear or awe I wasn't sure. "You have shown great kindness. Your thoughtful deeds and words will forever be as treasured as a precious stone." Her voice was soft and her eyes were gentle. But when she whirled around to face me, her demeanor darkened. Every bone in my body was telling me to run, but I was paralyzed. "And your words of cruelty will forever be *poison*." On that last word, she vanished in another spectacular flash of light.

Though our mobility had returned, Pennah and I stood frozen to the spot for several minutes. Just a few moments ago I was sure it was my fate to die of starvation. But now, I could hardly believe I had survived to see that day. Finally, I heard a quiet voice say, "Sable?" We both looked down at the bucket full of water. A glimpse of red had caught my attention and I saw that the red was a rose petal that had fallen into the water. There hadn't been a live rose anywhere in the area for months. "What's that?" Pennah asked, reaching for the soft petal I was rubbing between my calloused fingers. I saw two more red rose petals land in the bucket. This time, I realized they had fallen from the folds of Pennah's threadbare dress.

"It must be because of the fairy," I told her, trying to keep my voice light so she didn't worry. "We should go home. Mama needs the water."

Pennah cringed and let out a tiny squeak as she pointed to my neck, where I suddenly felt a tickle. I brushed at my throat and a small spider landed on the ground.

Chapter 1

SABLE: PRESENT DAY

"Kill her!"

"Burn her!"

"Witchcraft!" The villagers I had grown up with were all suddenly against me, their eyes full of rage to cover the fear.

"Please! It's not witchcraft, I've just been cursed!" I tried to explain. Somehow, believing I—a girl this entire village had watched grow up—was a witch was easier than grasping the idea of a fairy curse. Witches were seen more often than fairies, I supposed, but these people knew me. Or I thought they did.

"Get her!" Two men grabbed me. Thin snakes with red and black stripes slithered out of nowhere, draping across my shoulders and hissing at the men until they jerked away.

"I promise, it won't hurt anyone!" At home while explaining to Mama, none of the snakes or spiders bit us. The only time was when I called the fairy an ugly hag. A garter snake bit Pennah and it was painful enough to make her cry, but it wasn't venomous.

"Stop!" A steely voice rang out amid the chaos. It was my late father's brother, my Uncle Morrin. I had explained it to him first, and so far he was the only one to believe me. "A fairy from the forest cursed my niece. She is not a witch. Now leave her be." He held a sword, but I doubted he would use it in my defense to harm any of the villagers. The crowd seemed less sure of their safety, though, and they stepped away from the man with arms and shoulders muscled from years of working the forge.

It took a little more convincing, but eventually my life was secured and the villagers dispersed, grumbling and glaring as they went.

"Thank you, Uncle," *I told him once we were alone in the empty market. Yearning for someone to tell me it was going to be alright, I reached for a hug, but he stepped back.*

"This is all I can do for you," *he told me impassively, keeping a few feet of distance between us.* "Tomorrow I will be leaving."

"But . . . why?" *I was fifteen years old and I'd been taking care of my family for years, so why did I feel like a child again? Tears burned behind my eyes, but I held them back.*

"This whole family is cursed, Sable!" *he exclaimed, waving the sword around like a madman. Anxiety rippled across my skin seeing him do that, and I wished he would put it away.* "First my brother dies far too early of a sudden illness, then your mother took ill and hasn't left that cottage in four years. That second husband of hers, as despicable as he was—rest his soul—was murdered and now you are fairy-cursed. Pennah is unscathed for now, but I have no doubt that soon, she too will fall to the bad luck of this family. I am leaving while I still have my hide." *He stalked away, finally sheathing his sword as he left. Unwilling or unable to move, I wasn't sure which, I watched him until he was out of sight. For a moment, I was alone in the mulch-lined street.*

I was about to turn and head home, though comfort was scarce there as well since my mother was so angry with me for upsetting a fairy, when I caught a glimpse of dark hair and blue eyes peeking around the corner of a building. When I made eye contact with him, he flinched but didn't move.

"Godric, you're still here." *I let a smile show as I rushed over to where he lingered behind the wall. Godric had been my best friend since we were toddling about the dusty alleys of this town. When we were children, he taught me how to skip rocks in the pond. When I was thirteen, he was my first kiss, and last May he said as soon as I was of age he'd start courting me properly. Just a few months ago I turned fifteen.*

"Sable, I—" *He stumbled on his words. I shrank away, knowing what he was going to say.* "I just wanted to say good-bye." *Tears flowed down my face now, uninhibited. My eyes burned, more than they normally did when I cried. He was going to say more, probably about how truly sorry he was that I had been cursed, but instead a look of fear and disgust appeared on his face.* "What is that?!" *Before I could ask what he meant, he ran away, stumbling as he disappeared around the corner. A full grown man, nearly nineteen, was sprinting away from a skinny girl in terror.*

At first, I assumed a spider or snake I had failed to brush away was the cause, but when I wiped the tears off my face, my hands were covered in a dark purple liquid.

A few months later, I figured out my tears were venomous. Very deadly, too. It wasn't snake venom, though, nor any kind of natural poison anyone had heard of. It seemed to be my very own brand of toxin. When the baker's dog licked my teary face, he was dead in less than a minute. It was then that I understood what Mama meant when she said I looked like a demon when I cried, bleeding from the eyes.

With a shiver, I pushed the memories away and focused on packing my things. It was time to pick up more supplies, which meant braving the town again. I dropped my pig bladder canteen into the bag and slung the whole thing over my shoulder, strapping it over the scabbard already secured between my shoulder blades. The sword was heavy, but it was a comforting weight. It was the one thing my father had left me before he died. It was old and rusty and dull, but it hadn't failed me yet. I had been attacked before in the woods on the way home from the village. The first time I had only been armed with my words, which were deadly on their own, but the second time, when the villager thugs thought to gag me, I had come prepared with a real physical weapon. After that, there was only one more attempt to attack me, this time in a way I couldn't hope to defend again with a sword. One of the vendors in town—I'm still not sure which one—tried to slip belladonna berries in with the pastries I bought for Pennah's fifteenth birthday. Luckily, I ate mine first and all that happened was a long, uncomfortable nap. It was proof that I could suffer the pains of being poisoned to death without actually dying.

"Please, could I this once go into town with you?" Pennah begged me on my way out the door. She looked up at me through her dark lashes, her full lips pouting. I had managed to keep her on our secluded grounds deep in the forest and away from the village for three years. I wasn't giving in now.

I tied the knot around my waist that kept my pants in place, double knotting it for good measure. Ever since I had to sprint away from villagers in a dress, I realized pants were much easier to move in so they became a regular part of my wardrobe, something that Pennah also never understood.

"One of these days we are going to have to lock you in a tower and never let you down," I told her roughly. A large tarantula, having appeared out of thin air, crept up my arm before I brushed it off absent-mindedly. Over the last few years, I had grown used to the constant sight of snakes and spiders and scorpions. Unless my words were vicious, the creatures never were. "Besides, who else is going to take care of Mama while I'm gone?"

Pennah sighed and plopped down on the stool in our tiny kitchen, the old stool legs creaking under her weight. "Fine." She crossed her arms with a frown.

Satisfied, I left the house and grabbed the handcart. It was big enough to carry the supplies we needed back from town but small enough for one person to handle, though the journey was never easy.

The walk to town seemed especially long today. My physical exhaustion was only the start, though. As I always did in town, I stayed silent unless communication was absolutely necessary—that was the unspoken deal. I had written down everything I needed and showed the vendors in town my list and gave them the money. They were happy to help me first. So happy, in fact, they always added a new piece of parchment to my supplies so I could make a new list next time I came into town. That way, I was in their stores for the shortest amount of time possible. Only one woman screamed when a scorpion crawled over her foot. A man standing nearby smashed it quickly, and they both sent me withering glares. I would have argued that the thing was tiny and brown, and therefore harmless, but talking would have only made the situation worse. Just as I finished, I heard a small child squealing.

"Mama! Mama! Look at this!" I came in closer. Just as the mother pulled her child further away from me, as if I would harm a child, I caught a glance of a sparkling blue gem in the girl's grubby hand. Pennah.

Even if someone would speak to me, I couldn't ask anyone if they'd seen my sister. That would draw too much attention to her. Everyone already thought I was an evil witch holding her sister captive in the woods. Half of them assumed I'd killed my mother off already. The best I could hope for was that Pennah would reappear at home when I arrived.

"How was the village?" Pennah asked cordially when I got back, her amiable tone accompanied by the scent of roses. It wasn't surprising that she'd gotten home before me since I was dragging a full cart behind me.

"I don't know, how was it? You were there, weren't you?" I narrowed my eyes at her accusingly as I began unpacking the pile of supplies I had brought home with me.

"No," she continued to deny it, blinking her wide eyes in false confusion. "I was here with Mama the entire time." She lied without hesitation. After all, Mama was probably sleeping, so she wouldn't disagree. She may not have even realized she was alone for a few hours. What else had Pennah lied about?

I wiped the sweat off my brow tiredly. Summer was beginning to cool into fall, but high afternoon was still quite hot, especially when hauling a heavy load along the worn path to the house. "If you were going to sneak around in the woods, you could have at least helped me bring all the supplies home."

Pennah finally had the decency to stop lying and look guilty. "How did you know? I thought I was being careful."

I set down the sack of ground wheat in the corner of the kitchen and snatched up one of the ever-present jewels lying around the house. It was a good thing we never got visitors. I held the tiny ruby up to her face. "You leave a trail of very expensive bread crumbs, little sister. And people are finding them. This is the very reason we keep you here." I muttered the last part more to myself, but she still heard me.

"And how is that a bad thing? Making a few villagers a little richer? We could buy a castle with all the gems in the pond." Over the years, we had so many jewels spilling from Pennah's clothes, mouth and sometimes just falling from a nearby tree, as if a bird dropped it from its nest, that we had to put them somewhere. Unlike my venomous creatures, the gems didn't crawl or slither away. I had started bringing them to the pond just east of the well and tossing the piles of riches in. The dirty pond floor masked the sparkle and kept our secret hidden.

"Richer villagers would just be the start. There are selfish people in the world that would do anything to steal the gems." She couldn't comprehend that people would resort to anger and violence just to get their way.

"They can take all they want! We have plenty to go around. I don't understand what the problem is!"

"Of course you don't understand what the problem is! You're still a child!"

"I'm fifteen!" She stamped her foot into the dirt floor. "Technically I'm of marriageable age, but it seems that will never happen since I haven't seen a boy in three years!" Of course this was about boys.

"Oh, I'm sure you saw plenty of boys in town today when you blatantly broke the rules, acting like an ungrateful, childish fool!"

"Ow!" A snake had snapped at my sister's ankle, drawing blood. In a panic, I quickly checked the stripes on the thin snake. It wasn't venomous. I had let things go too far. I never meant to hurt Pennah.

"I'm sorry," I said, my voice faltering. The frustration I'd allowed to build up fizzled into shame.

Not saying a word she turned on her heel and went back to our room. I heard a *clink*. A small diamond tear had fallen and struck a stone on the floor.

Chapter 2

PENNAH

I knew exactly what Sable would say. She'd say I was sulking because I didn't get what I want and I should act my age. Ever since Mama got sick, Sable has taken care of me. So now I had two mothers telling me what to do. Though Mama usually let me do what I want. It wasn't as if she could stop me.

A small brown scorpion crawled onto my bed, struggling to clamber over the folds of my blanket. After all these years of sharing a room, house and life with Sable, all of her accursed creatures still gave me shivers. We had learned which ones were not venomous, though. The scorpion wouldn't hurt me, but it didn't mean I wanted it crawling on my bed. I brushed it off, pushing a few pieces of straw of with it.

I peeked out the small window, spotting Sable through the gap in our old shutters. She was practicing her sword forms again. She moved slowly, adjusting each stance until it was perfect, her figure just a silhouette against the twilight sky. The decrepit sword glided from one position to another, blocking the invisible strikes. I had once asked her why she bothered practicing. Our uncle had trained her a little to use the sword her father had made her, but now that he was gone, she had no way to practice real moves on anyone. She simply said no one would bother her if it appeared she knew how to wield a sword.

Sometimes Sable's logic was so beyond me, I didn't even bother trying to understand anymore. First of all, no one even talks to her in town; no one would initiate a confrontation. The villagers were all too superstitious to approach the girl surrounded by snakes and spiders, both of which were considered bad omens. Secondly, that sword was so old and rusted, I doubted it would strike fear in anyone's heart. A butter knife was probably sharper.

At a snail's pace, Sable struck a nearby tree lightly, leaving no markings behind. The tree didn't fight back of course, but Sable's focus on defeating the imagined enemy didn't waver. She implemented several more strikes before I turned away from the window.

Dead flower petals crunched under me as I laid down, trying and failing to put Sable out of my mind. Often I'd wake up surrounded by flowers and petals, but those didn't even faze me anymore. It was when I had particularly good dreams that sharp topaz and sapphires appeared, jabbing me in the back and waking me up.

We had so many riches from the fairy's curse that Sable had started throwing them away. In town, I had seen skeletal children trying to scrounge for food. People were starving and I had the power to help, but Sable was selfish and wanted to keep me hidden away. Even during the worst winters, when using just a few jewels could have had us eating like queens all year, Sable refused to use more than one at a time. She always said it would look suspicious if a family of three women who earned a living by selling vegetables in town suddenly had a wealth of gems. Sable's collection of serpents and arachnids helped keep the pests out of the garden, but not enough to start a full-fledged farm large enough to warrant the sudden manifestation of a small fortune.

After Sable apologized, I almost did too. But before I did, I realized I shouldn't have to. The rule keeping me at home shouldn't be there at all. I didn't talk much when I was in town. And if I dropped anything that sparkled, I kept a small bag with me to hide it away. Clearly I had missed one or two. At least some family would eat well for a while.

While I shifted on the bed, a purple gem dug into my arm. Standing up, I began pacing around the room, stepping carefully so nothing crunched underneath my feet. It was a challenge to move anywhere in this house without tripping over a gem or something skittering across the floor.

A little green snake twitched as I got close. It was tiny and harmless, so I picked it up. The creature did not appreciate the gesture, biting me the second my fingers were around it. With a jerk, I dropped it.

"You're just as paranoid as Sable," I told it as it darted out into the hall. After brushing the dead petals and sparkling rocks from my bed, I sat back down.

Paranoid might not be the right term. Worrisome, maybe. Either way, it made it incredibly difficult to deceive her. The only time I could sneak away from the house was when Sable's prying eyes weren't there. And that only ever happened when she was going into town. So I'd usually leave right after her, going the long way so she wouldn't see me because I knew Sable had the eyes of a hawk and the ears of a bat. I had secretly been going to town for two months now, and frankly, I was surprised Sable hadn't figured me out until now. It helped that everyone assumed I was being held captive by my wicked sister, which meant none of the villagers were going to tell her I was in town. Some even tried to "rescue" me, and it took some persuading to get them to let me go home.

Most of the time, I avoided the market, because I knew that was the only place Sable went. Sometimes, though, I'd watch her enter the market. I saw how the villagers treated her. She never spoke to anyone. But she watched everyone. She knew everyone from before the curse. Sometimes she would see Godric in the market with his wife and their new baby. Whenever his wife noticed Sable watching them, she seemed to mistake her sad eyes for malice and dragged her husband and baby out of the market. I could never tell if Godric truly regretted betraying my sister like he did when she needed him most because he never acknowledged her presence. I was tempted to set a garter snake loose in their house, just to scare them, but I knew they'd blame Sable. And leaving a ruby wouldn't quite have the same effect.

"Pennah?" Sable stood in the doorway, watching me like I was a fragile doll. Apparently she had finished her exercises for the day. "How's your ankle?"

"Fine," I mumbled. The small bite had already scabbed over. It didn't even hurt anymore.

"It's getting late. We should probably get to sleep soon," she told me. She spoke in a kind tone, but as always, she was telling me what to do.

"I'm not a child, you know," I reminded her, frowning.

"I know," she sighed. She looked so tired all the time; so dejected. Like she had already given up. "But you're my baby sister. I can't help thinking of you as a kid. It's hard to accept that you're almost grown up. I'm not sure what I'll do when you leave the house and decide you just don't want to come back."

"Oh, Sable." I stood and hugged my sister. I was nearly her height, but since I was finished growing, I would never quite catch up. "I'd never leave you behind." Despite the braid, some of the spider's silk that was always in my sister's dark, messy hair got on my hand. I tried to be subtle in wiping the webbing on my dress, but she noticed.

"Sorry. It's not exactly gold strands." She reached her hand out to me and pulled a thin, golden string from my soft, wavy hair, letting it drop to the floor. I knew the only time she let her own hair out of its braid was to wash it. The sticky webs tangled her hair too much if she let it hang loose like mine.

I sat back down on my bed. "So while you were in town, did you get another story?"

She rolled her eyes and sat on her own bed across from mine. "Didn't you just go to town yourself?" I had yet to commit such a heinous crime that Sable wasn't forgiving me by the end of the day, but it was still nice to see her lips give way to a flicker of a smile.

"But you tell the stories so much better than Ulrich." Ulrich was actually a superb story-teller, which is why everyone in town came to listen to his collection of stories, but Sable was too. She had been telling me stories for years and sometimes complained half-heartedly that I was getting too old. But you were never too old for stories. And I knew Sable loved to tell them.

She laughed. If it was me that had laughed, daisy petals would have fluttered to the floor. Instead, tiny spiders crawled out from under her shoes.

"Alright. Are you ready?" I nodded and she tucked her feet up onto her bed, getting comfortable. "You only get part of the story tonight. It's already getting late." I nodded again, eager to hear the story. I could read of course, Sable made sure of that years ago, but Sable telling it made it so much more exciting and keeping books in our musty old house where they could rot never worked well.

"Once upon a time," she began, weaving the tale with an enthralling light in her voice that all storytellers had, "there was a king with a beautiful garden. In the center of the garden, a special tree that bore golden apples flourished. It was the king's pride and joy. He counted the apples every day, but one morning, one was missing. He had his three sons guard this apple tree night and day." Sable's voice was much rougher than my own rich voice. It didn't make for pretty songs like mine, but it was very soothing. Something about it made the mattress I sat on ten times more comfortable. "The first night, the eldest son was on watch. He vowed to stay awake all night, but by midnight, he was fast asleep under the tree. The next morning, the king was furious to see that another apple was missing. The second night, the middle son stayed under the tree and made the same vow. The next morning, he was found fast asleep as well and yet another apple was gone.

"The third night, the youngest son stayed under the tree. At dusk, he saw a fox approaching the tree. Assuming this was the thief, he drew an arrow and took aim.

"'Stop! I am here to give you the same advice I gave your brothers,' the fox told him. The man lowered his bow. 'A golden bird is stealing the apples. At midnight, he will approach and sing his song. If you hear this song, you will fall asleep, like your brothers.'

"The man thought the fox was trying to persuade him to leave his post, since everyone knows foxes are the sneakiest of creatures. But before he could shoot the fox, it stole away, disappearing into the night. The young prince told the nearest guard to fetch him some beeswax. He put the beeswax in his ears and when midnight finally came, all the guards in the garden were fast asleep from the song he couldn't hear.

"Moonlight shone on a golden bird that perched in the king's beloved tree and stole another apple. The prince shot an arrow at the bird, but it was so quick, he only got a fallen feather for a reward. The next morning, everyone agreed the feather alone was worth half the kingdom, but the angry, greedy king yelled, 'What am I to do with a feather? I must have the whole bird!'" I could almost see the bird in my mind's eye. It would have had feathers that glinted in the moonlight like golden razors and eyes that shimmered like diamonds.

"The king sent his eldest son after the golden bird. After just a few day's walk, the eldest came across that same fox. 'You again!' The son tried to shoot the fox, but the fox scolded him, 'I have good counsel for you. I know you seek the golden bird. In the next town you will come across two inns. The one is beautiful and pleasant, but you should seek shelter in the poorer, smaller inn.' The eldest scoffed at the fox. 'What does a fox know about such things?' He shot again at the fox, who ran away into the woods.

"When the eldest son found the two inns, he remembered the fox's advice, but decided *why should I suffer in that rundown inn?* Laughter and singing was coming from the beautiful inn. The eldest ignored the fox's counsel and stayed in the beautiful inn, forgetting about his quest for the golden bird and about his own country.

"After a few more days of no tidings from the eldest son, the king sent his second son. The fox approached this son as well and gave him the same advice, but when the second son saw his older brother in the beautiful inn happy and having fun, he ignored the counsel and joined his brother.

"More time passed. The youngest son insisted he also join the quest for the golden bird, but his father would not be persuaded, afraid to lose his last son. Finally, though, the young prince convinced his father and set out for the golden bird. The fox gave this son the same words of wisdom. When the last son found the two inns, he abided by the fox's counsel and stayed the night in the shabby inn. The next day he set out again for the golden bird, the wise fox leading the way."

Sable was silent. I opened my eyes. "Why did you stop?"

She laughed quietly. "I thought you were asleep."

"No. I was just closing my eyes." The truth was, the details on the last little bit were fuzzy. I hadn't fallen asleep to Sable's stories in years. My argument that I was not a child was weakening by the minute. "You can keep going if you want," I prompted, but the yawn that followed seemed to undermine me.

"Sable!" Mama didn't have to shout so loud. There was only a thin wall separating our rooms.

"How about you go to sleep instead? I'll take care of Mama." I had to admit I was getting tired. Wrapping my wool blanket around me, I curled up on my straw-stuffed mattress and closed my eyes.

Sable didn't leave the house for three more days. This time, she took a load of vegetables to sell in town. She continued to insist I stay at home. When I told her I would follow her anyway and there was nothing she could do about it short of chaining me to a tree, she decided it was better if she could keep an eye on me. And maybe this way people would stop thinking she was holding me against my will.

"Think of it this way, now I'll help you pull the cart." I took the cart full of vegetables from her hands, taking a moment for my hands to get a good grip on the worn wooden handles. She smirked. For a while, I pulled the cart, but when my arms became too tired to go one, I let Sable take her turn and helped by pushing on the back.

The look on the villagers' faces when the two of us came to town together was priceless. I blushed and cringed away from their looks. When I was alone, I only got looks of concern. This was sheer curiosity and amazement. It made me fidget with discomfort under their scrutiny. I was beginning to see Sable's point. This would only be ten times worse if they knew what happened when I spoke. It was a good thing I was extraordinarily shy with anyone besides my sister. That tends to happen when you only interact with two other people for three years. I wondered if Sable was shy too with other people besides me and Mama. It was hard to tell since even if she was willing to talk to people, there was no one who would reciprocate. Everyone in town made a special effort to keep clear of Sable, even if it meant walking down a different street.

The walk through the main square was longer than I ever could have imagined, each dusty step drawing the attention of another person. Some of the old buildings lining the square quivered and let off clouds of dirt as their inhabitants slammed the shutters closed. It was so different from the first time I'd snuck into town. Now, the baker had closed his door so the smell of fresh bread was replaced with the dull scent of grit and dying leaves. The laughing children that usually play in the streets had been shooed back into their houses by mothers worried about nothing.

Sable ignored the way the crowd thinned and parted in front of her, keeping her eyes down as she led the cart toward a narrow side street. She stopped the cart next to a vendor selling jewelry near the tavern's back door. The small polished stones and bits of colored glass looked so dull and ugly compared to the jewels I dropped and spat out every day. When the vendor realized we were going to be here for a little while, he picked up his cart and relocated. Sable paid him no mind, but I couldn't help frowning after him. That was rude.

"I'm going to take the vegetables to Lilah. *Stay with the cart.*" I rolled my eyes. It wasn't as if I would run off chasing butterflies.

"Okay. Stop worrying." Sable gave me one more glare before grabbing the sacks of vegetables and precariously lugging them down the alley.

She was taking more time than I thought she would and the autumn breeze was chilly now that I was standing still. Just before I decided to see what was taking so long, some excited shouting came from the end of the road. After glancing down the alley one more time and not spotting Sable, I headed for the crowd of people that was developing at the far end of the square. A white horse's head reared back and the crowd moved away, giving it more space. The majestic horse was at least two heads taller than the tallest of the men in the crowd.

"Please step back. My horse doesn't do well in crowds." A deep voice came from the other side of the horse. Now I was close enough to touch the stallion's neck. My hand ran along the corded muscles, smoothing the glossy white coat.

"What a beautiful horse! Fit for a prince." I thought I was only loud enough for me and the horse to hear, but the man peeked around the horse to look at me. He had short dark blonde hair and a thick beard. We didn't get a lot of nobility in town, so I couldn't tell what his rank might be, but I knew it was well above my own.

"Not exactly a prince," he replied with a perfect smile. He was several years older than me, but very handsome. I felt heat rush to my face.

"Sorry." I bowed my head and quickly backed up into the crowd. Just before I was gone, he called to me.

"Did you drop something?" His eyes flicked to the ground. I followed his gaze and saw something sparkling in the dirt. My whole body clenched up and my mouth clamped shut. I shook my head and bolted away, hurriedly weaving through the thick cluster of people.

"Pennah!" Sable yelled as she saw me approach. A few scorpions skittered away from her as she shouted. She must have been muttering some unkind things.

Saying nothing, I ran to her.

"I thought I told you to stay by the cart." I mumbled an apology. She sighed angrily. "What was all that over there?" She motioned to the crowd that was thinning by the gigantic horse and its master.

I shrugged. "Let's go home." Her brow furrowed. I grabbed the empty cart before she could ask more questions and pulled it down the road, grateful it was so much lighter than before.

Once the town was out of sight, I decided I should tell Sable what happened. The last time I kept a secret from her, she nearly turned into a gorgon with all the snakes popping up everywhere.

"That man with the horse. I think he saw me drop a gem." I kept my eyes trained on the orange and brown leaves that crunched under my every footstep, afraid to meet her eyes.

"Are you sure?" she said, calmer than I expected. "There was a pretty big crowd."

"He looked right at me and asked if it was mine. He must have seen something."

"Well, it's not as if he knows where we live to ask more questions."

I didn't respond. I wasn't nearly as blind as Sable seemed to think I was. I knew it was a simple matter of asking around town and following our obvious tracks. Over the years, Sable had formed a nice trail to follow that the autumn and winter storms couldn't quite erase.

"It'll be fine," she said, but I couldn't tell if she was consoling me, or herself.

Chapter 3

SABLE

I triple checked the counterweight trap on the main trail to the house. It had never been tested on a person before, but my smaller versions worked well on the game nearby. The black wool string was nearly invisible across the trail, the ankle noose was hidden under fallen leaves and mulchy dirt, and the stakes were far enough away to be inconspicuous.

Satisfied, I headed into the house. First I checked on Mama. As expected, she was already fast asleep. Her stringy hair was pushed back into a messy braid, the brown color making her skin appear even paler. Mama's sleep was fitful, but at least she was sleeping. Some nights she kept me awake to care for her until dawn, and neither of us were happy the next day. After making sure the blankets on Mama's bed were thick enough, I came into my room expecting Pennah to be sound asleep as well. Instead, she lay awake staring at the ceiling.

"Could you finish the story?" I knew I should be happy that some sense had finally been knocked into my sister, but I wished there was some way to make her stop worrying. That was my job.

I took a moment to remember where I had left off. "Oh, yes. Just before the young prince came to the castle where the golden bird was kept, the fox warned him that he should keep the bird in its worn, wooden cage. When the prince found the bird, though, he saw beside the bird a shiny silver cage with jewels. He thought the wooden cage was not worthy of such a wondrous creature, so he tried to put the bird in the beautiful cage.

But when he did, the bird squawked and screamed until the whole castle had woken up and he was taken captive.

"He was going to be executed, but he pleaded with the king, saying he would do anything. The king agreed and said if he could bring back the golden horse from the next kingdom over, he could have the golden bird. So the prince set off, with the fox at his side, for the golden horse.

"This time the fox warned him again, saying to leave the old leather saddle on the horse. But when he went into the stables to steal the horse, he saw a new, ornate saddle, fit for a golden horse. He tried to put the new saddle on the horse, but it kicked and thrashed, waking up the stable hand, who alerted the guards. Again, he was approached by another angry king. The prince made the same plea.

"'If you can bring me the beautiful princess,' the king said, 'you can take my golden horse.' So the prince was off again, this time further away from his home to steal away the princess from the next kingdom over. The fox offered more of his unwavering advice, begging the prince to heed him. 'The princess will be in her tower, and if you give her a kiss, she will gladly come with you. But she will ask you to let her say good bye to her father. You *must not* allow her to do this.'

"The prince agreed to this, and climbed up to the window at the top of the princess's tower. The princess had wonderful, golden hair." I paused, stroking Pennah's hair, also a beautiful golden hue. The princess of the story always had golden hair, never black and spider-webby.

Pennah was lying down, but still wide awake. I continued. "The prince gave her a kiss, and the princess promised to go wherever he wanted. Before she left with him though, she begged to be able to say good bye to her father. Faithful to his promise to the fox, the prince declined. But the princess wept and wept until the prince gave in. When she found her father, he had the young prince arrested. To amuse himself and his court, he promised that if the prince could remove the hill beside his castle that blocked the view from his window, he would gladly give him his daughter. But the feat had to be accomplished in eight days. After that, he would be executed.

"Since his only other option was execution, he agreed. He worked hard for eight long days, but by the end, he had hardly made a dent in the gigantic hill. The fox, taking pity on the poor prince, said, 'Rest. I will work for you.'

"By morning, the hill was gone. The king begrudgingly gave the man his daughter, and he left happily. On his way out of the castle, the fox found him again and told him that by the end of the day, he could have the princess, the horse and the bird. 'But how?' the prince asked. The fox carefully instructed the prince on what to do.

"When he arrived at the kingdom with the golden horse, he told the king there would be no trade until he saw the horse with his own eyes, just as the fox had advised. The king brought out the horse, and the young prince mounted the worthy steed. As he galloped off, however, he whisked the princess away and they both rode off toward the kingdom with the golden bird. The man told the king the same thing he told the other king. Instead of handing over the horse, though, he snatched the bird, cage and all, and galloped off.

"He returned home, and when his father died of old age, the young prince became heir to the throne since the two older princes were never seen again. The end."

"That's not how it ends," Pennah objected half-heartedly. She seemed too tired to insist further. She was right. The older princes were to be hanged, but freed by the youngest. As the fox predicted, they betrayed him. The fox helped him yet again, and when the youngest truly did return to his kingdom, the fox asked the prince to kill him. When the prince finally agreed, the dead fox morphed into a man who had been cursed. In fact, the fox was the princess's own brother. But I hated including the morbid details. If I wanted a depressing story, I'd tell the Little Mermaid. Nothing was more depressing than a heartbroken mermaid committing suicide to save the man who betrayed her. Besides, the crueler stories I told aloud only incited more dangerous creatures and I didn't fancy sleeping under a blanket of serpents tonight.

"That's how it will end tonight. We both need rest."

I knew Pennah was tired when she lay down on the bundle of material scraps we called a pillow and wrapped up in her blanket without a word of argument. Knowing I'd be lucky to get even a wink of sleep, I laid down on my lumpy pillow, wrapping my fingers around the hilt of the dagger I kept underneath.

Pennah was silent for so long, I thought she had fallen asleep. But suddenly, she spoke. "Sable, I know you thought Godric was supposed to be the one, but he was a worthless coward. There's a real prince out there for you."

"I'm sure there is," I said, not believing a word of it. Pennah was far too idealistic for her own good.

I jerked awake in the morning and frantically scanned the room. Pennah was still snug in her bed. None of the bells I had placed in the forest surrounding our house had sounded in the night. Maybe the handsome, wealthy man from town really hadn't seen anything. Maybe Pennah had just overreacted.

"Sable?" Mama called from her room. At least she had the decency to keep her voice down, knowing Pennah was probably still asleep. I slipped out of bed, keeping the warm blanket around my shoulders, and entered her room.

"Yes, Mama?" I rubbed the sleepiness out of my eyes. It took a moment for my vision to adjust to the dim room. Mama insisted on keeping her shutters closed, no matter how nice of a day it was.

"Could you bring me my stockings? My feet are cold." I did as she asked, even helping her put them on. "And could you make some breakfast? I'm getting hungry." She pushed a tangle of chestnut- and gray-speckled hair out of her face as she spoke, and I took it upon myself to quickly tuck it back in a braid.

"Yes, Mama," I replied meekly, my fingers finishing off the braid with a piece of string tied at the end. I wasn't awake enough to argue. On my way out she reminded me I needed to do the laundry today. I acquiesced again and went into the kitchen to make some porridge for breakfast. It was a little thin and normally Pennah would complain about how we could afford a heartier breakfast if we sold a gem or two, but after the scare yesterday she might keep her mouth shut.

By the time breakfast was ready, the smell of warm food had woken up Pennah. I watched her sit down at the table and she looked at the thin porridge with distaste at first, but she said nothing as she ate the entire bowl. Maybe this man's suspicious appearance had a few benefits.

After we ate, I took Pennah with me to do laundry. Mama would have to fare on her own for a few hours. Some days, it didn't seem like she was ill at all, only using it as an excuse to make me do everything for her. Most days, I thought she was dying. But somehow, after all these bedridden years, she was still here.

Pennah hummed as we worked together. The creek was a little farther away than the well, so it was pleasantly clear of all people, including our mother. Scrubbing at the clothes in the icy water numbed our hands quickly, so we both had to take breaks often to get the blood flowing in our fingers again. As we stood on the river stones, our feet were completely numb as well, but that didn't seem to bother us as much. We'd have to get out and thaw our toes eventually, but for now we would survive the cold.

"Funny how there's always new laundry to wash," Pennah commented as she rubbed the life back into her hands. "I keep wishing it'll somehow clean itself."

"Well I know better than most that wishing something doesn't mean it'll happen. Life would be so much easier if it did," I said. There were so many stories about wishes coming true. Of course the tale that became my life was a story of curses and loneliness. Wishing on stars, blowing dandelion tufts. I knew for a fact that the well we drew water from was *not* a wishing well. I wasted one coin on that, and I wasn't going to do it again.

Pennah stopped humming and began to sing loudly, a song about springtime—though fall was nearly here—and beauty. The fallen leaves floating in the river were proof of summer's fading. The song was unfamiliar. She must have picked it up in town, because I had certainly never heard it before, and Mama never sings anymore.

"Beyond the rolling hills and into the glow of the mo-or-ning!" Pennah practically shouted.

"Pennah!" I laughed with her, my heart lighter than air. "You're dropping gems all over the place!" Unlike the pond it brushed up against, this river was as clear as glass, doing nothing to hide the sapphires and emeralds that bounced on the cobbled riverbed, making the icy water shimmer with crisp blues and greens. "It'll make people suspicious."

"I don't care," she giggled. "It is a beautiful day! And it deserves to be sung about!" She twirled in a circle, whipping a wet pair of trousers around her head. Our laughter stopped abruptly when she slipped, submerging under the icy river water. She burst up, gasping because of the cold water that now soaked her to the bone, and laughed all over again. Knowing she was unhurt, I couldn't help but join in.

"Glad to see you enjoying yourselves." A deep voice came from the other side of the river. A man sat atop his horse, watching us.

Our smiles fell in an instant. Pennah jumped up quickly, attempting to cover herself since the thin, sopping dress she wore clung to her every curve. I stepped in front of her protectively. From her reaction, I guessed this was the man from town. The one who saw what she could do.

"No need to call in the troops," he chuckled. His voice was pleasant to listen to, his laugh soothing, but I didn't relax. Appearances were deceiving. That was one lesson I *had* learned because of this curse.

"We have nothing, sir. If you are here for taxes, we have already paid them." I wasn't sure what else he could possibly be here for. Besides Pennah, of course.

"I am not here for your money," he said gently as he dismounted his horse and stepped into the shallow river. "Though I've noticed you have plenty to spare." He pointedly looked down at the jewels in the river.

"We have almost no money, actually," I told him, pushing Pennah back to the edge of the river.

"Maybe no coin, but I've seen plenty of jewels." He looked down hungrily at the sapphires in the riverbed. What did he even need jewels for? His clothes screamed wealth and his purse sounded full. There was even a crest emblazoned on his chest to match the symbol on his horse's saddle blanket, which meant he not only had wealth, but rank as well.

"Any jewels in this forest are because of the fairies and witches that roam these parts. The jewels are tricks for those foolish enough to try to take them. They are all cursed." I had thought of this lie before. I just hoped the threat of a fairy's curse was enough to deter him from pushing the issue. Just speaking of a curse of any kind caused a few spiders to unknowingly leap from the bottom hem of my shirt to their watery doom in the river below.

"But I've seen at least two families in town sell their gems without issue." He still wore his charming smile. I reached for the dagger I kept around my waist when a sword was too bulky to carry around. "Now, now, child. I mean you no harm. I have simply come to make an offer to your sister." One of his hands was tucked into his jacket, touching something that hung on a string roped around his neck.

"What offer?" Pennah asked. I nudged her hard, willing her to be silent.

"To come live with me at my castle. I know you have a gift for treasures, and I understand that you stay hidden in the forest to protect yourself. If you come with me, you can be with other people and I will protect you from those who would wickedly try to steal you away." I hoped against hope that Pennah did not believe his offer was truthful. I knew Pennah well enough to know that she had to be tempted. Somehow, this man had said just the right thing.

"I am happy where I am, thank you. I'd like to stay here with my family," she told him with a frown.

He advanced. "I don't think you understand what I am offering you, sweet girl." His voice grew grimmer and his handsome face grew darker.

"She's not interested," I told him fiercely, clutching the handle of my dagger even harder. He growled and stepped closer; too close for comfort. In one motion I drew my dagger and slashed it at him, mostly trying to get him to back away. I was as surprised as Pennah, who gasped when my blade met flesh. A line of dark red appeared on his jawline going all the way to the tip of his chin, dying his beard. At the same moment I drew blood, the mysterious man's entire form flickered, but I couldn't clearly see what was hidden underneath.

"What are you?" I asked, backing away. One thing was for sure, if he flickered like that, there was magic involved. Which meant he probably wasn't human.

He snarled and lunged, striking me down with the back of his hand. My surprise at his magic let him catch me off guard. It was pitiful how quickly I was rendered useless to Pennah. My head slammed into a cold, wet stone. For a moment, the river full of gems ran in a spiral across my vision, still sparkling in the sunlight. When I got back up, I could barely stand straight, let alone fight the magical man when he grabbed Pennah around the waist and slung her over his shoulder. The dagger was still miraculously in my hand, so aiming for his wide back, I lunged forward. I didn't stab him, but I could tell I sliced through his skin by his shouting. Through my blurry vision I saw Pennah kicking him and scratching at his face until suddenly she went limp once the man reached the edge of the river.

"What did you do to her?" I had dropped the dagger in the grass and I didn't see it right away. Before I could get up out of the river and onto solid ground, I saw his foot too late. My stomach exploded with pain and I doubled over, my face resting in the grassy carpet until I could breathe again. Finally, I forced myself to my feet, still seeing double, just in time to see the man galloping away with my little sister.

"Pennah!" I screamed. A trail of pink rose petals fluttered to the ground behind them. Before long, they were gone. Poisonous tears burned in my eyes, but I couldn't stop them. In a haze of desperation, I grabbed my dagger, leaving the pile of clothes abandoned beside the river. They would only slow me down. I knew following the trail of petals was foolish, and I had no hope of catching up. I had to talk to Mama. I had to go back to the house.

The path away from the river never felt long before, but it was an eternity of sprinting before the rickety cottage came into sight. I nearly tore the old door off when I burst in.

"Mama! She's gone!" Her sunken cheeks sagged into a frown. Tears coated her eyes, glazing them over. Without any details given, she seemed to know what I meant. Maybe she could tell from the dark tears that had dried on my own face from running the whole way here. The day we had dreaded for years had finally come. "A man came into town and found out about her. He grabbed her! I tried to stop him, but I couldn't." The failure stung and my voice caught as I tried to speak. Frantically, I paced around the room in circles.

"Gone?" Mama, who had been looking so strong this morning, seemed to fall into herself. Her blankets would swallow her alive if she sank further into the bed. "My baby is gone forever?"

Pennah truly was still a child. She may have been becoming a woman, but she didn't know the harsh realities of the world. Not like I did. She would never last out there. I had to go get her.

"I have to find her," I said, suddenly anxious to get moving. I grabbed my blanket and brought it into Mama's room, rolling it up and tying it off with some twine. It should hold. We had some food stored for the coming winter. I could bring that to travel with.

"No!" Mama yelled urgently as I neared her cot, grabbing my wrist with a renewed strength. "You can't go!" At first I thought she was afraid to lose both her daughters. Then, she said with despair lining her broken voice, "You can't leave me!"

I pulled my wrist from her grip. "Mama, you don't understand. I'll find someone in town to take care of you." She used to have friends in town. Surely one of them was loyal enough to come help for a few weeks.

"I forbid you from leaving!" she shouted, her voice hoarse with fear.

There was a moment of silence and my grief at losing Pennah was quickly turning into disappointment.

"You would have me leave Pennah?" Mama stiffened her jaw in a silent *yes*. "You would let your own daughter be taken?"

"She could already be dead for all we know." I put a hand up, stopping her from continuing. I couldn't think about that. She *couldn't* be dead. I couldn't lose her. It was my job to protect her and I wasn't going to fail now.

"You're willing to give up all hope, just like that?" I shook my head, saddened by the change I saw in my mother. I knew she was deteriorating here in bed, more concerned with her mortality than with her own daughters. But this was too far. I had listened to and obeyed every word that came from Mama's mouth my entire life, but this was a request I could not comply with. "I'm going. I'll find someone in town to—"

"No one will take care of a cursed woman!" she snapped harshly, fists shaking against her ragged blankets. The sickly circles under her red-rimmed eyes seemed to darken.

I froze. "You? Cursed?" My voice rose. "All these years, I've had to endure that village full of people just staring—always watching—and keeping their distance, scared and angry. I've been attacked time and time again for doing nothing! *You* are not the cursed one!" A hot fire blazed in my chest and I threw down the rolled blanket. I had never told my mother about the attacks. The announcement didn't seem to faze her. Did she even care? About me? Pennah?

"For doing nothing?" She let out a harsh, mocking laugh. Anger seemed to have energized my mother. She spoke with her teeth clenched. "I am cursed because I was given a daughter who did not even have a kind word to spare for a fairy in disguise. A daughter who has never learned to keep her mouth shut and just do as she's told!" Her face was twisted with fury.

"A daughter who devoted the last nine years to an ungrateful mother!" Trials were the true tests of love. And Mama had failed miserably. Tears fell from my face, but I couldn't tell if they were from the anger, the disillusionment, or the grief that swelled inside me like a bubble about to burst. The burning in my chest grew until I tasted bile, which only deepened the look of utter disgust I could feel on my face. "No one is around to care for you besides me because you are a selfish woman who doesn't even care that one of her daughters might be lost forever! Maybe if you had an ounce of love for your family, they wouldn't keep disappearing. My father is gone, Matthew is gone, your own brother-in-law left you years ago because he knew who you really were: a needy, self-centered parasite," I sneered, venom tears still glossing over my eyes, glad to see regret flit across her face before disappearing. A strange calm settled over me before I continued. "Soon no one will be left and you'll be all alone," I finished in an eerily quiet voice that didn't even sound like it belonged to me. My mother's greatest fear was to be abandoned, and I knew it. I had used it against her shamelessly and I felt a tinge of regret, but there was no taking back the words now. She was about to retaliate, crystal clear tears finally slipping from her sickly, red-rimmed eyes and running down her face, when the burning in my chest and throat became unbearable and I fell to my hands and knees, dry-heaving.

"Sable, what's happening?" Anger still laced the concern in her tone.

I couldn't respond. In fact, I couldn't breathe. I felt something moving through my throat, along my tongue. Scales. The muscles of my throat spasmed as my body tried to reject the reptile that was slithering out of my mouth and onto the dirt floor. It was an eternity before I could breathe again. Even then, my breath came in labored gasps and shudders. I brought my head up to see yellow eyes boring into me with malice. I knew I should be backing away slowly, but I remained frozen, still trying to get my breathing under control. With a serpent's speed, the brown, scaly creature struck. A painful fire erupted on my neck. I clutched at the pain, but there was nothing I could do. My own words, with the help of the fairy's curse, were killing me. I knew it was only a matter of time. But now I'd never be able to find Pennah.

I was wheezing now and my eyes wouldn't focus. In my blurred vision I saw the snake turn away and slither onto the bed. Mama was screaming for help. Screaming my name, and Pennah's name.

"No—" I could barely whisper. I reached and felt smooth scales against my fingertips, but the snake pulled out of my grasp. The elbow that was supporting my weight slipped and I fell to the ground, a puff of dust rising around me when I hit the dirt. I saw another glance of brown scales before everything was gone.

Chapter 4

PENNAH

My wrists hurt. I tried to rub them, but quickly discovered that the source of pain was ropes tied too tightly, binding my hands together. I opened my eyes to see a man staring down at me, his face emotionless. I jolted. He looked just like the man who kidnapped me, except this man was at least 10 years older and his eyes were a duller blue, almost gray. His hair and beard were both speckled with peppery gray, dried blood clumping on his right jawline.

"Why does my stomach hurt so much?" It felt like I'd been punched over and over again.

"That's from riding on a horse unconscious. Which is why I woke you. I'd rather have you without broken ribs. We've gotten far enough so your pesky sister can't follow, even if she wanted to." At the reminder, tears prickled at my eyes. I might not see her again. Diamond droplets fell to the ground.

"Astounding," he said as he crouched down and inspected a tear. As he pinched the tiny diamond between his fingers, a glint of greed in his eyes, I looked at our surroundings. There were trees in every direction. I couldn't even tell which way we'd come in on the horse.

After slipping the tear into his pocket, the man grabbed a strip of dried meat from the horse's saddle bag. "Here," he said, tossing the meat so it landed right beside me. "You should eat something before we get moving again." I carefully brushed dust from the meat and took a bite, even though my stomach was so cramped I wasn't sure if I was capable of digesting anything at the moment. Not sure when I'd eat again, I finished off the meat.

"Alright, let's go." The man got close again and I could see a dagger on his belt. My chest grew tight. I couldn't go with him. Somehow, I needed to get home. I needed Sable. That was it! What would Sable do? The man waited for a moment before reaching to grab my arm. Suddenly, I knew. While he reached out, I launched my heels into his face.

The man cried out and I rolled to the side, scrambling to my feet. Afraid to look back, I sprinted away. Before I got far, he grabbed the back of my dress and pulled me to the ground.

"We'll have to deal with a few broken ribs then," he snarled, blood dripping from his nose. He blew a shimmery powder into my face and an overwhelming urge to sleep overcame me.

Chapter 5

SABLE

Sticky tears coated my cheeks. Blinking was difficult for a few seconds while I reoriented myself. I gently grazed my fingers across my neck, which was pulsing in pain. A huge welt had risen up on my skin. So the snake bite hadn't killed me. I turned to the bed where Mama had been for years. Horror crept up my spine. Before I could speculate what happened, I forced myself to stand and pull back the messy covers, ignoring the spinning sensation that threatened to overwhelm me. Mama's face was pale and her opaque eyes still seemed to hold terror, even in death. I sucked in a hoarse breath and collapsed to my knees. My whole body was shaking as I began crying all over again. In one terrible day, my whole family had vanished.

Ugly sobs escaped me and I let the tears come. Soon, spiders littered the floor, crawling on my arms and up the side of Mama's bed. Suddenly, my tears of despair turned into anger and frustration. It was all because of this curse! I pulled out my dagger and stabbed down at the nearest spider. My quick motion made the rest of the spiders skitter away. I lifted the blade to my cheek and let the rest of my tears dribble down my face and drip onto the blade. I would save this for the man that took my sister. And then I was going to find that fairy.

Once the tears stopped, I sheathed my now poisonous dagger and grabbed my pack. I took all of the food we had stored for the winter and put as much as I could fit into the pack. I rolled up my blankets and tied them on. The next stop was the pond. But first, I went to the back of the house and grabbed our shovel.

I knew one day I'd have to bury my mother, but I never thought it would be my fault. Digging the ditch was numbing and it allowed me to put the worries from my mind for a short time. Once the grave was deep enough, I had to resist the urge to just sit down and cry until nothing was left. Unfortunately, I already had nothing left, so I went inside and wrapped my mother's body in her blankets and half carried-half dragged her outside. Rigor mortis had already set in, so moving her proved difficult. Once she was in the grave, I stood above, looking at the pile of blankets that covered Mama's body. I had told her she would die alone, which wasn't quite true. At least she had someone to bury her. And now, I was the one who was left alone. I was the one who repelled everyone and everything.

I had no way to make one, so my mother was left without a tombstone. It wasn't the funeral I'm sure she wanted, but I didn't have much left to give. For a few self-pitying minutes, I sat at the head of the grave, looking at the tiny cottage I'd grown up in. My own father had lived here, years ago. I was born in this house, as was Pennah a few years later. I had repaired the thatched roof and the frail shutters with my own hands more times that I could count. Pennah and I built our lives here. It was trivial to attach so much sentiment to a worn collection of timber, but it was the only home I'd ever known.

As I grabbed my pack and sword and walked away, I kept telling myself I wasn't leaving home, but going towards Pennah, the only home I had left.

It didn't take long before I arrived at the pond. The pond itself wasn't exactly picturesque. Bare, tortuous trees loomed at its edges and the murky water was so dark, it was impossible to know that a kingdom's worth of treasure lay at its bottom. I set the pack and sword down against a half-rotted tree and stripped down. The rest of my clothes were still sitting in a sopping pile at the river. I'd get them after, but for now, I needed something that was dry.

The water was cold, but I continued in, edging deeper and deeper until I couldn't reach the ground anymore. Once I had gotten close enough to the pond's center, I dove down and grabbed a big handful of jewels. Careful not to drop them, I carried the jewels back to shore and put them in my leather pouch. Once they were secure, I quickly redressed. My clothes were slightly damp now, but I was still warmer in them than I was in the nude. Suspiciously close to the moment I finished dressing, a man's voice called out.

"Hello?" I raced to put my shoes on and I tied the sword and its sheath to my back, slinging my pack on over it. Once I was ready, I drew my sword and moved towards the voice, making plenty of noise so the man knew I was coming. I muttered a few curse words, ensuring at least a few venomous creatures were around. Hopefully my sword or the appearance of snakes and scorpions would scare away this inconvenience.

I stood at the ready as a man emerged from the bushes. "Stay away from me," I told him. He had brown skin and nearly black hair. Underneath the layers of dirt he'd accumulated, he was quite attractive, but the worst kinds of men always were. Clearly he'd traveled quite a distance from home. He was probably just a lost traveler. When the man spotted me and my sword, he drew his own. Unfortunately, in a match of appearances his sword was the winner, by far. There were huge jewels encrusted in the hilt and the blade itself was curved and it looked sleek and sharp. Traveler was now out of the question. This was definitely a thief, and I prayed he was a lone thief and not part of some band that was about to jump out at me.

"I just need directions. I am searching for the Black Forest," he assured me in an accent I didn't recognize. Likely story. Everyone knew where the Black Forest was. It was the forest infested with magical creatures. In fact, our town was on the outskirts of it. I didn't respond, and the stranger felt the need to continue speaking. "You have a good stance for a woman." If only I knew more about sword fighting than stances and the most basic of blocks and attacks.

"And you have a good sword for a traveler," I spat. Neither of us lowered our weapon.

"Alright. I may have stolen it, but the owner had no right to it either." He sheathed his sword, smiling a little, as if we were friends. "And actually, it's a *sosun pattah*. Her name is Amani. It means wish." Not every sword carried a name. Usually, naming a weapon meant it was special. Eyeing the gaudy hilt, I flattened my lips. Special indeed.

After a moment, I put my sword away as well. If this was a thief and if he was watching me get dressed, not only was he a despicable person, but he also probably saw the large handful of jewels I now held in my pack. I considered reasoning with him, but only for a moment. Finally, I came to a decision. Just when the thief thought I was ready to talk, I sprinted away, back towards the house.

"Wait! I won't hurt you!" he shouted as he ran after me. The fact that he was chasing me made me doubt his words even more than before. I glanced back to make sure I could still see him, but I wasn't going to have to worry about losing him. In fact, he was right on my tail, though he was weighed down with just as much luggage as I was. Finally, we reached the main trail that led to my house. I sprinted down the trail, leaping over the black wool string that went across the walkway. I didn't slow until I heard a yell of surprise. Turning around, I ran toward the yell and saw the dark skinned man hanging upside down by one of his ankles. His pack had slipped to the ground, but he was trying to cut himself down with his sword, or sosun pattah, or whatever he had called it. Using the flat of my own sword, I smacked the weapon out of his hands and held the tip of my rusty, dull-looking sword to his throat. I stayed there for a moment as I caught my breath.

"This is incredible," he told me. "How did you do this? It completely caught me by surprise." Was he talking about the trap? He really wasn't from around here. This wasn't an uncommon animal trap. "It looks like that rock over there is a counterweight of some sort. But how did you raise it up?" He was still trying to figure it out.

"Enough!" I shouted at him impatiently. Didn't he ever shut up? "Now tell me what you are really doing here." I pushed the tip of my blade into his skin, drawing a little bit of blood.

"Wow, that thing is sharper than it looks." He appeared genuinely surprised that I had drawn blood. I was a little surprised as well. I wasn't even sure this sword was sharp enough to cut hot butter.

"Tell me now, you dirty thief, or you'll be covered with snake bites before you can speak another word." As I said the threatening words, more snakes appeared and circled underneath the man's fingertips which hung down. He paused, watching the snakes. He didn't seem afraid though, only curious. Then, he looked back at me, seeming to inspect me.

"You have no more control over these snakes than I have over you." He crossed his arms. His stiff, dirty hair hung down, away from his face. He was actually quite young. Maybe even as young as I was. "If you did have the control, then you wouldn't have a bite there on your neck. It looks new. Painful." I could almost feel my face reddening in anger.

"Regardless, I am still the one with the sword." I smirked a little, still seething. He sifted this over in his mind as a few of the snakes below him snapped before slithering away to hide.

"Fine. I heard about a special girl who lives on the edge of the Black Forest. A girl who makes jewels appear out of thin air. I thought it was just a rumor at first, but as I got closer, I heard more stories."

"And what would you need a girl like this for?" I asked, though I knew the answer.

"My kingdom is very poor, and I came here so we could prosper again." He sounded genuine, but all thieves did.

"Not for personal gain, I'm sure." He was about to continue lying to me, but I stopped him. "Besides, she's gone. She's been taken."

"Taken?" He sounded truly alarmed. His acting skills were quite impressive.

"Yes, taken! Someone stole her before you could." I shoved him and he swung out his arms, but he had no balance to regain. Instead, he resigned himself to simply swaying.

"I was never going to take her. I was simply going to ask."

"Of course. That's what the other man did too. But when she didn't want to go, he stole her." I started pacing, unable to help thinking out loud. "And he had some kind of magic."

"Well there you go; I can't use magic. See? Different. Besides, I wouldn't have taken her. I would have just taken some jewels. She has plenty to spare, doesn't she?"

I considered telling him I had a pond full of riches, but I might have use for him, if only I knew I could trust him.

"How badly do you need those jewels?" I asked him. His face was beginning to turn dark red and the veins in his forehead were protruding a bit. The swaying back and forth didn't seem to help. If I didn't cut him down soon, he'd probably pass out.

"Desperately."

"Would you be willing to help me get her back?"

"So you know where she was taken?" He blinked hard, tried to make his vision focus.

"Not yet, but I intend to find out," I assured him.

"I will help you, then," he agreed. "But you realize this means you will have to cut me down. I'm feeling a little light headed."

"Swear to me you won't hurt me or my sister."

"Your sister?" It was hard to tell through the strained expression on his red face, but he looked taken aback.

"Swear it!"

"Alright, fine." He lightly gripped my sword blade with his right hand, drawing a small line blood from his palm. He pressed his now bleeding palm to his heart and said, "I solemnly swear on my life that I will not intentionally cause harm to you or your sister. Now cut me down, my vision is blurring." I had hoped for a simple oath, assuming that, despite the man's status as a thief, he had a sense of honor. This was much more than an ordinary oath, however. According to legend, if you broke a life oath, you died. It was just an old wives' tale, but most people were too superstitious to risk it.

As soon as I recovered from the brief moment of shock at his promise, I sliced through the taut rope and the thief fell to the ground, severely lacking grace in his landing.

"Servans," I told the thief. I didn't often use the sword's name, but I always remembered it. Every time I held it in my hands, its name was hovering in the back of my mind.

"Is that your name or the sword's?" His eyes were closed, but the redness in his face was fading to his normal coppery skin tone.

"It means 'watching over.'" I sheathed my sword. He sat up slowly, holding one hand to his head. When he opened his eyes, I noticed how dark they were. He fixed his focus on me and I briefly wondered where he could be from before I reminded myself that even though we were allies now, it did not mean we were friends.

"So, the girl with the gift is your sister? Does that mean you have a gift too?"

"Yes, the gift of a sharp tongue along with a knack for traps," I barked.

"And a quick wit, apparently." He stood and picked up his sword and the pack that had slipped off his back when he was flipped upside down.

"Do you have enough supplies in your pack? No one's going to be here while I'm gone, so we might as well not waste food." My mind went back to the unmarked grave I had just finished, but I pushed that thought away and I focused on Pennah and my quest. I couldn't possibly fit all the food we had in my own pack. He admitted he was running low on rations, so we restocked his bag. As we did so, he asked what I knew about the man who stole my sister.

"Not much. I know he is some kind of magical creature. And there was some kind of family crest on his horse's saddle blanket. I think it was a dragon." Either that or a bird, but most birds didn't have long, reptilian tails and arms as well as wings. "There are about a million crests out there though, but they have a collection of historical records in Payton. It's the largest town nearby, only a few days walking distance." The records should have some sort of crest log.

"No need. No one has had a dragon crest in over a century. It's considered bad luck; people are afraid a symbol like that might incite a dragon attack. The only one I can think of is the crest of Cornelius the Dragon Slayer—it was a picture of a dragon with a sword in its chest. He and his younger brother slayed a dragon, with the help of several knights of course, and some incredible luck, and ever since then, they boasted they could tame the world of magic. In their arrogance, they built a small kingdom deep in the heart of the Black Forest. It only lasted a decade or so before the forest and its creatures took over the kingdom. Ever since then, it was thought to be abandoned."

I stared at the man incredulously. This thief was more educated than I was. "Thanks for the history lesson. Now let's get a move on." I led him out of the house, but he paused in the garden.

"Don't you have a horse or mule or something?" He looked around as if the alleged animal would crawl out of one of the nearby leaf piles. Did I look like a princess?

"Other than rescuing my sister, what could I possibly need a horse for? I grow vegetables. It's not exactly mass labor." I was, however, proud of how much my tiny garden had grown since it first began. It was a shame I had to abandon it now.

"Isn't the town relatively far away?"

I shrugged, tiring of this conversation already. I just wanted to be with my sister. A horse would be nice, but it was not an option. Even if I could get one, it would just be spooked by the excess of snakes I was constantly surrounded by.

"I have legs. Didn't you walk all the way from wherever you came from? Why didn't you bring your horse?" I pointed out.

He paused a moment. "Valid point."

Finally, there was silence. Until he ruined it again.

"It's Karim, by the way. My name." I said it in my mind: *Ka-reem.* Definitely foreign. I didn't respond, and more silence followed, interrupted only by the soft sound of our footfalls. "Generally, this is the point where you tell me your name."

"If you're going to be chatting the whole way, soon you'll regret not having me make an oath too." I decided reaching for my sword or dagger might be a little excessive. He'd promised he wouldn't hurt me, so he shouldn't make it so tempting to pummel him.

"Oh, you can't harm me," he said, matter-of-factly. While I was thinking the same exact thing, I was still offended that he didn't believe I could beat him in a fight, especially when he swore he wouldn't hurt me. He went on as if no offensive words had been spoken. "If you give me your name, I will be quiet for an entire hour."

It felt like I was selling my soul to the devil, but I needed some quiet. "My name is Sable."

"See that wasn't so bad. Sable." My name sounded different with his slight accent. I glared back at him. He smiled and shrugged apologetically. True to his word, he was silent for the next hour.

Chapter 6

SABLE

"I realize you probably like the flamboyance of your sword, but we'll start to see more people on the road soon. We are approaching Payton, and it might arouse suspicion if people see someone looking like you and someone like me traveling with a sword like that. Use this to cover up the hilt." I tossed a long leather cord to Karim. It was meant to be one of my extra shoelaces, but I'd have to make do without it. Not only would it make the humans suspicious, but according to the stories, a great number of magical creatures seemed to be attracted to shiny things.

"Why are we going to Payton? I thought we were going to the Black Forest." Karim began wrapping the cord around the hilt of *Amani*, carefully making sure all traces of the shimmering wealth were hidden.

"You may seem to know the detailed geography of this land, but no one knows how to get through the Black Forest." He had been prattling on for the last day and a half on random subjects, one of which was his extensive knowledge of a land that was not his own. "Fortunately for us, if the man we're looking for is actually staying in the Black Kingdom, there is a road that leads right through the forest to the city's gate. And the main road starts at Payton, the largest city on the outskirts of the Black Forest."

"Seems logical enough. The road has really survived all these years?" I winced, but he couldn't see it on my face. "Survived" was a relative term. I just hoped there was enough road left to follow the whole way.

Soon, the road was busy with travelers, vendors, and anyone with any reason to come to or leave Payton. For once, the stares we received were not intended for me. Karim was clearly not from around here, and he seemed uncomfortable surrounded by so many wary eyes. As a thief, he probably preferred melting into the shadows. Most skirted around us on the road, so we kept to the edge. I hoped they all thought the snakes that tangled around my feet were from the bushes that trailed along the side of the road. People from bigger cities didn't exactly believe in magic. They thought anything magical was a myth from small, superstitious villages. They all knew the Black Forest was a dangerous place, but they had no idea what dangers lurked beyond the treeline. Until I saw one myself, I hadn't even really believed that fairies were real. Fortunately, once the road got busy, Karim and I both quieted down, and fewer words meant fewer venomous creatures.

Relief washed over me, and Karim was also visibly happier, when we saw the shambled road heading west towards the Black Forest in the distance. Payton itself, or at least the enormous wall surrounding the city, was also now looming in the distance. As the day turned to evening, fewer people were leaving Payton and the traffic going the opposite direction as us dwindled to nearly nothing.

Hypothetically, the road coming from the Black Forest should have come up to the West gate in Payton's wall, but the last time I got word from Payton, only three gates were opened every morning and closed every night: South, East, and North. Due to this inconvenience, we would have to walk around the wall. It was just as well, though, since I didn't feel like being gawked at by even more people inside the walls.

The moment we stepped foot off the main road, Karim's silence vanished. "Are you following a trail?" The path around the city wall was barely more than a game trail and it was mostly covered with weeds and brush since no one dared go this way. As he asked, I realized had strayed from the actual path. I subtly went back to where I guessed the path was, Karim faithfully trailing behind me all the while.

"Yes," I told him, hoping he didn't realize I'd strayed again.

"It's very hard to see it." As if I needed him telling me that. At least the road leading into the Black Forest was visible now. Even if we strayed from the path, we'd still end up in the right place.

"Are you afraid of the snakes?" As I spoke, some tall, grassy weeds a foot away shivered as something slithered by.

"It was less disturbing when I could at least see them." He paused. "If you don't mind my asking, is there a particular reason you always have snakes following you around? I've also noticed many spiders, and even a few scorpions. They don't seem to bother you much."

I sighed and didn't answer for a moment. He deserved to know if he was going to be traveling with me for who knows how long. "When Pennah received her—" I almost choked on the word, "*gift*, this was what I got instead. We weren't born like this, you know. It was a fairy."

When I stopped talking, he asked for more. "How did it happen?"

I stumbled on a rock I couldn't see through the thick brush. We had left the rough path completely, but the road wasn't far now. "It doesn't really matter how it happened. The point is, if you're squeamish about the snakes, I suggest turning back now."

"Actually, I had a pet snake once. It was a—" He stopped himself abruptly before finishing the sentence. "A small green one. He ate crickets."

If he was going to make up stories, I almost suggested he put some thought into them ahead of time, but I honestly couldn't care less if he had some pet snake or not.

I hesitated before taking the last step onto the old cobbled road. Dry weeds, nearly dead from the heat of summer's end, popped up between the stones. Once I was on the ancient road facing west, the dark trees of the Black Forest were suddenly so close, so real. How far did it go? It couldn't go on forever, so there had to be something on the other side. But how could any city on the other side thrive and hope for better days when the sun rose every morning from such a dismal place?

"I've never seen anywhere that looked so . . . hostile," Karim put it. The Black Forest's trees, though still some ways down the road, already seemed to be looming in over us, the bleak branches sharp and crooked like bared teeth.

"Like I said before, now is the time to turn back," I reminded him.

"I'll manage," he said easily. "But it is almost dark, and while I do admit I am putting off the inevitable a little, I also think it would be wise if we sleep here."

For a moment, I considered leaving him behind and charging after Pennah. The Black Forest was in sight, and the castle couldn't be more than a week's walk from here. However, the idea of heading into the Black

Forest alone was not very appealing. My odds were much better with Karim's help.

As I lay down to sleep, I realized that we were, ironically, the safest we would be on this trek since we left my home. The main road often had thieves, none of which would be on this particular road, and our surrounding area wasn't crawling with magical creatures yet. The dry weeds even made for a relatively comfortable mattress. Despite all this, it was still difficult to sleep, knowing Pennah was imprisoned in the middle of this awful forest. Not only that, but we were going into unknown territory tomorrow not even knowing for sure if she was inside that castle. But then again, why else would that man be brandishing a long-dead dragon slayer's emblem?

A maelstrom of thought like this bombarded me until I was finally overcome with sleep.

"Sable!" An unfamiliar voice whispered my name loudly and urgently. The ground had never been so comfortable. I moaned sleepily and rolled onto my side. "Sable, get up."

Couldn't Karim just let me sleep? He called my name again. I sat up and rubbed my eyes.

"What?" I said. The gaudy sword in his hand was pointed at my feet where a rattlesnake had started to stir. I must have had a nightmare or been talking in my sleep. This particular snake, while its bite could injure an average adult, as I had seen it do to the village butcher, had almost no effect on me, other than a mild headache. I simply slipped my feet out from under the snake and stood. The rattlesnake, interrupted in its nap, slithered away into the thicker brush.

"You woke me up for that?" I rubbed my eyes tiredly.

"It was venomous! And it was *on* you."

"Nothing that comes in my sleep will kill me, or even hurt me much." At least nothing had so far. "It might kill *you*, but I'll be fine." I rolled up my blankets and packed up. I had slept in the same house as Pennah and Mama for years and neither of them were ever injured due to any nightmare-induced creatures. The chilly night air also made my cold-blooded friends more sluggish than usual. Karim would be fine.

"Are you ready?" I asked him after we finished eating a morsel of food for breakfast.

"After you." He gave an exaggerated bow. I went first.

"I don't think that is considered gentlemanly when we are heading into that." I gestured to the grim road ahead. Karim frowned, and with two longer strides he was even with me.

"Together then." Was it evil of me to hope that some of his unrealistic cheer wore off in the depths of the Black Forest?

Generally speaking, forests began as trees spread out before thickening and becoming a true forest. That was how it was near my house. Here, the trees came abruptly, like a thick wall. It was from chopping down all the trees that approached the walls of Payton, effectively moving the treeline of the forest. I expected the midst of the Black Forest to be more dismal. It was less bright than the open road we had traveled before, but it didn't block out the sun entirely. In fact, there were even birds chirping. We entered the forest wary and jumpy, but towards the end of the day, when nothing of even remote excitement or danger happened, our guard slowly went down. The wariness returned quickly, though, as darkness settled over the forest.

"You sleep first," I told Karim. He half-heartedly objected, but walking all day was very tiring. It wasn't long before he gave in and went to sleep.

There were moments I thought I'd doze off, but then some noise woke me right up. A crunch of leaves. A growl that was probably just trees creaking. Sometimes I'd see a glimmer of something in the distance, but I would stare after the glimpse I saw and nothing would reappear. I'd never been this far from home before, and I'd never had to stay up standing guard. It was very lonely, and very boring. Every once in a while I stood up and paced around to wake myself up. I only wished we could make a fire, but Karim and I had decided that while a fire might scare away the earthly creatures we were used to, who knew what might be attracted to the flames in the Black Forest?

My chin slipped off my elbow and I jerked awake. I had fallen asleep. My heart raced and worst case scenarios filed through my mind in a rush of thought. I shook Karim's shoulder. He didn't move and I began to panic. Did something sneak up and kill him in his sleep? Or maybe my nightmare snakes were not as lazy as I had thought. I shook him harder and he finally moaned as he sat up. Relief filled me like a breath of fresh air.

"You sleep like the dead," I said.

"Is it morning already?" His accent was thicker than normal in his groggy state.

I didn't have the energy to roll my eyes or make a sarcastic comment. My near heart attack had sapped what little alertness I had left.

"It's your turn to look out for monsters," I told him, taking his spot on the bedroll once he stood up. Of course I had my own, but I wasn't going to set it up when his was just sitting there unused. He didn't say anything in argument, so I settled in, using my own blanket.

Chapter 7

PENNAH

I was woken with a jolt to my tailbone and I looked up to see my kidnapper staring down at me. He had dropped me in a pile of hay, but there hadn't been enough cushioning atop the stone floor to prevent pain from shooting up my spine. The new pain made the aching of my ribs seem duller, if only for a moment.

"Where am I?" I asked the man. "Who *are* you?"

"You are in my home, in the Black Forest. Go ahead and see for yourself." He gestured to the window. Cautiously I edged towards the window, standing up only when I was within reach of the outside. He wasn't lying. Trees reached out farther than I could see, stretching up past my window. I looked down and immediately regretted doing so. Instinctively I braced myself against the wall. We were so high up. A fall from here would surely kill me. And yet, the trees were still taller than my window. It was as if just to spite the architects, they refused to stop growing even once they reached the height of an average tree. My room seemed to be at the top of a tower set on the corner of a dark gray stone castle. I didn't even know the Black Forest had kingdoms in it. From the ivy and cracking on the stone, though, I had to assume the castle was made decades ago and since abandoned. Which meant I was probably all the way out here alone with my kidnapper.

I stayed facing out the window, afraid to look my captor in the eyes again.

"You should know, dearest Pennah, that your door is not locked. You are free to go wherever you want in the castle. However, the halls are filled with doors that are nearly identical. One is obviously the exit, but the rest are occupied, and I'm sorry to say that my pets aren't as gracious of hosts as I am. If you choose the wrong door, you'll ruin their appetite for dinner, and we wouldn't want that." He may have been disguising his face earlier, but his voice was the same sweet tone as before. It made me sick.

I leaned my head out the window and let a few diamond tears fall down the side of the tower. At least that way it wouldn't be easy to collect them.

"Speaking of dinner, yours will be ready shortly. Make yourself at home."

Chapter 8

SABLE

Unlike me, Karim appeared to have stayed awake for his entire watch. The sun was already up when I awoke and Karim was munching on his breakfast. It didn't take long to clean up our meager campsite and once we finished, we headed west again.

So far, the road was in one piece. Some cobbles had slipped away, separated by a bit of greenery that forced its way between the cracks. It wasn't the best road for walking on, but it was easy to follow, and that was more than I'd hoped for. As we traveled, the scenery didn't change much. There were trees and there was dirt. It was turning out to be a perfectly boring journey.

"I must say, I expected some kind of delay before now," Karim mentioned about halfway through the day. "If it continues like this, we should have your sister back in no time at all."

"I don't mean to put a damper on things, but we still have a long way to go," I pointed out, trying to be a little more realistic. He nodded in agreement but still wore a slight smile.

"So tell me about Pennah. What is she like? She must be strong willed to put up with a sister like you." His smile grew so I knew he was only teasing.

I would have kept my mouth shut, afraid to share any information that might be used against us, but since his oath to not harm me or Pennah was binding, I figured it didn't hurt.

"She is strong willed, but not in the same way I am." I was stubborn and harsh, I knew it, but Pennah . . . "She's more gentle and kind. And she's always been the prettier one. As a child, one of her smiles could win anyone over."

"I have a beautiful sister as well, but I'm afraid she is quite scheming. Growing up, she had boys at her beck and call. My parents didn't know what to do with her," Karim told me. I had assumed that he was an orphan without brothers or sisters at all, though I suppose thieves could have families too. "As a young man, I was terrified that all women were as conniving as Maram. I was glad to discover that this was not the case."

"You have just the one sister?" I asked.

He shook his head, a few big, brown curls shaking too. "I actually have four older sisters. Three of them are married." I almost laughed. Four older sisters? No wonder he turned to thieving. That many sisters would have driven me away too. "If you don't mind my asking, what about your family? Why are you making this trek with a stranger?"

My urge to laugh vanished. My family tree was a tragic one. My father died long ago. Pennah's father, who abused me and neglected her, was killed as a result of his gambling habits years ago, though I doubted he would have helped anyway. Uncle Morrin abandoned us when the curse came. And Mama . . .

"Pennah is my family," was my only reply. Karim could read my face enough to know that was all I'd say on the matter.

Karim attempted to revive the conversation several times before giving up. Afternoon eventually dimmed into evening. I squeezed the last bits of water from my canteen. I had been rationing the last of it, hoping to find Pennah before I needed to resort to drinking the water provided by the Black Forest. My hesitation to go near a river around here stemmed mainly from the stories I had heard of water nymphs and kappas drowning anyone who got too close to the water's edge. Unfortunately, now, I didn't have much of a choice.

"We should get more water before it gets too dark," I suggested, assuming Karim was also nearly out of water, if not already carrying empty canteens.

"The creek that follows the road shouldn't be too far." Karim headed off the road to the north and I followed. The trees seemed spread out and open while we were on the trail, but the moment we left the path they grew closer together. I couldn't stop thinking that anything could be hiding out there in the dense foliage. After several paces, I stacked a few small rocks to mark the trail. All along our way I left a line of cairns and sticks protruding from the ground. I knew it was just a matter of heading south after, but I also knew the forest played tricks. I wasn't about to stake Pennah's life on the bet that nothing strange would happen during our excursion to the creek.

"Did you hear that?" Karim's head tilted as he listened to the faint burbling of the creek.

"We're almost there." We kept going until the narrow creek was in sight. This part of it seemed much too small to house any dangerous creatures. Despite that reassurance, I drew my dagger and held it in one hand as I dunked my canteen into the creek with the other. I filled the two canteens I had brought with water and I withdrew my hand from the creek without incident. I hated to think it, for fear of jinxing our journey, but the Black Forest had fallen short of my expectations of magical attacks at every turn. Karim also filled his canteens without any webbed hands yanking him under.

Now, the final test. Karim and I were both inspecting our canteens warily. We had to drink the water or turn back now, and going back was not an option. Even if I did plan on returning after packing more water, knowing now that the trek would last more than two days, there was no way I could carry enough water there and back for myself and for Pennah for the journey home.

"I'll test the water first to make sure it is safe," Karim offered. How very noble. But if the water was poison, not only would it be less likely to kill me, thanks to the curse, but I couldn't just walk away. If the water made the trip impossible, at least Karim could go home and steal some other jewels. Instead of arguing with Karim, I took a deep swig of the water before he could object.

"Sable!" He froze. I froze. I felt nothing unusual, and there was no pain. If it was poison, while it might not kill me, I would definitely still feel its effects. We stood there for several minutes. When I didn't combust or turn into a monkey, Karim spoke.

"So . . ."

"I think it's just regular water," I told him.

"I suppose we could wait until morning to make sure."

"As far as I know, magic happens quickly. I think it should be safe." And I would know. It only took a moment after the fairy cursed me for spiders to start appearing. If the water had some deleterious effect, it wasn't great enough to bother us.

"Then I suggest we drink our fill before returning to the road." Grateful yet another obstacle was avoided, I agreed and drank until I couldn't drink anymore. The water tasted fresh and crisp. Though I was now bloated with water, I felt lighter. I must have been dehydrated before. When I was refilling my canteen, I noticed that the water seemed to sparkle a little more than before. I shrugged it off. Yes, water sparkled. It was *water* and the sun was just reflecting off the ripples.

Karim refilled his canteen as well and we headed south, following my trail markers. We started out walking beside each other, but Karim drifted a few steps behind me. I was staring at the next cairne when I noticed that it, like the water, sparkled a bit. I ignored it and kept going. The lightness I had felt earlier was fading and it was replaced with a pull that had me dragging my feet. I had slowed so much that Karim bumped into me from behind. There was a light tug at my braid.

"Sable . . . your hair." I turned to see him inspecting my dark braid. There was something different about Karim. Something off, but my thoughts were lethargic and hazy so I couldn't quite figure what it was. Also, my hair wasn't its usual color. Well, it was still dark, dark brown, nearly black, but there was something new about it. "It's glittery," Karim pointed out. Ah, yes. That's what was new. He looked up into my eyes and let out a small gasp, followed by a smile. "Your face is glittery too!" His words were slow, like he was drunk. He released my hair and instead cupped his hands around my face. Normally, I would have pushed him away, and I was slightly confused as to why I wasn't doing that now.

"So is yours." As I spoke, I realized the truth of what I said. Karim's face, in fact his whole body, had the same sparkle as everything else around me. Actually, he shined a little brighter than the trees and rocks. He let go of my face and set his hands on my shoulders, keeping a tight grip to steady himself.

"Why are you moving?" He wore an innocent look of confusion on his sparkly face. I was about to tell him that *he* was the one moving when I noticed that I had grabbed his elbows because we were *both* swaying like drunkards.

"I think . . . the water . . ." The thought escaped me before I could finish it.

"You are . . . you're . . ." Karim finished the sentence in a mumble, not that I knew what language he had started speaking anyway. Finally, he slipped to the ground. I knelt beside him and tried to shake him, but it was no use.

"Stupid humans," a deep, growly voice came from above us. "Drinking more water from the Black Forest than their puny bodies could handle."

"At least the wait was worth it," another gravelly voice said. "They're like suckling babies now."

I looked up to see two looming figures, both covered in sparkles, though not nearly as much as Karim and I were. One, underneath the shimmer, had bluish-gray skin and the other one was more brown. Both, however, were ugly and covered in lumps it seemed. Not only that, but they were far taller than a man. They must have been at least ten feet tall. The blue one grabbed Karim roughly and slung him over his shoulder. The brown one objected.

"I told you, *I* wanted to carry the sleeping one." The blue one ignored him and began walking away, his joints grinding like boulders with each step. The brown one growled, but settled on carrying me. The wind was knocked out of me when my stomach hit his shoulder. Why wasn't I struggling to escape? I just couldn't bring myself to care enough. I couldn't even remember what I was doing here in the first place.

I must have fallen asleep, because the next thing I remember was waking up with a new clarity. Now that I had the presence of mind to escape, though, my hands were tied. Karim was lying beside me, still passed out. I thought back to what happened after we drank the water, when everything started to glitter. The mossy rocks littered about the cave, the creatures, and Karim were still faintly sparkly, but it wasn't as vivid as before, and I didn't feel drunk like before either. I remembered the two creatures. They were just blurs earlier, but now as I looked at them sitting a few yards away I could identify them as ogres. The plated skin, hard as iron, and ability to speak gave it away. From the stories I'd heard, I knew ogres were not the most brilliant, but they weren't simpletons either. Over our heads, there was a stone ceiling littered with what appeared to be icicles made of rock. We were in a cave. It was plenty tall for the ogres, though I guessed they had to crouch at the corners.

"Do we have to wait for them? Can we at least start the fire?" the brown ogre complained in a deep, oafish voice. He was sitting on a giant rock next to the blue-gray one, both of them between us and the cave opening. Neither of them noticed that I was awake now, but I was sure if I somehow got untied, I'd never run fast enough to escape.

"They won't be much longer." The blue one used a giant stick, more like a small tree, to itch a spot between his shoulder blades. Pieces of the tree splintered away, ground down by the ogre's thick armor.

I had to think of a way to get out of this. If I died here, Pennah would remain trapped. I scooted closer to Karim and nudged him. Nothing. I plugged his nose, but then he just breathed through his mouth. I would have dumped water on him, but our packs were right next to the blue ogre's rock. I couldn't slap him; the noise would have been noticed. Instead, I clubbed him in the stomach with my bound hands. His eyes shot open and he let out a lungful of air. I quickly covered his mouth so he didn't shout at me.

I shushed him quietly before removing my hands and pointing to the ogres.

"Are you awake?" I asked him.

"Of course I'm awake, I was just punched in the stomach," he whispered back, glowering at me.

"No, I mean from the water. Can you run?"

He blinked hard. "I think so. Everything is still glittery, but I feel better. More in control." He halfway reached for his sword when he realized it wasn't there. "Amani . . ." He spotted it lying in the dust with his pack by the ogres.

"Take my dagger." I pulled at the hem of my shirt so the dagger's handle was visible. Karim drew it and cut my ropes and the ropes at his feet. Before he could give me the poisonous blade so I could release his hands, the blue ogre's booming voice interrupted us.

"You think that little thing will help? That puny blade can't even pierce my skin." He grabbed Karim's arms and dragged him towards the fire pit. To test the ogre's claim, Karim stabbed down at the ogre's arm, but the blade was deflected by thick-armored skin. Just a little prick would kill him, or at least incapacitate him, but the armor was too thick and it covered every part of him, so finding an exposed area seemed impossible. The ogre laughed loudly.

"Care to try again?" He tossed Karim into the cold fire pit and ash puffed up around him while my dagger clattered harmlessly to the side.

The blue ogre picked up the dagger. It looked like a child's toy in his hand. He was going to use it on Karim.

"You're right!" I shouted, grabbing his attention. "That little knife is hopeless against you. It's no more than a toothpick."

He chuckled. "I like you. I'm sure you'll taste sweet. You're not quite a child anymore, but you're still youthful enough for my tastes."

I nearly gagged then. He liked to eat children? How had I forgotten that part of the stories? Why else would they have been keeping us here? We were still alive because they wanted us fresh for cooking.

The ogre nodded to Karim. "Go over there with your friend where I can see both of you. And don't try anything." Karim obeyed and stood by me, his hands still bound. The blue ogre turned to the brown one. "What are you waiting for?" he bellowed. "Get the fire ready! We are eating sweet meat tonight!"

Chapter 9

SABLE

The blue ogre was twisting the dagger on his kneecap flippantly as the brown one stacked wood chunks in the fire pit. Karim and I were silent.

"You've got a little . . . *flesh* . . . in your teeth." I gestured to my own teeth, wincing at the ridiculousness of my attempted ruse. If I could get him to prick himself or something in his mouth where there was no armor, we might be able to make a run for it. He ignored me, but Karim was glaring at me, willing me to be silent. I spoke again. "No, really, it's just—"

With a stamp of his foot that made the cave shake, the ogre stood and approached me menacingly, dagger in hand. Apparently food that spoke was amusing at first, but quickly became irritating.

"I don't like you as much anymore," he said. His face was remarkably similar to a man's. He had two gray eyes, a knotted nose and a mouth with frighteningly large teeth. His body as a whole was almost twice my size. The bluish, lumpy plates on his face made his sneer uglier.

The commotion distracted the brown ogre from his work. "Hey! You said we couldn't kill them until the others got back!"

The blue one shoved me into the rock wall, a jagged stone digging into my back. His open palm didn't quite reach all the way around my rib cage, and even though my hands were untied, I knew I stood no chance against such a giant. "I won't kill her. I just want a little taste." Karim stepped closer, as if he were about to protest, but what could he do against this creature?

The ogre poked the center of my chest, piercing through my shirt and drawing blood. He dragged the dagger along my skin until blood was seeping in a thick line all the way to my shoulder. I struggled to stay silent. It stung, but no more than a dagger should. The poison on it, since it was my own, had no effect on me.

"Not another word from you," he said menacingly. With a grin, the ogre, still holding me against the wall, brought up the dagger and licked the blood from its tip. Now it was my turn to grin. I could tell from the ogre's face that my poison acted much quicker when ingested than it would have if my dagger had cut him.

He stepped back, his hand dropping from my waist and the dagger slipping from his fingertips. I quickly snatched it up, ready to use it again if the poison didn't do him in. The ogre's face reddened. The poison seemed to be closing up his throat. He swung a sluggish fist at me, but I dodged it easily. The other ogre was beginning to notice just as the blue one fell to his knees, clawing at his neck.

"Brother!" the brown ogre screamed in alarm. Then, he whirled on me. "What have you done?" His brother wasn't dead yet, but he seemed to be as good as. The brown one came charging at me and I readied myself with my dagger, but unless I could reach his neck or face, there didn't seem to be any other unprotected skin for me to use the dagger on.

"Wait!" Karim shouted. This brown ogre wasn't as bright as his dying companion, so he stopped in his charge. "She's a witch with poison blood! Didn't you see what she did to your brother? You can't eat her."

If Karim truly believed my blood was poison, I'd have to remedy that. I didn't want him thinking he could kill other enemies next time by telling them to eat me first.

"I can still kill her!" He resumed in his charge, but I lunged to the side, barely avoiding him.

"If you kill me, I'll put a curse on you!" I told him, going along with Karim's witch theory.

"You are no witch!" the brown ogre bellowed. "It is *fairy* magic I smell on you! And you are no fairy either." He was about to charge again when a loud *clink* of metal on stone sounded. He turned to see Karim wielding his sword, an awkward task since his hands were still bound together. The noise must have been from Karim hitting the ogre on the back of his knees.

Though the sword couldn't have caused him any pain, the ogre hollered and wheeled around on Karim. "Perhaps I should eat you first then!" Karim stumbled to turn around, but before his footing was sure, the ogre swatted the curved sword away and grabbed Karim's upper arms, lifting his whole body. The ogre's mouth was wide open like he was going to take a gargantuan bite.

"No!" I screamed, but there was nothing I could do. At the last second, I turned away. The loud crunch of breaking bones echoed in the cave. Karim yelled out in pain. Just as I forced myself to look, the ogre also cried out. I watched him drop Karim's body to the cave floor and I rushed over to him, surprised by the lack of blood.

"Aaagh!" Broken chunks of bone clattered to the floor as the ogre continued screaming, until the screaming was abruptly cut off. After looking at the ogre's face, I saw that the broken bones weren't Karim's. They were the ogre's shattered teeth. Blood began dripping from the monster's mouth and he was convulsing as he fell to the floor. He was choking on the shards of his own broken teeth, shards that were also tearing up his throat.

Karim groaned loudly as he sat up. He recovered quickly, grabbing Amani and thrusting it into the ogre's throat. I wasn't sure if he wanted to end the ogre's suffering, or make sure he never recovered. Blood flowed freely down the ogre's neck and the convulsing stopped. Karim raised the sword and faced me, at first I flinched, but then Karim wiped Amani on the ogre's trousers and slipped the weapon into his sheath.

"Care to cut me free?" He held his wrists out to me and I sliced through the ropes with my dagger. A bright shimmery shield coated Karim's right shoulder, but it was fading quickly. I tried poking the shimmer, but there was nothing physical to poke.

"What just happened?" I said, gaping. The only response Karim gave me was an uneasy smile.

"We'll talk about this later. For now, we need to leave before the ones they were waiting for get here. They must have heard all this noise."

"Karim, you can't—" Before I finished speaking, a deafening roar shook the cave. Two more ogres, each holding a dead deer, stood at the cave's mouth. Karim drew Amani again. The ogres dropped their deer and rushed at us, the larger green-brown one heading for me and the red-brown one storming after Karim. I sprinted for my sword.

The green ogre was directly behind me when I reached my sword, which was carelessly dropped on top of the packs, so I blindly swung it out at the ogre, hoping at best for this to distract the giant. Instead, my sword sliced cleanly into the ogre's shin, shocking both of us. I seemed to have cut right through the rock-like plating on his leg. He bellowed and swatted me aside. I tumbled over rocks. Once I stopped rolling, I scrambled to my feet and grabbed for my sword again, swinging it at the ogre, who blocked it with his forearm like he always did. However, he was used to his forearm deflecting a blade's blow, but Servans slashed through his armored skin like paper, eliciting another roar from the ogre. Before he recovered from his surprise, I lunged and buried my sword deep in his stomach. He twisted away from me, wrenching Servans from my hands. He pulled the blade out and dropped it to the ground, a heavy flow of blood following.

Satisfied my opponent was distracted, I turned to see Karim barely dodging the other ogre's swinging fists. For some reason, Karim's sword couldn't pierce the ogre's skin like mine could. While rolling away from the beast's hands, Karim thrust his sword into the top of the ogre's foot. It didn't deflect like I expected, but instead buried itself deep into the foot. A scream erupted from the red-brown ogre. The spot Karim pierced wasn't actually covered by plating. It was scarred over, but there was clearly some old injury that left an exposed area of flesh.

The ogre stumbled and flung his hands out to catch himself. As he fell, Karim cut his throat. The ogre died quickly.

Karim wiped the ogre's blood on the fur vest the now dead ogre wore. In that moment, he seemed frighteningly ruthless. I reminded myself that not two minutes ago, I too had killed one of the ogres. Two if I counted the poison. Remembering my own sword, I cleaned the blood off and sheathed it.

After sheathing the sword that still carried small streaks of ogre's blood, Karim grabbed his pack and offered me mine. For a moment, I didn't take it. We had just killed four ogres. It had all happened so fast. I knew I would encounter danger in the Black Forest when I chased after Pennah, but I never expected this.

"I don't think any others are coming, but it might be wise to move on," he suggested, dropping the bag into my waiting hand. I pulled the heavy pack on and nodded. On the way out of the cave, Karim paused by one of the dead deer. I hadn't noticed my hunger until then.

"We wouldn't want it to go to waste," I commented. Stealing from the dead was never a good idea. But since they were ogres, did the rule still apply? And it wasn't as if we were stealing money. It was just a dead deer that happened to be in the home of dead occupants.

"I agree." Using a long, thick branch from the ogre's wood pile and the scraps of rope that we had been tied with earlier, we fashioned a kind of spit to carry the deer until we had walked a good enough distance from the cave. Since neither of us knew where the road was, we settled for walking west, the general direction the road seemed to go in anyway. We mostly followed game trails, but when they veered off toward the water again, we had to forge our way through the brush.

After clearing an area to camp in for the night, we agreed that a fire was necessary to cook the deer, and we decided to keep it burning as long as we could. If anything suspicious came along, we could always put the fire out and move on.

"I don't suppose you're going to finally tell me how you killed that ogre?" I asked Karim across the fire. It was dark outside, but we were still eating as much of the deer as we could stomach. Who knew when fresh meat would be available again?

Karim paused in his meal. "It's not fair to expect full disclosure when you are so hesitant to tell me anything about yourself." The moment the immediate danger was passed, Karim had returned to his normal, chipper self, chatting away as we carried the deer through the woods and set up camp.

"We are traveling together. You must tell me something about your magic. Are you immortal?" Now that would truly be a curse. Who wanted to live in a world like this forever?

He laughed softly. "Hardly." After a pause, he continued. "If I tell you, do you promise to tell me how you came upon your fairy-curse?"

"Fine." It couldn't hurt telling him the details.

"Alright. It happened when I was a baby, nearly two years old. My four older brothers had all died by this time, none of them reaching sixteen years of age."

"How did they die?" I interrupted.

"Different reasons. Khayri was trampled by a horse as a child. Naveed was killed when a gamble went wrong." He trailed off. Matthew, Pennah's father and my stepfather, was killed in a similar way. He owed many people too much money. I don't think they meant to kill him, but the beating was too severe for Matthew to survive. "Anyway, my father wanted to protect me. He thought this was best accomplished through dark magic. He tracked down a genie, and an exchange was made. The price for my immunity to anything that would kill me was much steeper than he expected though. My family lost everything they held dear. And that is why I am here, with you. I am hoping Pennah can help us."

At least now I knew his reasons weren't purely selfish. Now, he was silently waiting for me to fulfill my half of the bargain. Reluctantly, I told him the story of how Pennah and I came across the fairy and how I was cursed. I told him nothing of how my Uncle Morrin abandoned us when he found out or how, because of the curse, my mother died.

Karim watched me carefully as I told my story. At the end, I met his eyes and found, of all things, sympathy.

After my father had died, when Mama was married to Matthew, I would walk in to town with bruises lining my arms and covering my face at times. He never touched Pennah, in fact he mostly ignored her, but to him, I was nothing but an unwelcome mouth to feed and body to shelter. When I was covered in bruises, people looked at me with this same look. But since my fairy curse, I had *never* been looked at with sympathy. Squirming and unsure of what to do with this look, I stood and took out my canteen and salve to prevent infection. Using as little water as I could manage, I washed the cut running across my chest as well as I could under the given circumstances and sparingly dabbed some salve on the wound. It was shallow, and after the water and salve, it didn't even really hurt anymore.

Before returning to the fire, I took a deep drink of the magic infused water. After leaving the ogres' cave, Karim and I slowly sipped the water. We discovered that the effects weren't nearly as strong in small doses. In fact, the more water we drank over time, the less intoxicating its effects were. The sparkles never went away, but they did get easier to look past.

Fortunately, when I sat back down, Karim's sad eyes had disappeared and he was now watching the flames dance against the darkness.

"You should get some sleep," I told him. I silently vowed not to fall asleep this time.

He nodded and he laid down on the shoulder that hadn't been chomped down on by the ogre. Apparently, while nothing could *kill* him, he could still be hurt. No doubt his shoulder had a giant bite-mark shaped bruise.

It was harder than last time to stay awake. I didn't have the same ever-present gnawing hunger to keep me alert. I hadn't been this full in ages. For the next few hours I entertained myself by stoking the fire and cleaning my own blood from my dagger, not to mention the ogre saliva, taking care to leave as much poison as I could on it as I cleaned. I momentarily wished I could tear up on command so I could replenish the poison coating. When I was really bored, I antagonized a hairy spider I found crawling on my shoe until it ran away into the forest.

Around the time I could barely keep my eyes open, I decided to wake Karim, who groggily switched places with me.

Chapter 10

PENNAH

"Raaaa!" I shouted and swatted at the sprites that were always in my tower room. They flew in from my window and always stole the smaller gems that my captor missed. I wouldn't have bothered shooing them, except they were infatuated with my hair. They pulled it and poked me. Sprites were obsessed with shiny things, I was coming to discover.

The neon blue sprite closest to my face hissed and bared its tiny, sharp teeth at me. In the end, there was only one way to get rid of a sprite.

"You are pretty little things, aren't you? With shiny, dragonfly wings, and your tiny hands are adorable." I spit a small sapphire into my hand and held it up for the sprites to see. They zipped through the air straight for the jewel and followed it when I flung it out the window. That should last an hour or so.

"Hideous wretches," I muttered once they were gone. A small emerald clanked to the floor. That was strange. I held it up to the light. Before I was taken to this castle, every gem I produced was perfect, unflawed. This one had a spiderwebbed opaque center. I tossed it at the door where my host would easily find it.

For the first full day and night I cried on and off for hours. I missed Sable. I missed Mama, and the way she used to lay with me when I had nightmares as a child. There came a certain point when Mama stopped doing that and Sable was the one I went to, but I'd never stop missing Mama. I just wished she wasn't stuck in bed all the time. I could barely remember a time when she wasn't cooped up in her room all day long. I even missed Sable's snakes. I had forgotten what a problem rats could be when there were no snakes around to eat them. I'd wake up in my tiny tower room to find the rodents skittering about, gnawing on stray gems, my clothes, or sometimes even my toes, only making me cry more. My dress wasn't quite long enough to cover my bare feet when I slept, so even when they weren't spattered with little bites, they were aching with cold.

Yesterday morning, I made a decision I didn't think I was capable of. I decided to stop wasting my tears on *him*. My nightmarish kidnapper. He only appeared once or twice a day to bring me food and collect the various gemstones lying around my room, many of which were diamond tears. Last night, he was sullen to find no more crystalline teardrops. I had never been so happy to disappoint someone before.

Often, like now, I'd find myself staring at the door. I had checked; it was unlocked. Should I try my luck? If I only peeked through each door, would some monster still bite my head off? What kind of creatures could he house here? There was always the chance he was bluffing, but I had heard enough strange noises to doubt that. At night I heard howling, growling, screeching, even screaming that sounded far too human. Were there other cursed humans here like me?

Without knocking, my host walked right in. He saw the flawed emerald on the ground and didn't bother picking it up.

"Pennah, you were providing me with such beautiful gems yesterday. What happened?" He looked younger again, and the blood was completely washed from his beard, but I knew the youthful, handsome face was just an illusion.

"I don't like giving you the satisfaction." I folded my arms, more in defense than in defiance. This man scared me without doing a thing. "Besides, don't you have magic of your own? Why don't *you* make the jewels today?"

"Magic has its limits, Pennah," he instructed bitterly. He opened his palm to reveal an opal, only to tilt his hand and drop it to the ground. It landed unnaturally and silently. Then, it vanished. It was just an illusion.

"So you are telling me that you are a glorified magician?" I said as I stood up.

"Well, it's nice to see you still have some beauty left in you." He crouched to pick up a rose I hadn't noticed. As he grabbed it, he immediately dropped it and inspected his hand. It was bleeding. Strange. My roses never had thorns before.

He crushed my rose under his boot, thorns and all. Without another word, he left.

Being so deep in the Black Forest somehow affected my curse. Normally, gems wouldn't appear unless I spoke or did something kind. Now, just thinking how much I missed Mama and Sable, dark opals with hidden rainbow flecks clanked to the floor. Sometimes I'd throw them out the window, but I knew he'd get them somehow, so half the time I didn't bother touching them. I hated to think it, but I could really use a deadly viper right now.

"Nice to see you looking well." In the last few days, I'd discovered that his voice was deceptively smooth, which wasn't surprising for a master of illusions. He set a tray of food on the floor and opened the door behind him wider until I saw three more figures. All lethargy from earlier vanished as I jumped to my feet and backed into the wall, which suddenly didn't seem nearly far enough away.

"What are those?" Fear shook my voice. The three stubby creatures behind him had warty skin that varied in blotches of dark green, gray, and brown, leading me to believe that if we were in the forest, they would have been invisible if that was their wish. Though they were shorter than my waist, ferocious claws hung at the end of long, gangly arms that almost scraped the floor. Their legs weren't short enough to make them slow and when I yelled out, they all bared their long, curved teeth. Their protruding lower jaws made them seem even more brutish.

"Goblins." The man snapped his fingers haughtily and all the creatures looked to him expectantly, their growls silenced. "Continue," he told them. One of them, the one that stood apart because of the small pearl that was somehow attached to the hollow of his throat, produced a low, hiss-growl before they proceeded to lug a washtub into my room.

He gestured for the creatures to follow him out and the door closed behind him.

I resentfully ate the food he left for me. Ironically, I ate better here than I often did at home, but I was never sure if I was eating an illusion. For all I knew, my captor had the ability to make rat meat look and taste like fish.

Once I finished eating, I figured I might as well wash my face and hair while I had the washtub here. Before reaching into the bin, I stared at my reflection for a moment. I felt like I should be seeing someone different, but I looked exactly the same. My golden hair gleamed, even in the duller, warped parody the water showed me. Dirt obscured my small nose and pink lips. The overall grime almost made my skin the same tan shade Sable's always was at the end of summer. Tired of watching myself, I slapped the surface of the water, ripples distorting the image. I watched as the water slowly returned to its previous glassy form. I reached again, this time to actually wash myself, but before I touched the surface a stream of water jetted into my face. What was that?

With cupped hands, I reached for the water again. This time, a face appeared in the surface and shouted in a whiny, gurgling voice, "Go away!"

I screamed and accidentally hit my knee against the basin as I scrambled away, jostling the basin and sloshing some water onto the floor.

A face formed again, sounding like a burbling creek as eyes, a nose, and a mouth became more distinct, but this time it peered over the edge of the basin at me, its fingers clutching at the side.

"Do you mind? I don't have much water to begin with," the small voice said. This time, I recognized that it was a young girl. And she was made of water. I leaned forward, but she dissolved back into the basin.

"Wait! Who are you?" I pleaded. She remained silent.

I waited, asking again every once and a while, but she said nothing for the rest of the day. I began to think I might have imagined the whole encounter.

Chapter 11

SABLE

After another half day of walking, I was seriously beginning to doubt we'd find the road or creek again. We'd run out of water in the next day or so.

"We need to climb a tree. Maybe you can see the castle from above the treetops," I suggested.

"Alright. Pick the tallest tree you see." We looked up. Every tree in sight was extraordinarily tall. They were all so close in height that it probably didn't matter which one we picked. I chose the one nearest us with decently sized bark chunks, making good footholds. It also had some lower branches, which would be helpful.

"Would you like to go, or should I?" I asked him.

"Well, seeing as I've never climbed a tree before in my life, I think having you do it is a good idea," he told me, like it was nothing.

"Never?" I gaped. I had been climbing trees since I was a child. I'd assumed everyone had had a similar experience.

"Have you ever been to Sukkad? It isn't exactly known for its tall trees. Also my parents were highly protective," he said, matter-of-factly. "If they knew where I was now, they'd each have a heart attack."

"But what if I fall and die? Wouldn't it be better if you did it, since you won't die no matter what happens?" I truly didn't mind climbing trees. I was never afraid of heights. Karim's hesitation to climb one was very entertaining, though.

"If you feared death, you wouldn't have come running headlong into the Black Forest," he said before adding, "I will wait here at the bottom and catch you, but I suspect you are quite adept at climbing trees."

I rolled my eyes and shrugged off my heavy pack. I unlatched my sword and set it at the trunk's base with my bag. The tree was easy enough to climb. The bark was rough, so I never once thought I would slip. It was a strangely tall tree, so it took a while, but eventually, I made it to the top. Out of breath, I looked out, but saw only treetops shifting in the wind. Who builds a castle in the middle of a forest and fails to make even the watchtower taller than the trees? I did one more scan and while I saw no castle, there was something suspicious off to the north. Dark storm clouds seemed to be moving quickly toward us.

I clambered down the tree and reported what I saw to Karim. "We have a little time before it gets here, but we should try to find some kind of shelter," I told him.

"We could always try to find the ogres' cave again," he suggested.

I considered it for a moment before rejecting the idea. "Not only would it take us too long to go back, but I'm not sure we could even find it again, unless you are some kind of tracking expert."

"Tracking is nearly useless in the desert, so it isn't exactly a highly valued skill where I'm from, unfortunately."

I sighed. A small part of me had been hoping that part of the curse meant the bestowal of the ability we desperately needed right now. This trek was looking more and more hopeless every day. "West it is, then." And we started off again.

After about an hour of uneventful walking westward, a slow drizzle began, adding an immediate layer of moisture to the low brush.

"This isn't so bad." Karim held out his hands palm up, letting the soft rain patter onto his skin. A loud screech sounded in the distance followed by the deep rumble of thunder. In a split second, his curved blade was out and ready.

"Was that an animal?" I wondered aloud, a slight edge of panic in my voice. The screech sounded again, and another round of thunder ensued. A huge wave of wind struck us from the side and we both stumbled to regain our balance. The rain was heavier now, and much louder. I had to raise my voice to be heard.

"Look!" I pointed ahead of us. Several deer darted past us, fleeing from the incoming storm. Rabbits and squirrels scrambled away as well. Rain was falling in thick sheets now and the wind was relentlessly hitting us, wave after wave. The screech and thunder, much closer now, was accompanied by a flash of lightning. I thought back to the stories of legendary monsters I heard as a child and realized what was happening.

"I think this is a stormhawk!" I yelled to Karim. I wasn't sure if he heard me. Suddenly, no explanation was required. A humongous bird with wet, black feathers that shimmered silver with every lightning flash descended below the treetops. With the flapping of his wings to approach the ground, a gale knocked us off our feet. We both sat in the mud for a moment, just watching the terrifying scene unfold. The stormhawk's white striped tail feathers flared and its talons, each as thick and sharp as a spearhead, flashed as it grabbed for a small deer that barely escaped the predator's deadly grip. Instead of ripping through his prey's flesh, the stormhawk's talons dug deep into the soil, creating a ripple of thunder that shook the ground. The creature that could have used my entire house as a nest took off again, rising above the trees. As it reappeared between trees, I noticed the layer of sparkles under its skin, like a ghost within the creature. These sparkles seemed to be everywhere. What did they mean?

Figuring staying in place wasn't a good idea, I stood up, the mud trying to keep me glued in place every step of the way. Karim sheathed his sword and I gave him a hand up. Another screech filled the air, this time so high pitched it hurt my ears, and the stormhawk reappeared, talons bared. And it was headed straight for us.

"Move!" I screamed, but I could barely even hear myself over the crash of rain. We tried to bolt away, but the mud was impossible to move in, holding onto us like sticky hands. Karim managed to get out of the mud patch first, but the bird was so close I could see the reflection of lightning in its glassy black eyes. I lunged, reaching out for Karim, but slipped face first into the molasses-like mud. The stormhawk's talons grabbed the air just above my backpack before swooping away for another attack. As Karim dragged me free of the mud, I could see a small brown scorpion struggling in the puddle, suffering the deadly fate I narrowly avoided. Once I was up I wiped as much sludge from my face as I could and we ran.

My clothes and pack were already waterlogged, making it ten times more difficult to run away from the stormhawk. At least the rain was washing off some of the mud that covered every inch of me. We dodged one more strike from the beast. Hopefully, it would give up on chasing us and go after another terror-stricken deer. The trees gave us cover, but the stormhawk's eyes were keen, even in the middle of all the rain and wind that made it hard to see anything more than a few feet away.

"Sable!" Karim's shouting sounded far away, but he was right beside me. "Over there!" He pointed to a small canopy of trees that seemed to protect a patch of grass from the raging storm. We sprinted for it, barely able to move in a straight line because of the winds that constantly swept at us, threatening to knock us over again. Just when the screeching and lightning sounded dangerously close again, we entered the eerily quiet haven.

Amid the thunder I hadn't heard our heavy breathing, but now it was the only sound there seemed to be. The rain was a soft background noise and the stormhawk, apparently having lost track of us while we were under the canopy, seemed to be flying away. Of course the storm would remain for a while, but there was no immediate threat anymore.

For a moment, we just stood in silence while we caught our breath. Drops of water slid down my face, collecting on my nose and chin until I wiped the moisture away. For the first time, I was conscious of the scent of rain and soil. When we weren't running for our lives through slick mud, the smell was actually refreshing.

"What a strange place," Karim observed, pulling off his backpack and jacket, both of which needed to be wrung out. Even the wind was less intense, thanks to the wide tree trunks and thick shrubs encircling us. I also removed my pack and jacket, knowing we might be here for a while waiting for the rain to stop. After wringing out all the clothes I could afford to take off, including my shoes, stockings, jacket and a light sweater I had put on when I first saw the storm approaching, I hung them on various knots on the tree.

I knew we were hopelessly lost and now we might never find the castle Pennah was being held in, but I was so tired I decided to worry about it after having rested for a while. Karim and I laid out our bedrolls and blankets, but it was clear that the slight chill that remained in the small haven was preferable to sleeping under a sopping wet blanket, so we both ended up sprawling in the soft, tall grass. I nuzzled my face into the meadow ground, noting the way each blade glistened. Ever since we drank that water, everything seemed to sparkle like that.

The ring of trees looked like they had woven their branches together, creating a blanket of cover, revealing none of the stormy sky above it. Everything about this place was peaceful. It felt like the blades of pale green grass were hugging me. They smelled fresh, like spring. And there was something else. Something I hadn't felt in a long time.

I felt safe.

Chapter 12

PENNAH

Every time I left the room, I made it maybe ten minutes before a goblin scared me back into my isolated tower dungeon. However, I didn't stop trying. Today I left the girl in the washtub to walk around the castle. So far I hadn't made it down enough stairs to get close to where the exit probably was. I dodged several goblins and eventually made it down to a main level, maybe the third floor.

I pressed my ear to one door after another, trying to gauge what creature could possibly be hidden behind it. One door held human voices. My heart leapt in my chest, fluttering excitedly. A small sunflower even fell out of my sleeve, adding a flash of yellow to the grim, stony castle whose colors had all muted after years of disuse. As it turned out, I had excited myself for nothing.

"I'm tired of living out here in an abandoned castle. You promised me riches, and power!" a woman's voice snapped. I didn't recognize her voice, but the response was familiar enough to send chills across my skin.

"I told you it was a matter of time. We will get there. You must be patient." It was the man who kidnapped me. Apparently, he was not the only one who lived here of his own free will.

"I have been patient for fifteen years!" she seethed.

"Then I suppose one more will feel like nothing!" A loud crash accompanied the man's shout, as if he had thrown something. Stomping feet headed this way. My throat seized in fear. He was coming! With no thought for what lay on the other side, I threw the neighboring door open and jumped inside, closing it behind me as quickly and as quietly as I could.

A sleeping mound of fur blacker than the night opened one silvery eye and watched me as I stood frozen in terror. With a low growl, the beast got up on its haunches. It was a bear, but it was bigger than any I'd ever seen. Its paw was as wide as my torso. The sound of metal scraping against metal rang in the room as the short claws extended into razor sharp knives that sung when the bear shifted, cutting through the air. Its silver eyes narrowed on me, fierce and angry—as if I was the one who trapped it here and killing me would set it free. With a roar that shook the room, the bear's claws lashed out at me. Just before I was turned into a spool of human ribbon, the back of my dress was pulled out through the now open doorway. The man who had kidnapped me tossed me against the banister, slamming the door into the face of the gigantic bear and looming over me.

"That was close." He gestured to a small hole in my dress. "A Black Ursa's claws can cut through any physical object. Fortunately for it, I haven't figured out how to harvest the claws yet. If they are disconnected from living tissue, they last a week at most before decaying away into useless bone.

"Next time I catch you snooping, I'm going to let whatever friend you find have their way with you before I come to your rescue. Understand?"

I gave a tiny nod. "Good." Out of nowhere, a troop of goblins appeared. "Please return her to her room," the man ordered.

Chapter 13

SABLE

My eyes fluttered open.

The rain had stopped and the canopy that was water-tight before somehow let the sunlight in. It felt so warm on my skin, like the whole glen was a bubble made of sunshine, separate from the rest of the world and perfect beyond compare.

Karim's honey colored skin glowed in the light, his dark hair curling on his forehead just a little. His eyelashes were long and his lips were curved up in the slightest as he slept.

I smiled.

It was nice here.

Chapter 14

PENNAH

"Get lost!" I swatted at the sprites. Some were grabbing at my hair, stealing a few strands of gold along with real hair they had yanked from my scalp, some were fawning over the jewels scattered about the room, and the others were watching the almost imperceptible ripples the faint breeze sent across the wash basin's surface. I flapped my hands at the ones watching the water and they bit my fingers before joining their comrades staring at an opal. I grabbed all the gems I could find and tossed them out the window. The flock of sprites trailed after.

"Thanks," a small voice bubbled from the basin. The water girl was peering at me again.

"Don't disappear again," I told her gently, desperately. She had remained silent for three days. There were times I knew she was watching me, but every time I looked at the water, she was gone.

Staying visible, she drifted to the back of the wash basin, her shoulders and knees peeking up above the surface like she was *in* the water rather than part of it.

"What are you doing here?" she asked. "You're just a human." As she spoke, her face became more solid, taking on a pearly hue. Her hair was plant-like, the purple tendrils cascading down until they became water at the ends. If I had to guess, I'd say she was nine or ten, in human years at least.

"A fairy curse gives me the ability to make jewels when I speak."

"I thought humans liked jewels." She was wary still, but at least she was speaking to me. I was tired of sitting in silence.

"That is why I'm here. That man . . ." I still didn't know his name, "wanted the jewels."

"Yes, but then why do you call it a curse?" Her eyes had become a very solid shade of blue that seemed to ripple as she watched me.

I paused. I called it a curse because that's what Sable always called it. I couldn't say I hated it. If I had control over it, I might love it. Then I could be with people, in the world, and not have to hide. And I could help people.

Instead I answered truthfully, "Because nothing good ever comes from it." After a moment of silence, I continued. "Why are you here?"

"Do you know nothing?" She shifted in the water, sitting more upright. "I am a water nymph. We are very powerful beings." There was pride in her voice, a trait that I had learned to associate with the worst kind of people, my current captor included.

"So powerful that you've been caught in a bathtub?" I immediately regretted saying it, suddenly afraid she might disappear again.

She slouched, thoroughly humbled. "This foolish human invention. Nature provides rivers and ponds and lakes and oceans. Why do you need more?" She continued sinking until only her eyes were above the water.

"What kind of power do you have?" I tried to reengage her in the conversation.

She had to bring her mouth out of the water to speak. "I don't have any." Her cerulean eyes rippled. "My mother is very strong with dominion magic, though."

"Dominion magic?"

"The pearl you saw at the goblin's throat?" I nodded in recognition. "That was my mother's magic. It allows the wielder of the twin pearl to control the goblin. And since that is the king of that tribe, whoever controls the king can control the entire tribe."

"And that man has the twin pearl?" I guessed. That would explain why the goblin followed him like a dog.

"Marcus," the water nymph spat, like the name tasted rancid. "The warlock keeping us all here." So he was a warlock. That explained the power of illusion. He must have had some magical creature for an ancestor, maybe a fairy or a dryad.

"What other creatures does he keep here?" I asked her, almost afraid to know the answer.

"How should I know? I'm stuck in this ugly bin," she said with a frown. Apparently once she stopped being shy, this water girl was very haughty, especially for a nine-year-old. She went on. "I think I heard a griffin a while back, crying."

"But now that he has the pearl from your mother, he has what he wants. Why doesn't he just let you go?" Did water nymphs have other magical gifts Marcus wanted to exploit?

Angry steam rose from the water girl's skin. "Because he's human. And humans never have enough power." She disappeared into the now boiling washtub.

Chapter 15

SABLE

The crackling and popping of a fire slowly woke me. It felt like my head was stuffed with wool. I forced my eyes open and the morning sky hung overhead, hazy with purples and pinks. My head lolled to one side and I saw Karim in his natural state: sleeping. Not yet ready to sit up, I shifted my head to see to the left. A stout creature wearing an ornate blue tunic poked at a fire and rotated the squirrel it had speared on a roasting stick. I should have been more alarmed, but I could barely see through the heavy fog that had settled on my mind.

"Stupid heroes, making amateur mistakes . . ." The creature's pointed, floppy ears swayed as it shook its head. ". . . hate meddling . . ."

I tried to say 'Excuse me' but all that came out was a dry cough. I hadn't realized how parched I was. Now, my throat suddenly felt as if it had been scoured out with sand.

"So the heroine finally awakens." The creature turned and squinted at me with wrinkled eyes. He itched at his beard before taking a bite from his roasted squirrel. He snatched up a canteen, *my* canteen, and held it to my lips. Halfway through finishing, I found the strength to hold it myself. With the last few droplets, I splashed Karim. He stirred, but slept on. I sealed the canteen and threw it at him, hitting the side of his face. His eyes opened and he began taking in our situation.

I sat up all the way on my bedroll, which sent my head swimming. The last thing I remembered was falling asleep in the small glen.

"Did we intrude on your home? If so, I'm sorry." My voice was hoarse.

"Home? Do they teach you humans nothing nowadays?" He spoke like an old man. In fact, if his skin weren't so grayish and wrinkly with such an odd, squished nose, I might have guessed he was just an extraordinarily small old man. "That was the Bosk Snare. Every fool should know not to go in there. It's like a Venus fly trap. From the moment you enter it, it begins lulling you into a sense of security and it puts you into a sleep so deep you may never wake. Unless of course some friendly gnome happens to be following you and drags the two of you out on your bedrolls."

"Venus what?" I asked, my brain still sorting through the excess of unfamiliar words this strange old-man-like creature just threw at me.

"Gnome?" Karim sat up as well.

"The name is Grem," the gnome responded with a bow, roasted squirrel still in hand. "And since you two seem to have some serious gaps in your knowledge of legends and lore, I have taken it upon myself to inform you.

"Gnomes are great collectors of tales and legends. Stories with no survivors are told by gnomes. In fact, most stories humans tell were brought from magical places like the Black Forest by gnomes. Sleeping Beauty, Little Red Riding Hood, Jorinda and Jorindel, The Frog Prince—all brought to humanity by gnomes. As a general rule, we stay hidden and we do not meddle in the affairs of main characters, or even minor characters. However, I have never been one to always keep the rules, and I haven't told a really good story since Snowdrop. And I've had glimpses, so I know yours will be one of the greats. Passion, intrigue, secrets, death."

"Passion?" Karim's face was still sleepy, so I couldn't read his expression, but that was not the part I was concerned with at the moment.

"Death?" I whispered.

"Yes, yes. Keep up. Gnomes have glimpses of the future, but that hardly gives us the entire story. To know that, we must follow our heroes from the shadows until the very end."

"You know the future? Can you tell me where Pennah is? How do we get to the castle? Can you get her out?"

"A little, yes, I'll get to that, and no. No meddling."

"But you meddled by getting us out of that snare."

Grem's face turned serious. "Would you like me to put you back?"

Karim, now more alert, shook his head. "No, we appreciate what you've done already. Did you say you could take us to the castle?"

"Of course." He took another bite from his squirrel and continued speaking, allowing the rest of us to see the squirrel meat in his mouth. "I know every inch of this forest."

"Then let's go!" I leaped to my feet and the world spun in response.

"Oh, please. It's only been two days since the Bosk Snare started sucking away at your life force." Grem scrutinized my face. "You didn't think that was *grass*, did you? It was the Snare's tendrils. They would have slowly eaten you until you were just a husk. You will need a while longer to recuperate."

I got to my knees and began rolling up the mat I had slept on, noticing the drag marks behind it for the first time. Though the thought of eating made me nauseous, I snatched a piece of sodden bread Grem had been soaking and began chewing the stale meal with difficulty.

"Generally, one companion asks another before laying claim to his food," Grem commented, though he made no motion to stop me.

"Heroes fainting from hunger don't often make a good story," I retorted, ripping off another piece of bread. Grem, thoroughly entertained, clapped his hands and rubbed them together.

"Off we go!" He snapped his fingers and the fire snuffed itself out, making me wonder what other hidden talents our odd friend had. "Out of bed, prince charming. A lady knight needs her squire." Grem whipped the blanket off of Karim's sleeping body.

"Squire?" he pouted. I could imagine the sound of creaking bones that had lain stiff for two whole days as Karim stretched his arms and legs out before carefully getting to his feet, cautious and unsteady as a newborn foal.

"Pennah is *my* sister," I pointed out.

"But I have a quest here too." Karim gathered his things. "I like to think of us as partners."

"Fine, *partner*, let's get going." I hefted my bag onto my shoulders, putting a hand on a tree when blackness edged my vision and my knees weakened. Karim said nothing as he also got situated. Finally, once my vision had cleared, Grem led the way.

Now that day had returned with clear skies, the Black Forest didn't look nearly as frightening. It was amazing what a small amount of sunshine will do. There was no path, but our gnome guide seemed to know exactly where he was going. He spent much of the time recounting the part of the story we'd already lived through. Apparently, he had a glimpse of me, Karim and Pennah several months ago with whatever psychic powers gnomes had, and simply waited and followed us until the story began to unravel.

"When Pennah was taken, the roses were just the perfect touch. Very mysterious and beautiful, just like Pennah. Of course, the response your mother gave when you told her what happened was tragic, traitorous even—"

Shame at the memory of my mother's death ripped through my gut like claws. A sudden realization dawned on me. "You were there? For everything?" He was lurking somewhere nearby while my mother was dying at my hand. He has magic. He probably could have stopped it. I almost said this in my outburst, but Karim was here. It shouldn't matter if he knew since he couldn't hurt me anyway, but I couldn't let Grem tell him about my mother. No one needed to know how black my soul truly was.

"Of course I was there."

I pushed down the shame and focused on my frustration with the wrinkly gnome. "You just watched while that man took Pennah and you did nothing?" I grabbed Grem's tunic to force him to look at me when he answered, but the second I felt cotton in my hands, it was gone. Grem's voice came again from behind me as a patronizing growl.

"It is not my job to protect *your* sister. I am a gnome. It is in my nature to simply watch. I helped you only to satisfy my own craving for the end to your story, whether it is happy or tragic. Do not mistake my favor for benevolence." In that moment, I realized that making enemies with a gnome would prove fatal. We were not friends. He just wanted to know the end of the story and he wanted to see us live to the climax.

Karim, somehow always lighthearted, continued walking. "So Grem, were you really there for Snowdrop?"

Grem's genial nature returned as if nothing had happened, making his abrupt but ephemeral anger even more frightening. "Yes, yes. But mankind always has a way with warping truths. There were only six dwarves. Humans seem to favor the number seven, though. No story ever retains its integrity for long. In a hundred years when your story is being told, who knows. Perhaps Sable will be the villain." He looked at me with a knowing twinkle in his eye. Biting down on my guilt, I averted my eyes. I decided I didn't care if I was the villain in Grem's silly stories. My soul was already filthy. I just wanted to save my sister.

Chapter 16

SABLE

"I'm starving," I muttered to Karim, who had spent most of our walk indulging Grem and his story telling. Karim's stomach growled as if in response. Grem was in the middle of explaining how the prince discovered Rapunzel when I spotted a pear tree. Somehow, morning dew still clung to the plump fruits, glittering with temptation. My mouth watered and before I knew it, I was at the base of the tree plucking a pear about to take a bite.

"NO! No no no no no! Stop, you foolish girl!" Grem's gnarled, gray hand came out of nowhere and swatted the pear from my grasp.

"What? I'm hungry and we've been walking for hours." And we had very little food left in our packs, so anything we found along the way was more than welcome.

"Look at that tree. You've had enough water to see it clearly. What do you see?"

"Lunch," I told him as I pulled another pear from the tree. He swatted it away as well.

"The water allows you to see magic now."

"Is that what the sparkles are? Magic?" I looked at the tree again. It was indeed covered with sparkling bits. Most things in the Black Forest were, though I had noticed some things sparkling more than others. The stormhawk, the Bosk Snare, and even Karim sparkled more than average. I had started getting used to it and more often than not, I just ignored it. Perhaps I should pay more attention.

"Yes. You know nothing about this tree. There are many plants in the Black Forest. Some bestow great strength, healing, or other magical gifts, but others can be deadly."

"Poison won't kill me." I grabbed a third pear. What could a little magical pear possibly do?

"I can assure you that an exploding stomach will," he said matter-of-factly. I dropped the pear. "These are Infinitum Pears. They are extremely delicious. In fact, anyone who takes even a single bite cannot resist eating and eating and eating until their stomach bursts and they die." The way he said it made me feel like a child being told that fire is hot. "Just don't eat anything magical unless you have suicide in mind. And most deaths wouldn't be as enjoyable as one by delicious pear." He picked up a pear and took a bite.

"But, you just said—" I half expected him to start ravenously shoving his face with pears, but he continued through the forest, munching on the pear contently.

"I'm a gnome," was his response, as if that explained everything.

I rejoined Karim behind our guide and he just shrugged sympathetically. Eventually, we found a non-magical tree with a fruit I'd never had before. It had brown fuzz on the outer skin, but the inside was green, juicy, and sweet. We grabbed a handful of the fruits and put them in our bags. I just hoped we got to Pennah before they started rotting. I knew she'd like them.

When the sun had dropped below the trees, warning us of the coming dusk, Karim suggested we make camp.

"We're about an hour away. Did you want to infiltrate the castle by day, or in cover of darkness?" Hope, an unfamiliar feeling, swelled inside me at Grem's words. An hour away? I had expected a week-long journey. Either gnomes had an uncanny way of traveling quicker or the castle was much closer than I had planned.

"I don't suppose you have a map of the castle, or some sort of building design?" Karim asked Grem, who just stared back unemotionally. "I didn't think so. Do you know where Pennah is being kept in the castle?" Another blank stare. "Lovely." Karim turned to me expectantly.

"Don't look at me. I make snakes appear, and that won't do us much good. And unfortunately, I doubt there will be a trail of jewels leading us straight to her."

"We'll have to decide once we're there then." I didn't like the idea of fleeing through the Black Forest at night with Pennah in tow behind us, but we seemed to have no other choice.

An hour later, the last bits of sunlight had faded and only the half moon lit our way. Anticipation sent ripples of energy through my veins. We were almost there. I could almost sense Pennah's nearness.

"Grem?" Karim's whisper broke through the silent night, making the lack of forest sounds obvious and eerie. Karim and I glanced around. Grem was gone.

"Some help that old gnome was," I muttered. A small snake slipped across my shoe and slithered back the way we came. "We've got to be close." We took no more than ten paces forward when the giant looming Black Castle appeared. It was a mystery how such a large castle remained unseen in this forest until we were right upon it. Vines imbued with magic striped the façade that hung directly in front of us. Even in the darkness I could tell that the Black Forest was still in the process of swallowing the castle whole. Assuming there used to be more to the kingdom than just the castle, it seemed like the forest was almost finished erasing the Black Kingdom from existence. Trees grew right beside the wall pulling up some bricks at the base and some branches had burst right through some of the windows. Even the Black Castle wouldn't last much longer.

"Do you think he's living out here all alone? Or do you think he has guards?" Karim said quietly.

"We can walk around to the front and find out. I don't know how he'd convince people to come out all this way to guard an empty castle though," I muttered back to him. We carefully crept through the thick copse of trees lining the entire castle's perimeter. We had reached the end of the wall and were about to turn the corner when we heard unfamiliar words coming from the brush. It was a very throaty language with sounds I didn't think a human could even make. Karim looked to me questioningly, as if I would recognize the strange sounds. I just shrugged and peeked out, hoping to glance what it was.

Karim saw the figures before I did. "What are those?" he breathed, and when I felt the warm air on my neck I realized that he was close enough for his shoulder to be pressed up against my back. I stepped away from him and looked at the figures he saw from the other side of the tree we hid behind. The silhouettes were squat, barely at hip level, with no neck to speak of. I froze when one angled towards us, not quite looking at us. The same gurgling sounds came from his mouth, revealing a wide, lipless mouth full of sharp, gleaming white teeth. He had tiny eyes that shone in the darkness and small floppy ears similar to Grem's. I pulled back behind the tree, fear making my insides go cold. Realizing Karim still watched them, I pulled him behind the tree and out of sight.

"I didn't think they were real," I murmured, horrified. A shiver ran up my spine.

"You know what they are." It wasn't a question.

"Goblins. There are plenty of stories about them. They are notorious for kidnapping babies in the middle of the night and eating them." I searched the depths of my mind for every fact I knew from the stories. "They have terrible hearing and they have very good eyesight at night, but only close up. I think we should be far enough away right now."

"There are only two." He leaned out but I pulled him back in.

"Goblins travel in hordes. There are never just two. They don't act as an army, but as a single unit. The second they see us, the rest will come. Each one will take a single bite until there is nothing left."

"So I'm guessing we can't take the front door." Karim pursed his lips. I narrowed my eyes at him. How did I get stuck with a man who never took anything seriously? Dragging him behind me, I went back to the unguarded wall we started at.

Where the first floor would be, there were no windows, but higher up there were windows cut large enough to fit a person. It seemed impossibly high and a bush lined the bottom, making starting off more difficult, but the walls were sufficiently crumbled to provide enough hand- and foot-holds. I slipped my pack off. Climbing with it would be difficult and fleeing with it even more so, but I knew putting it down now meant I might never see it again.

Settling amongst the trees, I started eating some of the smoked meats and the green fruits we had packed.

"If I had known we were going to give up once we got to the castle, I would have told Grem to just leave us where he found us." Despite his uncertainty, Karim sat down across from me and also began eating.

"I can't scale a wall with this whole thing and when we get Pennah, we will have to leave quickly. We will need the canteens though." In mid-bite, I pulled out the two pig bladder canteens, one mostly empty and the other full, and fastened them to my waistband. Karim followed suit. I did a quick inventory: I had my sword, dagger, water, money-purse and jacket. I'd have to do without the bandages, salve, blanket and other travelling supplies I had brought.

"Are you ready?" I asked Karim. He was still chewing the jerky, so he just nodded. "Try not to cut yourself on the wall. I think the goblins can smell blood."

"I couldn't cut myself if I tried. No harm, remember? It was part of the deal."

I had forgotten my companion was invulnerable. Maybe he could march in and let the goblins break their teeth on him while he freed Pennah. Although it wasn't impossible to capture him, which ruled out that plan. I tested a nearby vine, which snapped off. "I hope you are less afraid of climbing than you were a few days ago."

"I was not afraid. I just knew you could do it faster." To prove me wrong, he started climbing first, and I was indeed faster.

Most of the vines were not as sturdy as they looked, but a few thicker ones were clinging to the castle wall as hard as we were, so they made for good footholds. We were about halfway to the nearest window when I heard the gurgling goblin language below us. I shushed Karim and we both froze. My muscles already ached, and we still had a long way to go. Holding still was agony; my feet were barely supporting me on narrow cracks in the wall. Karim had found an arrowslit just wide enough for his foot, so he had no problem staying still. Finally, the goblin guards moved on and we continued upward.

I arrived at the window first, and before climbing in, I silently prayed that this just happened to be Pennah's room. With shaking arms I heaved my body into the window frame, awkwardly wiggling head first through the narrow opening. In a tumble, I landed on the floor, quickly jumping to my feet and searching the area. When I met eyes with the room's occupant I jumped back, knocking my elbow against the stone wall. A fiery bird stood chained in the corner with its wings bound, staring at me with sad orange eyes. It had to be two feet tall, larger than any bird I'd ever seen, besides the stormhawk of course. Dried blood was smeared at its feet.

A soft mewing from the other end of the room drew my attention. It was the same bird, only smaller. This one tugged at its chains, attempting to cross the room.

"A phoenix," Karim whispered as he slipped in through the window.

"Two, actually." Karim turned to see the younger bird. He moved toward it.

"We should unchain them," he suggested.

"But they'll just be caught and put back in here. It's not as if they can fit through the window. At least the big one can't." And I had a feeling the baby phoenix wasn't going anywhere without its mother.

"They might get out, they might not. But either way, two birds running rampant in the castle might give us some extra time." He made a valid point. We carefully undid the chains that tied down the little bird's wings and we broke through the chain that held it to the wall. Immediately, the baby phoenix scuttled across the room to nestle into the flaming feathers of its mother's breast. The mother phoenix didn't move as we approached and pulled at the heavier chains that held her down. As we pulled, I noticed the extra shimmer the chains carried. Magic. They must have been enchanted to hold the bird, which also explained why it didn't burn our hands, though the bird's hot feathers brought a sweat to my brow.

"No distraction then." Karim dropped the chains, crestfallen. The phoenix seemed to understand that we were as powerless as she was to undo the chains.

"We're sorry," I muttered to the creature. The bird's beak warmed, but did not burn, my hand as I stroked it sympathetically. A pearlescent tear steamed as it dribbled down the bird's face and onto the cold stone floor. Legends said that a tear of a phoenix could heal any illness or injury. For a moment I imagined touching the fallen tear and my curse disappearing, but I knew it was not that easy. My curse was no illness and it wasn't going anywhere anytime soon.

"We should go." I tugged at Karim who was still watching the birds huddle together in the damp corner.

Fortunately, the door was unlocked. Apparently the kidnapper trusted the enchanted chains to contain his prisoners. I pictured Pennah shackled to the stone wall, and just the thought of it sent a shiny, black scorpion skittering out the door I had partially opened.

"Wow," Karim balked, criticizing the state the castle was in. I, on the other hand, didn't even notice the spiderwebs, grime and rust until I had completely taken in the grandeur. A huge chandelier glimmered above the fanning staircase that had a worn red rug running down it and into the foyer. The rug led to a set of doors large enough for an ogre to use with ease, but the doors were sealed with chains and wooden bars. The goblins and their master must use a side door. However, each and every door was designed to look the same. The crumbling staircase was the only thing that kept me oriented.

"Where do we even start?" The hope I felt when we neared the castle was beginning to fade.

Karim pulled Amani from its sheath and carved a notch in the lower right corner of the door frame. Using the curved blade he pointed to the door to the right. "We start here. But we should move quickly." He was right. There wasn't time to free every creature held captive in the Black Castle. We checked door after door. Many of the creatures were asleep, which was just as well since often times they had sharp teeth.

After about fifteen or sixteen doors, we heard the telltale gurgling language of the goblins. Karim reacted quicker than I did and he shoved me into the nearest room. We did a swift survey of the room to make sure nothing was about to attempt to eat us. This room was very different from all the others we'd seen. Either a very prominent prisoner stayed here, or this was not a dungeon. A large dining table with an empty plate at the end sat nearest to the door. Several candles lit the room and a fire was popping in the corner near a cluster of velvety armchairs that were probably more comfortable than anything I had ever slept or sat in. A feminine gasp pulled my eyes to the chair that sat beside the fire. Only this chair was occupied. Karim and I simultaneously pulled our swords and pointed them at the extravagantly dressed woman, who stood in alarm and dropped the cross stitch she was working on.

This woman, though her sliver-streaked hair was intricately done in beautiful plaits and her dress was satiny with tiny gems sewn in, was not beautiful. She wore a derisive sneer on her middle-aged face and the dress didn't fit quite right. Several small things like this made her seem out of place. She shifted and the firelight caught in her gaudy diamond necklace. I zeroed in on the necklace and my arm slackened for just a moment before my grip retightened and I strode over to the woman, sword in hand. Panic replaced her haughtiness as I approached. I relished the fear I saw in her face.

Keeping the sword pointed at her black heart, my free hand clutched her throat and harshly pushed her against the mantle.

"Where is the girl you got this from?" My hands shook with fury.

"Got what from?" She had the boldness to say that? I ripped the necklace from her throat and held it up for her to see. The tears sparkled with light and Pennah's magic, and a soft chime seemed to echo in the lavish room when the diamonds clinked against one another.

"This! Where is Pennah?" I pushed the sword against her skin where a few droplets of blood dripped onto the white lace trim on her bodice. I felt Karim come closer behind me, but he made no motion to stop me.

"My husband gave that to me." I could see the fear in her eyes, but she still didn't answer the question. I threw the necklace to the floor where it exploded against the stone.

"Where is my sister, you witch!" I moved the edge of the blade against her age-spotted throat. A long-legged hairy spider crawled down the flat of my blade, nearly brushing against the faux queen's skin. That seemed to finally get to her.

"The tower. North wing." Bitterness still tinged her voice. The hatred that burned in the pit of my stomach didn't abate, but Karim and I used the decorative ropes from the curtains to tie her to a chair and gag her. I made sure the ropes securing her hands behind her were pinching and pulling her shoulders uncomfortably. Hopefully no one found her for a few days.

After checking for goblin patrols, Karim and I sprinted to the north end of the castle and found a servant staircase. We had climbed up three flights in leaps and bounds when we heard gurgling echo ahead of us. My arm was nearly pulled from its socket as Karim yanked me out through the nearest door.

We sprinted past doors and Karim pulled me around a corner . . . where we met the beady eyes of a pair of goblins. A low growl came from their throats, and I could almost feel the responding growl of the rest of the goblin horde throughout the castle.

"No," I whispered. Karim's hand squeezed mine because he knew the same thing I knew.

It was over.

Chapter 17

PENNAH

The castle walls and floor vibrated with a feral growl. What was that?

Taking a chance, I left the west tower room. The water girl emerged slightly from her wash basin.

"What is it?" she asked in her burbling voice.

"I'm not sure." I left the door open so I knew which one it was and meandered down the hallway. The growling continued. Normally, I would have seen a few goblins by now. If they were all distracted by something, now could be my chance to escape. I already knew where the main staircase was, but I hadn't gone all the way down. Goblins had always stopped me before I got far.

Most doors I passed held captive creatures. Even if some were friendly, the nymph girl told me most of the creatures were chained with enchantments that only Marcus could undo. If I could save myself now, maybe I could come back with more people. Maybe Sable could let some vipers loose on the goblins. A piece of black amber clattered to the floor. Recently, black amber gems had appeared when I thought of my sister. I had discovered that in daylight, the jewel just looked plain and dark, but in firelight it shimmered with green and gold. I picked up the amber and clutched it tightly as I ran down the stairs.

I made it to the ground floor. There were still no goblins to be seen anywhere. The large front doors were sealed shut, but Marcus had to get in and out somehow. I checked several doors, but with no luck. One held a giant scaled creature that roared and lunged at me before I slammed the door shut. Another held a sleeping tree nymph. None of the rooms had windows either, so aside from finding a cannon and blowing through a wall, the door Marcus used was my only hope.

Unfortunately, I didn't find the right door before I heard pounding footsteps rushing down the main stairwell I had come down. I heard a man's voice yelling, but it wasn't Marcus. There were other humans here? I moved towards the stairs until I saw a man with brown skin and a curved sword slashing through the few goblins that had run ahead of the main horde. One fat goblin bit down on his calf as he kept running along the second-floor balcony. He yelled out in pain. Another voice joined his. A more feminine voice, hoarse with exertion, shouted out.

"Karim!" And then I saw Sable swipe her sword clean through the goblin, which detached itself from the man's seemingly unharmed leg.

Tears of joy dropped to the floor. "Sable!" My sister had come for me!

Chapter 18

SABLE

"Pennah!" I lashed out at another goblin with Servans, aiming for its ambiguous throat area. In desperation, I looked around. The horde of goblins was piling down the staircase, blocking the only path to my sister who stood alone on the bottom floor. Karim, fighting beside me, also surveyed the situation.

"We can't get to her," he told me.

"No, we have to—" I looked back at Pennah who was also realizing there was a blockade between us. There were a hundred goblins headed straight for us, all gnashing sharp teeth and swiping after us with their claws. How could I have believed we could do this on our own? How could I have been so stupid?

One of the goblins had gotten ahead of the others and it was loping toward me. Its razor-sharp teeth snapped at my forearm, grazing my skin just enough to draw blood before Karim kicked it aside. The goblin bit down on Karim's arm instead, shattering its own teeth. Karim cried out before finishing the creature off with a slash of his sword.

"Sable!" I had never seen Karim so serious. He grabbed my upper arm and jerked me to face him. "We will come back. But we can't win this fight." We had only seconds.

"I'm sorry Pennah!" I yelled back to her before following Karim down the hall back to the room with the phoenixes. There was no way to block the door, so we headed for the window, not giving the birds a second glance. Karim helped me through after we sheathed our swords.

Climbing down was much easier than coming up, but goblins were built for climbing and we only had a moment's head start. Fortunately, goblins weren't exactly master strategists, so none waited at the base of the wall for us.

Ominous growling buzzed against the wall as the goblins skittered out through the window one by one like a trail of carnivorous ants. Karim and I were now half falling and half climbing. About fifteen feet from the ground, a vine snapped under my hands and I slid several feet before my foot caught on a crack. As I scrambled to cling to the wall, the stone crumbled under my weight and I slid further until my hand found another vine. The vine slowed my fall but snapped, and I fell the last seven or so feet into a thick bush.

Just as I was rolling out of the shrub, Karim leaped over the bush and pulled me along.

"I really hope Grem saw that," he told me. Despite everything that was happening, I laughed, but it sounded pained.

We spared a moment to look for the bags, but we resumed our pace when we couldn't immediately find them.

Our full out sprint eventually became a jog when the goblin horde began thinning and slowing. When we couldn't see them anymore, we just walked for a few hours in silence, which was surprising considering Karim's need to fill the quiet with words.

There was enough tree coverage to block the stars, so I wasn't even sure which direction we were walking. All I knew was that we were getting farther away from Pennah. She was the only thing I had left, and I had to leave her behind. I ran away and left her there!

The burning in my eyes told me poisonous tears were about to start streaming down my grimy face. My mother was right. My curse damaged everyone around me. It ruined lives. *I* ruined lives. All of this pain. If I had just let Pennah give that fairy the piece of bread, this all might have never happened. I would be caring for Pennah and my mother, probably married to Godric never knowing that he could betray me the moment things started to look bleak.

When Mama got sick, she told me I had one responsibility: to take care of the family. Now, Mama was dead, and Pennah was still trapped in that awful castle. I had failed.

A picture of that woman's necklace was etched in my brain. There were more than fifty teardrop diamonds strung up. I could remember the hint of sparkling magic in each one, pieces of the curse manifesting. Pieces of Pennah.

Karim's dark hands rested on my shoulders. I hadn't been aware of dropping to my knees. My fingers wove into my spidersilk-ridden hair and clenched into fists as purple venom stung my eyes and slipped down my cheeks. Spiderwebs stuck to my hands as I let them drop when Karim pulled me into his chest. I locked my hands together around his back and on top of Amani's sheath.

"We'll go back." His words vibrated in his chest against my cheek.

"That necklace was made of her tears." I inhaled roughly and pulled against Karim harder. In that moment, more than ever before, I was glad I didn't go after Pennah alone. "What are they doing to her?" Karim didn't respond.

We stayed there until our knees hurt. Then we moved up against a tree with a wide base and I huddled into his side while his arm stayed wrapped around my shoulders. I scrubbed at my face with my jacket sleeve until all trace of my tears was gone and my face was raw. Without a blanket, it was easier to feel the coming winter, but Karim's arm blocked much of the cold.

I could feel the moment he fell asleep. His breathing became much steadier and the full weight of his head rested on my own. The sound of wind and nocturnal insects filled the forest in an ambient symphony of noise. At one point my breathing had synced up with Karim's. Not long after that, I fell asleep.

Chapter 19

SABLE

I had originally planned on staying awake and keeping watch, but I didn't feel too bad when I woke well after dawn and Karim was already awake and neither of us had been eaten in the middle of the night. As I stayed still in Karim's half embrace, I tried to think back to the last time I had cried in front of someone else, even Pennah, but I couldn't remember.

"Sable, do you know where the Winterwood is?" Since he already knew I was awake, I sat up and shifted away to face him, but his arm still stretched to reach around my shoulders.

"It's just the northern part of the Black Forest. Why?" The Winterwood was probably already snowy, which was weather we were not prepared for now that we had no blankets or bedrolls.

"At dawn, there were voices coming from the trees. They said the first of the fairies were gathering for winter solstice." At this point, I wasn't even surprised that the trees were talking now. I did wonder why fairies were gathering already. Winter solstice was over a month away. But that wasn't my biggest concern.

"Why do you care about fairies?"

"Maybe they can help us."

I removed myself from Karim's arm. "We don't need the help of fairies." That would only make things worse.

"Sable, we can't get Pennah on our own. Especially now that they know we're coming. Also, we have no food and I'm not sure either of us can hunt with a sword."

"Fairies don't take requests. They barge in and do what they want. Humans are no more than pets for them." A memory of a beautiful, but terrifying, pale woman flashed in my mind. I could remember how she looked at me with such contempt. "Actually, we're more like stray dogs. Some of them think we're cute and give us a little treat, but they'd just as soon slash our throats."

It was clear from his expression that Karim understood the nature of fairies, either from my own experiences he had heard about or perhaps there are fairies just as bad from wherever he came from.

"Do you have any better suggestions?" he asked, and I remembered the teardrop necklace. I had several cuts on my arms and legs where the goblins barely missed clawing or chewing a limb right off. If we went back in there without help, I'd probably come back out missing a chunk of flesh. Or worse, I'd end up locked in one of those rooms. Maybe Karim was right. We had to do something, and this was the only choice we had left. Unless Grem decided to pop out and help us again, which was highly unlikely.

"Depending on how far north the Winterwood actually is, it might take us days to get there."

"Well, north is that way." He referenced a stick he had placed on the ground, presumably at sunrise, that pointed north. Interestingly enough, the stick was pointed away from the direction we had come.

"Were we traveling north all night?"

Karim, unfazed, shrugged. "We could have been running in circles and wouldn't have known it. It was pitch black and the trees all look the same."

It was strange not to have to pack up any campsite. We just brushed ourselves off and left, northbound. The farther north we got, the colder the air became and the more magic everything seemed to have. We didn't find a non-magical fruit tree until the following morning. This time, we ate bananas. I had seen the yellow fruit a few times, but often it was browned already and far too expensive. At first, I enjoyed the taste. By the time we had eaten our fill, however, I hated bananas.

"Are you sure you don't want any more?" Karim was gathering a bunch to take with us until we found another source of food. He knew I had already eaten eight, and I had told him just the thought of bananas made me slightly nauseous. Instead of responding, I finished off the last of my water to get rid of the lingering taste of banana.

By late afternoon, we finally came across a creek. It was less than ten feet wide, easy to cross but deep enough for some magical creature to lurk in. On the bright side, it was also wide enough to wash up in. Almost a week-and-a-half's worth of dirt, sweat and goblin blood had built up, and who knew when we'd next see a washbasin?

I rolled up my pants and waded into the crystalline creek until the icy water was just past my knees. With Karim's back to me several feet away, I pulled off my jacket and tunic and prayed no lewd creatures lurked nearby. After washing my arms, face and neck as well as I could around my breastband, I carefully undid my hopelessly knotted braid. I washed out my hair as best I could, pulling out a few spiderwebs, though I knew they'd reappear, and I rebraided the thick mess. Goosebumps prickled my skin all over from the icy water, but I was beginning to feel clean again.

"Don't feel rushed." Karim's voice almost made me drop the shirt and undergarment I was hastily washing, but he was still turned around. Even though I had put on my winter jacket, I hadn't closed the buttons so I wasn't exactly decent. "My feet are killing me." Karim finished speaking as I buttoned the jacket, just to be safe.

"We can camp nearby," I told him as I squeezed the water from my clothes. "By the time we finish, the sun will be setting. You can turn around," I added.

He turned and looked me up and down before pulling his shoes off and dunking his aching feet in the cold water, followed by him ripping his feet back out.

"How do you stand it? This water is freezing." A small smile broke onto my face. I had somehow forgotten that he was from the desert.

"I don't suggest lounging around in it, but you won't lose any toes washing up."

Karim hesitantly dipped his feet back in the water, slower this time. He rolled up his pants and scrubbed the dirt from his legs. Before I realized what he was doing, he pulled his shirt off and began cleaning off his arms and chest. I quickly busied myself with tending to the blisters on my feet and not thinking about the flash of honey-brown skin tone I saw.

In the corner of my eye, I could see Karim, still shirtless, washing his hair in the freezing water. I was laying my shirt on a dry rock when a large, rough hand wrapped around my leg and hauled me under the water.

Before I could yell for help, I was deep underwater—far deeper than I had believed the river was. Thin claws dragged down my calf before the hand released me. For a moment, I was paralyzed, helplessly floating in the water as a pair of slitted cerulean eyes drifted up until they stared into mine. The paralysis seemed to wear off and I began flapping my arms, attempting to reach the surface. The hand clawed at me through my thick jacket several more times and I felt the venom my body was desperately trying to fight off.

Limbs thrashing, I scrambled to push away from what I now presumed was a kappa, a tortoise-like creature that was known to mutilate its victims as they drowned. Finally, my foot made contact with the soft underbelly of the creature. The kappa gave me a last disdainful glare before swimming off, its tortoise shell leaving a streamline of bubbles behind it. Once the kappa had disappeared, the surface seemed much closer. I broke through and hastily clambered to the shore.

Karim stopped where he was frantically digging through the shallow river several feet from where I came out of the water. He could easily stand up in the center of the creek—though his pants were wet now—which made me wonder how the kappa created more space to drown me in.

"But, how did you—? Are you alright?" His wide eyes swept over me from top to bottom, assessing the damage. I could feel the sting of several scratches, but only a few were actually bleeding enough to be concerned about, a fact that confirmed my guess that the kappa had some kind of paralytic venom that didn't work as well on me.

As Karim got closer, I stood and sloshed through the creek to where I had left my weapons and my clothes, ignoring his questions.

"When our clothes dry, we should keep moving." I hung the sopping material on a tree and began gathering firewood to speed up the process and rid myself of the bone-deep chill that had developed inside me while I was under the water with the kappa.

"I really think you should take a break. Those scratches don't look good," Karim told me for the tenth time.

"I'm fine," I finally snapped, turning away from him to put a cool finger to one of the itchy scrapes on my arm. Though disconcerted, he began clearing away a space for a fire pit while I gathered sticks to burn.

Irritated and anxious from the kappa attack, I snatched up small pieces of wood like they were the ones that had attacked. Eventually, I had a decent bundle. When I looked down at the pile of firewood I had collected, hot, sticky blood dribbled from my palms, the red ooze bubbling up between logs. With a startled gasp, I dropped the wood as if it were a corpse. Suddenly, Karim was beside me again and the blood was gone.

"Are you sure you're alright?"

"I'm fine. It was just a sliver," I told him shakily as I retrieved the wood.

Our clothes dried over the flames and I waited without any more hallucinations, but this river was obviously not safe, so I still insisted we should continue on tonight despite the lateness in the day.

Karim slowly laced his shoes. He had made it clear that he wanted to stay here for the night. On the other hand, I had also made myself clear when I said I'd leave here tonight with or without him, but that didn't stop him from slowing us down as much as possible.

"You look pretty scratched up. I still think we should get some rest before going on." By the fire, I had counted seven clear sets of claw marks ranging from my neck and shoulders to my ankles, but they were all shallow and barely even stung. Each one had already scabbed over, but many were flaring with a soft ring of red around them. Hopefully they didn't get infected.

"We can't just sit around doing nothing," I reminded him. Suddenly, a woman screamed my name somewhere in the woods, her voice so penetrating my chest tightened at the sound of it. My head whipped around, but I couldn't see anything.

"Did you hear something?" Karim inched forward and I tightened Servans's sheath-belt before moving north. Since sunset was approaching, it was easier to make sure we were headed in the right direction.

"It's nothing," I brushed him off. "Let's go."

We moved in silence for a bit before Karim inevitably began talking.

"I've been thinking. I've never heard any goblin stories, but maybe there's something in a story you know that can tell us how to stop them from guarding the castle, or distract them somehow." I heard my name again, but this time it was just a choked whisper. The voice sounded like it was standing right beside me, but Karim was the only one nearby and he continued to prattle on, oblivious to the voices I was hearing. "You said they swarm like bees right? Acting as one unit instead of a hundred separate creatures. Do they have some kind of queen bee? If we kill their leader will they all die? Or if the man is paying them with jewels from Pennah, maybe we can distract them with more jewels. Do the stories . . ."

The whispers grew louder and louder until I couldn't hear Karim anymore. As suddenly as they had begun, the whispers stopped and the new silence hung heavily around me. I looked at my surroundings. Karim was gone.

"Karim?" Where did he go? Just a moment ago, he was right beside me. Now, I was standing alone in the Black Forest. It was pitch black with no moon or stars to speak of. I called his name again, but there was no response.

"Sable—" a woman choked out my name. I jumped at the sudden appearance of another person. I turned, astounded by who it was.

"Mama?" She looked distraught, standing barefoot in nothing but a nightgown, the mulchy soil staining her feet. Her face had a ghostly glow, the only source of light in the dark night. I reached out for her, and there was blood on my hands, etched into every crevice of my skin and dripping down my arm until I was up to my elbows in it. Looking back at my mother, I saw that her nightgown was soaked in red, and her face was twisted into hatred.

"Sable. *You* were my curse. You killed me. You killed my sweet Pennah. You are a plague, bringing death to everything you touch. Everyone you ever loved. You're a murderer!" My dead mother lunged at me, wrapping her bloody hands around my neck until I couldn't breathe. I pushed her off and tried to move away, but I slipped in a slick puddle of dark venom, landing flat on my back.

A gentle, delicate hand helped me up.

"Sable, are you alright?"

"Pennah?" I sighed with relief and pulled my baby sister into a tight hug. "I've been all over trying to find you." I stepped away from the hug and looked into Pennah's angelic face. Fear spread over her soft features and she let out a blood-curdling scream.

"What? What is it Pennah? I'll protect you!" And then, she pointed at *me*.

"You're a monster! Get away from me!" She stumbled backward.

"Pennah, it's me! I'm your sister." I grabbed her wrist and she screamed again at the scaly hand that had grabbed her. In shock, I released her. What happened to my hand? There were hard, green scales where flesh used to be.

"How could you do this to me? I thought you cared." A blotchy, purple blossom spread from the spot on her wrist where I had grabbed her until she was gasping for air and clawing at the dark veins crawling up her neck. Her eyes turned black. "Murderer . . ." she choked out, then collapsed. Dead.

"No," I muttered, quieter than a whisper. The world was spinning. More corpses were strewn on the floor. I recognized my mother, Pennah, Godric and his family, Karim, Uncle Morrin. I even saw my father, or at least I saw the man I pictured as my father since I have no real memories of the man. Their dead, black eyes all looked at me, the accusation undeniable.

And then I screamed.

Chapter 20

PENNAH

"I warned you," Marcus cackled. His hands were covered in the same blood that dripped from his butcher's apron. "After this, there won't be any more chances."

Marcus's form shifted like a pile of clay in a sculptor's hands until he was a giant bear: the Black Ursa. Shiny claws glinted in the moonlight as they swiped at me.

I awoke in a sweat. It was just a dream. I looked around, disoriented for a moment, not recognizing the room. Then I remembered. After Sable's rescue attempt, I was moved to a different room and my watery friend, whose name I had finally extricated as Daria, was moved along with me. I was fairly certain we were on the fourth floor, still higher than any building I'd seen. This room seemed to have been a bedroom at one point. There was a decorative tapestry on the wall—all other decorations had been removed at some point—and there was a bare fireplace with a large, musty cushion in front of it. Despite the molding, it was quite comfortable. And there were far fewer rats, so it was an overall improvement. This room's windows still had no bars, but I'd never survive jumping or attempting to climb the crumbling wall. I had maybe a day or two of peace, but the sprites were able to find me again, poking and prodding and stealing without mercy.

Daria and I spent most of our time exchanging stories of our lives before we got here. I learned more than the stories ever told about every kind of nymph there was and every water creature that existed in the Black

Forest. Daria rarely spoke about her mother, though. I could tell she missed her. Even though she had given Marcus the pearls, both water nymphs were still trapped here.

"So a kiss from a naiad lets humans breathe underwater?" I had never heard that before, which made sense when most stories with nymphs included a poor drowning human seduced by a beautiful woman.

"Generally, we stay away from humans, but there have been a few forbidden loves in our lore about naiads falling in love with humans. Unfortunately, humans get far too attached to their mates and naiad loves are strong but short-lived, so it never really ends well for the human."

"What about stories with true love? Don't you have those?" I thought of all the stories that ended in two lovers living happily.

"Naiads live for a very long time, and no one wants to spend hundreds of years with the same person. Marriage is a very human idea, because humans are afraid only one person would ever love them so they settle for the first person they feel deeply for. When my mother and father were together—"

"There are male nymphs?" The stories only ever had females.

"Water spirits, actually. Naiad is general, like human. Nymph is female, like woman, and water spirit is male, like man. Anyway, if I were a water spirit, I would have lived with my father, but since I am a nymph, I was raised by my mother. After I was born, my father stayed for the first few years, but my parents parted ways eventually."

It was so strange to hear such a different perspective. Love and marriage are so valued for humans that I assumed it was for everyone. I had always dreamed of finding a true love, but at this point my chances were slim unless Marcus found an extraordinary man with a magical talent and chose to lock him in the room next to mine, replacing whatever creature was there now screeching at every hour of the night.

"You loathsome creatures!" Daria squirted some sprites staring at their reflections away from her tub. They returned in full force. Combing my fingers through my hair I pulled some loose gold threads out and tossed them into the corner where the sprites followed and fought over each strand. One sprite began coiling a piece so it reflected more light. Its hands buzzed and glowed on the gold, and when it finished, the thread was fused in place, almost shaped like a miniature rose.

"I didn't know sprites could do that."

"Oh, they love to tinker, but only when it suits them. They make the most wondrous jewelry, but it is nearly impossible to find something more beautiful to trade for it. Persuading a sprite to do what you want is like trying to change the tides. It's doable, but not usually worth the effort."

"You can talk to them?" I had been thinking of them as little more than bugs.

"They might act like vapid insects—actually, they are vapid insects—but they know what you're saying. Most of the time, they just don't care."

"What about goblins? Do they understand us too?"

"Enough about what I know. Tell me some more stories about those handsome knights."

Recalling the way Sable used different voices for different characters and the way her inflections always seemed to give life to a story, I started telling Daria about Sir Rosborn and how he slayed the Great Beast that was plaguing his town by stealing maidens every new moon for his supper.

Chapter 21

SABLE

"Are you finished now?" Residual paralysis prevented a word or even a nod, but Karim seemed to understand and he pulled his hand from covering my mouth and unleashed me from his tight embrace to move in front of me and look into my panic-stricken eyes.

"Are you awake? Can you hear me?" Blinking, I felt some control return. My head bobbed once. "Good. What happened? You just froze for ten minutes. I couldn't get you to budge. And then you started screaming. I'm sorry I covered your mouth like that, but it's getting dark and I didn't want anything unsavory to hear you."

So I was actually screaming. That explained the raw throat.

"I think the kappa normally paralyzes its victims with fear before drowning them." The words came slow and in a raspy voice at first, but they quickly became stronger. "I'm immune to most poisons, as I am quickly discovering, but some still have an effect, or belated effect, on me." As I spoke, I focused on moving my limbs. A few fingers twitched and I shifted my weight from one leg to another.

"What was it that made you so afraid?"

"A living nightmare." With jerky movements, I began walking again as if nothing had happened. Or at least I was going to continue walking until my sword strap tugged at me, halting my forward momentum.

"We aren't going anywhere until morning. I'm exhausted, and we'd only get another half hour of walking before dark anyway and since it looks like you can barely move, we wouldn't make it far."

I angrily pulled the sheathed sword out of Karim's grasp. However, he wasn't holding as tightly as I had expected and I ended up whirling around and falling onto my tailbone. When I saw Karim's amused smile I bolted up and pushed him away, half stumbling into him with the too quick movement.

"You think this is funny? I'm trying to save my sister!" The leap to my feet left my breathing ragged and labored. Fighting off the venom must have been more draining than I realized. Karim's smile slipped away and his expression became infuriatingly soft.

"We saw Pennah. She wasn't hurt. She wasn't bleeding or bruised. We are still helping her, but we can't kill ourselves in the process."

"Of course you don't care if we take our time. She's just the answer to your money problems, and you're just a thief," I snapped. The worst part about this argument was how calm and diplomatic he was being.

"I'm still a human being. I do care if she gets hurt. And I care if *you* get hurt, which is exactly what will happen if you don't reign it in." He set his hands on my shoulders and this time I didn't have the energy to pull away. "And don't even think about going off on your own while I'm asleep."

My eyes drifted down to my shoes. I would never admit it, but that thought had crossed my mind. Deep down, though, I knew I'd never make it alone.

"You can sleep first." Karim gestured to the patch of ground he had cleared of twigs and padded with dead leaves. I shook my head at the offer. After the kappa-venom dream, there was no way I could fall asleep until I absolutely couldn't keep my eyes open. With a shrug, Karim untied his canteens from his belt and unhooked the sword from his back, setting the weapon beside him before he laid on his back with his hands twined together on top of his stomach. Since I met Karim, I had become jealous of his gift of falling asleep in an uncannily short amount of time.

It was easy to stay awake for my shift since I was dwelling on the kappa-induced hallucinations all night. Much of the incident had become blurred, like a dream, but some parts had been carved into my memory. I remembered the way Pennah looked at me in horror and fear as she realized I was killing her. I couldn't stop seeing my hands covered in blood while Pennah's poisoned corpse lay in front of me. It was so real.

Finally, my physical exhaustion from the kappa ordeal began weighing down my eyelids. Karim and I wordlessly exchanged places. Using my arm as a pillow, I curled up and let sleep overtake me, desperately hoping that no nightmares found me while I slept.

The next morning I was awakened to the scent of bananas. The combination of lightheadedness and the hungry burning in my stomach actually made my mouth water. After three bananas, however, my foul opinion of the yellow fruit had returned.

By the end of the day, we had found a giant hill that turned out to be a sleeping troll (fortunately trolls sleep deeper than Karim), a magic-infused banana tree surrounded by small dead animals and half eaten bananas—further supporting my stance that the fruit was that of the devil—and a rabbit hole we were able to flush out with a few snakes. The rabbits were small but filling, and far more savory than the bananas Karim still ate.

Halfway through the following day, Karim stopped in his tracks, spotting something at the base of a tree.

"Look." It was a small pile of snow, sheltered by the shade of the tree. Karim picked up a handful of the dirty snow and stared at it as if that was the most magical thing we had seen so far.

"Haven't you seen snow before?" I picked up some cleaner snow and placed it in my mouth. It gave me goosebumps, but we were running out of water and my throat was dry from hiking all day.

"Only a few times in my life. It rarely happens in Sukkad. And there's actually a drought right now . . ." He dropped the now wet ball of slush.

"Well, that has got to mean we're close to the Winterwood." Unfortunately, the farther north we got, the colder it would get. Last night was chilly, but bearable. Sleeping in the snow would be impossible, so we would probably have to keep going from here until we ran into fairies.

As we continued walking north, more and more frost and snow appeared and the inclined hike steepened little by little. Soon, breathing felt like prickly snowflakes were slicing my throat with each inhale.

I was stepping over an icy log when Karim jumped in surprise with a gasp. I was met with an odd look when I glanced over to see what was the matter.

"What?" I asked.

"Did you just get pinched?" he asked quietly. I raised an eyebrow and shook my head. Giggling came from above us. We turned our heads up, but then Karim jumped again.

"Gah!" He took a step toward me. Prepared to continue up the hill, I turned to face forward but a tanned nose hovered an inch from me, the creature's extra height placing it directly in my line of sight. Above that nose was a pair of neon green eyes staring unblinkingly into my own.

"Who are you?" The odd girl cocked her head inquisitively, her pink hair flopping to the side as she did. Tiny green lips pursed into a condescending smile and the girl stepped back. Strips of bark seemingly melding with her skin kept her from being completely nude, but just barely. She leaned in again. "What are you doing here?" I lifted my hand to push the girl out of my face, but before I touched her, she vanished.

"Who's that ugly girl?" The high pitched whisper came from behind Karim. We both turned to see a bright red-haired woman with white and black aspen-bark skin hovering directly behind Karim. Both women had inhuman eyes. No iris or pupil, just solid color.

"They're wood nymphs," I spat, ignoring their insults. I told myself that they called all humans ugly, but the way they stared at Karim seemed to disprove my theory.

"Are you the ones who keep poking me?" That explained why he was being so jumpy. Judging from the flush in Karim's cheeks and the strange look he gave me earlier, I deduced that it had been a *friendly* kind of poking.

"Wait, you thought that was me?" Now it was my turn to give him the astonished look.

"So you're the one bringing all the spiders in. I've had snakes in my roots all day," the pink-haired one pouted, materializing in front of me again. When I turned back to Karim, the aspen and a new evergreen nymph with verdant dreadlocks were both pressed up against him, holding him tight as he tried stepping back. The aspen's snow-white lips were a breath from his and she was peering at him through her icy lashes. A fierce blush crept down his neck as he strained to pull away.

"I don't suppose you ladies know how much farther away the Winterwood is. We're looking for the fairies." He seemed out of breath, like he'd been holding it. Karim just stood there, his posture as stiff as a board as the evergreen nuzzled closer into his shoulder, cooing over him.

I didn't hear a response to his question, because a dainty hand attempted to rip the braid off of my head. As I turned to face my antagonizer, I drew my sword.

"Back off, cherry blossom!" The magenta-haired nymph gasped, a mixture of terror and enmity on her face. I wasn't used to my rusty sword creating such immediate fear. Maybe she didn't see many swords in the depths of the Black Forest. She was a tree, after all, and a sword was only a short step away from an ax.

"You shouldn't have brought that bloody sword here." That was all she said before disappearing. I swung around, sword still in hand to face Karim just before the other two stricken dryads vanished.

"It could have been worse." Karim smiled nervously.

"Worse? It looked like they were about to ravish you." I scowled before sheathing Servans. "Or maybe they're used to men tripping all over themselves to come willingly."

"Well, looseness isn't exactly my selling point." He chuckled, but he still stood stiffly and awkwardly.

"And what, exactly, *is* your selling point?" I meant it half-jokingly, but when Karim's shoulders relaxed as he watched me, I realized I didn't want to know the answer, so I didn't wait for one. "Nevermind. Did they tell you if we are almost there?"

He blinked and blushed again. "No, they didn't say."

"Then we'll just keep going." I marched onward, not waiting for Karim to follow.

The nearly full moon rose and we still hadn't seen any signs of fairies. The last glimmer of daylight sparkled on the patches of snow that now sprawled across the forest floor. At least we didn't have to worry about water anymore. The snow should eventually melt in our canteens.

As darkness engulfed the forest, broken only by the moonlight that managed to leak through the tree cover, I could distinctly feel where each rip from the kappa's claws let the frigid air reach my skin. The brisk wind bit my exposed leg, chilled me through my jacket, and made my eyes water. We were even reduced to jogging every so often just to warm up. I just hoped we made it to the Winterwood soon.

"Is that a path?" Karim pointed out. There indeed seemed to be a path cutting through the steep, snow-covered pass. "We must be getting close." He started up the hill, following the narrow trail.

"Something doesn't look right," I muttered, slowing down. The hill seemed completely ordinary, but there was a nagging sensation that held me back.

"It doesn't look strange." Karim shrugged, looking at the hill. Then, something clicked into place.

"There's no magic. Anywhere." Every corner of the Black Forest was draped with glistening magic. Every corner except this one. The trees and rocks surrounding the path were oddly absent of the normally present sparkles. Even the snow that covered everything in spots seemed to lack its usual luster. "If we were getting close, wouldn't there be more magic?"

Karim's face scrunched as he eyed the hillside. "Did we take a wrong turn?"

"I don't see how we could have." We'd been heading straight north all day. It didn't take a genius to know directions.

"Maybe we should go back." Karim started back down the hill. I was about to join him when the ground beneath our feet began to groan. We looked down at the soil. It seemed to be . . . rippling. Carefully, Karim took hold of my arm. Together, we slowly stepped down the hill. We'd taken two steps when the ground dropped from under us.

When we landed at the bottom of the pit that had appeared, Karim rolled right and I rolled left. The dim moonlight was barely enough to see this far beneath the ground's surface, so I couldn't tell what kind of creature approached from the darkness. No sooner had I drawn my sword than a giant paw came to swipe me off my feet. Servans was buried deep in a pile of soil, out of my reach. I scrabbled to it, but the same broad paw thrust me to the ground.

"Sable—" Karim yelled out, but was cut off with a grunt as another paw slammed him into the ground as well.

A deep rumble of delight came from the creature. "Mmmm." A snuffling sound grew louder until a twitching snout came close enough to ruffle my hair. "Two delectable options." The snout took a big whiff of me as soft, moist tentacles groped around my face. I cringed away, but the huge paw held me in place. The creature sighed. "Fairy magic," he grumbled. "Powerful, but unremarkable. You on the other hand . . ." More sniffing. I couldn't see, but judging from Karim's disgusted groan, the snout was probably on him now. "Genie magic. I haven't tasted genie magic in centuries." There was a deep inhale and Karim made a quiet noise of protest. Then, the creature sneezed.

"Of course it protects you." More sniffing. "But what is this? Didn't your mother teach you not to take blood magic lightly? I can smell your life oath as clear as your genie magic."

"Let us go!" I shouted into the darkness. The moment the words had been spoken, I regretted them. They sounded so foolish, but what else was there to say?

"There is a possibility of that. Have patience," the shadow said calmly, crushing my chest with his paw. "But that is to be determined by him." The creature removed his paw from Karim's torso, allowing him to leap up and draw Amani.

"Release her," he demanded.

"If you believe you are the one with the upper hand, you are sadly mistaken." The shadow pressed against my chest and I cried out in pain. "You may keep your sword. All I want is a deal. And judging from the smell of you, your family likes to make deals."

Karim paused. "How do you know that?"

"If the dryads are the heart of this forest, I am the stomach," the creature rumbled. "The Ravenous Pit, the Hunger, the Mole." It leaned forward until the moonlight shone onto his furry face. It looked like a mole, but it was far larger than any I'd ever seen. And the proportions were different; almost human. "Would you like the deal or not?"

"What deal?" Karim asked. I tried to tell him that making deals with magical creatures was never a good idea, but the pressure on my chest was too much to talk through.

"I will leave her alive and even set her free if you harm her. Nothing more than a scratch, nothing deadly."

"The life oath," Karim realized aloud.

"Yes, yes. I can smell it. *I solemnly swear on my life that I will not intentionally cause harm to you or your sister.* It is an interesting loophole in an otherwise airtight spell. Genies may believe their magic is the most powerful, but blood magic trumps all others. The one form of magic I cannot destroy, and the one form that can destroy you."

"But . . . why? Why destroy me?"

"Humans," the mole muttered. "Must I spell everything out? I suppose so, if I'm to convince you to make a deal. I feed on magic. Why do you think I set a trap for passing fairies? Unfortunately, magic is interwoven with life, so I cannot take it from you while that genie spell protects you. Harming her is the only way to override the genie magic. Now, make your choice. Either you die and she goes free, or she dies now and I hold you here until you die of old age. Choose, human."

Karim hesitated. "You have made your choice, then." The mole's deep voice held a smirk I couldn't see. The weight of the paw was removed and I could finally breathe again. Before I was able to stand, the mole's snout pressed up against my chest, the fleshy rays tickling my chin and shoulders. It inhaled loudly and a stabbing cold formed in my heart. I gasped in pain. The coldness grew until it was all-consuming. I vaguely noticed Karim behind the mole, striking at the monster with his sword. He cut through flesh, but the mole was undeterred. My whole body shivered, but there was nothing I could do. When I thought I had no more left to give, the warmth returned in a wave and the mole backed away from me. I sat up, only to realize that there was a shallow cut on my arm.

Karim faced the mole, his weapon in hand. Suddenly, Karim swayed and stumbled to his knees, the consequences of the broken life oath coming into effect. Amani fell from his hands and Karim clutched at his heart. A dark chuckle emanated from the giant mole and it leaned in until its star snout was pressed to Karim's chest.

"No!" I shouted, struggling to my feet. The mole paused to look at me.

"Do you think your measly fairy magic can stop me? Fairy-cursed humans in these parts are as common as leaves in a forest. You are not special and you are powerless against me." The mole placed its snout on Karim again, and a steady stream of sparkling magic flowed from Karim's body and into the mole's where the shimmer dissolved into the void.

I was still dizzy from whatever the creature had done to me, but the mole didn't even flinch as I drew my knife and approached it. Even when I stabbed my small dagger deep into its thick neck, it was so focused on sucking the life from Karim, it didn't even notice until the poison on the blade began taking an effect. It released Karim and stumbled back, landing in a confused heap on the other side of the pit.

"I don't understand . . ." the mole muttered, finally snapped out of its feeding. As it died, it still stared at me in disbelief.

There was barely any glimmer left in Karim. With a shaking hand, I sliced a line across my palm using Amani's sharp edge. I placed the bleeding hand on Karim's chest.

"I release you from your oath."

At first, nothing happened. Then, the magic inside him seemed to explode, refilling him with stars of magic and he jerked up.

"Did I save you or did you save me?" he asked, dazed.

"Yes," I replied. We both got to our feet.

"What happened?" He picked up Amani and I fetched Servans.

"You broke the oath, which apparently does kill you if you break it, and that thing tried to eat your magic." I used the bloody dagger to point to the mole's body. "I bet you didn't think that oath meant much when you made it. Considering the genie's spell." I kicked the giant mole's body. It seemed sturdy enough, and it was tall enough that I could probably reach the top of the pit if I stood on top of the furry mass.

"Well, I never thought this would happen, but I still meant it. And I'd make it again."

"Please don't," I snapped back. The last thing we needed was a repeat of tonight's events. "I trust you enough without the oath." I shrugged as I began to climb up the side of the mole, using its coarse fur as handholds.

"You trust me?" Karim began climbing beside me. I rolled my eyes.

"I trust you won't try to kill me at the very least," I amended, but he still smiled like I'd handed him a gold brick. I wound my fingers together and gave Karim a boost to the top of the pit. He pulled me up and we followed the pit until we were back on the path, headed due north.

Chapter 22

SABLE

The sun was long gone and the air was brittle. Unwilling to let any other pesky creatures of the Black Forest hinder our journey, we relentlessly pushed onward.

Karim was in the lead when a pale figure dressed in moonlight appeared in front of him, causing him to stumble back into me, nearly knocking me down the hillside.

"Genie magic. You have come from a very distant land, boy." The shirtless man glowed faintly blue. How on earth could everyone else tell what kind of magic we were tainted with? "And you." He turned to me, his stare not nearly as piercing as I remembered from my last fairy encounter. Regardless, the sight of this fairy man left my yearning for revenge sizzling out like a spark in the snow, a raw fear in its place. As much as fairies made me angry, they also terrified me. "You have bright fairy magic, but you do not belong here. You also bring blood magic into the Winterwood. What is it you seek, humans?" Blood magic? He must be mistaken. The life oath was broken, and that was the only blood magic we'd brought with us.

Karim recovered quicker than I did. "There is an evil man in the Black Castle who has kidnapped many magical creatures as well as her sister." He gestured to me, and I just nodded. "We want to free the captives and defeat the man, but we are only humans and we need help."

Any moment, I expected him to laugh in our faces and toss us out to freeze to death. But he didn't.

"You seek the Trader then. She is the only of our kind here that will help you."

"How can we find this trader?" I asked when he made no move to show us the way.

"Follow the gnome." A gnome promptly popped out from behind the fairy-man's legs, ducking under the man's arctic blue wings that hung behind him like a cape.

"Grem?" Karim asked, unsure if this was our story's narrator. The gnome gave Karim a dirty look. "Sorry, we've only met one other gnome. Do you know Grem?"

"Do you know every human in existence?" The shocked look on Karim's face was perceived as a no. "My name is Gromulus. Humans." He muttered the last part, obviously making it loud enough for us to hear. Without further ado, Gromulus stalked off.

The moment we crossed the threshold that the fairy was guarding, the air immediately warmed. There was still snow on the ground, but it didn't feel like winter anymore, thank heaven. I think my toes were at the beginning stages of hypothermia. An audible sigh of relief came from Karim, who I realized hadn't complained once about the chill despite his penchant for warmer weather.

Fairies of all colors and sizes were scattered about the woods. Some peeked out of white tents, but most were collected around fire pits. All, however, watched us with varying reactions. Most were shocked. Apparently they didn't get many humans in these parts. Many fairies had their lips curled with disgust and some watched with curious fascination. A few looked ready to skewer us, making me cringe and step a little closer to Karim as we walked. I stumbled a few times, distracted as I tried to take in every fairy, each with perfect features and a luminescence that shone bright under the waxing moon.

We followed Gromulus past a pale, sleeping fairy who lay on a mat near a fire. The only one I could see that wasn't staring. Recognition registered and I froze, a tumult of emotions building up inside me.

"This is her. This is the fairy that cursed me. And Pennah." I was honestly surprised that I recognized her. In the crowd, they were all beginning to look the same. Even the men looked effeminate enough to appear similar. But this was the one. The one I had dreamed of for so many nights. Fear, anger, hatred and confusion churned in my heart. I had imagined a whole collection of scenarios, ranging from tracking this fairy down and slitting her throat for cursing us to kneeling at her feet and begging for her to take it away. But I also had nightmares of this terrible beauty throwing me in a pit of snakes. And here she was, the fairy at the top of my list of most despised people. Followed closely by Pennah's kidnapper, of course, but without this fairy, Pennah and I would be safe at home. And Mama would still be alive. And the accursed fairy was just lying there, completely helpless.

Surrounding fairies edged away as vipers and venomous scorpions crawled over my boots and slunk across the catatonic woman's wings.

"Reina," Gromulus named the fairy that destroyed my life. "She's a young fairy. It is mostly the young fairies that meddle with humans, thinking they are acting as the hand of justice in Reina's case, or sometimes just causing mischief."

"Why is she like that? She looks almost dead," Karim commented. I stopped myself from saying *good*, not wanting the extra attention of other fairies within earshot.

"Many years ago, she cast a spell on two humans, one presumably being you. What are the odds?" He chuckled and I withheld my snarl. "Young fairies are incredibly powerful, but a spell that intense and permanent is difficult. Not only is it a difficult spell to keep up, but she did not account for amplification."

"What—" I started to ask the wrinkled gnome what he meant, but he foresaw my question and interrupted before I finished asking it.

"Humans are seen as inferior by most magical beings because it is believed they have no magic of their own. Most creatures discount the indirect magic all humans hold however. This magic is seen in human emotion. As you well know, magical creatures have little to no empathy or capacity for love. When Reina's magic was imbued into you, she could not have foreseen the way human emotions can amplify such a spell. Every time the spell is activated, which seems to be a lot with you . . ." He too stepped away from the venomous creatures at my feet, a look of distaste on his elderly face. "It pulls from her life force. She must stay in the Winterwood to survive. Young fairies eventually learn from their experience and limit their spells."

"Why doesn't she just undo the curse?" That would solve both of our problems.

"A spell cannot simply be undone. And to discourage you from acting on any violent, human compulsions you may have, you should know that if Reina were to die, the price of the spell would draw power from you, and you would die soon after," Gromulus said flatly. It physically hurt to have to walk away from the culprit of my curse, knowing I'd probably never see her again or ever be able to do anything about. Her pale figure remained unmoving as Karim and I followed Gromulus.

When we stepped into a gazebo with a fountain in its center, Gromulus vanished as gnomes could. Assuming this was our stop, I called out.

"Hello? Trader? We need help."

"How peculiar." A woman's intrigued voice came from behind us, presumably the Trader. "A strange, dark boy with the Sosun Pattah of Sukkad carrying a genie's wish and a fairy-touched killer carrying a blood magic sword." I glanced sidelong at Karim, but he seemed intent on giving no reaction to the fairy's accusation.

"I'm not a murderer," I told her, wishing it were true.

"I didn't say you were. You are a killer," she restated matter-of-factly.

Refusing to argue further, I changed the subject. "What is blood magic?" All I knew was that a life oath was one form blood magic took, but what could that possibly have to do with my sword?

"You don't know? Did you think an ordinary sword could cut through an ogre's armor? Or pierce a genie's wish?" I thought back to the moment Karim was swinging upside down, caught in my trap. I had poked him with my sword, drawing blood, before I knew that no blade should be able to pierce his flesh.

"But it's just an old sword." The words felt like a lie the moment they left my mouth. I went on. "How do you even know all that?" A smirking Grem waved from behind the fairy before disappearing again. I glared at the spot where he stood.

"There are three types of magic," the Trader continued, ignoring Grem's brief appearance. "Simple magic is made up of minor illusions and parlor tricks. Raw magic, like the spell of a fairy and the wish of a genie, is inherent in magical creatures who draw strength from magical corners of the world, like the Black Forest. Dark magic, part of which is blood magic, involves a much higher cost: either blood, life, soul, time, pride and so on." She glanced at Karim at the end before turning back to me.

"When you were born, your father vowed that nothing would harm you." This was beginning to sound like Karim's life story. "But he had no money and no power. He was just a lowly blacksmith. But, he heard rumors of a sword that could be forged in blood. A sword that would never break, could cut through anything, both physical and magical, and could only be used by the forger, or those of shared blood. I do not know much about dark magic, but I know forging that sword cost him dearly. Ten years of his life, to be precise. But he never could have known that his fated death would be in twelve years, leaving him only two more after the sacrifice."

Tears burned my eyes but did not fall. My father gave up ten years I could have had with him, ten years-worth of memories, for this stupid sword? I supposed he couldn't have known how little time he had left, but that was dark magic. Why did he feel that was the only way to protect me? I suspected that while the Trader somehow knew what happened with my father, there was no way she could tell me his reasons beyond what she already had. Head spinning, I heard Karim speak to the fairy.

"I don't suppose this information will be free."

"My boy, the information itself is to prove I can help you. And by knowing what the sword you call *Watching Over* can do, you can better help me in return."

"So you can help us." I was still stunned, but recovering.

"Of course, child. It's what I do. And for that, there *will* be a cost."

"And what would that cost be?" Karim asked, suspicious—as he should be.

"Have you heard of the love story of Salim and Anarkali?"

I shook my head at the same time Karim said, "Of course."

"Enlighten us," the Trader urged him.

"Every child in Sukkad knows this story. Salim, Emperor Akbar's son, fell in love with a servant girl. The emperor found out and tried to make the servant, Anarkali, fall in the eyes of the prince. Salim discovered the sabotage and tried to usurp the emperor, but the emperor's armies were far greater. Before the final battle, Salim secretly married Anarkali, but they were caught at the battle's end and the prince was sentenced to death. Anarkali renounced her love for the prince to save him, and she was entombed alive while Salim was forced to watch. He died of a broken heart the next day."

My face was agape by the time he finished. "That's awful," I whispered.

The Trader went on. "The cord used to bind the lovers in marriage is said to have magical properties. It was cut in the attack, but if two people retie the cord around their wrists, their fates would be intertwined forever. This cord is called the Heartstring of Salim. If you retrieve this artifact for me, I will ensure you can get into the castle and past the goblins."

"Don't you have your own magic? Why do you need the Heartstring?" I shouldn't be asking questions, but I didn't want her backing out when she realized she could probably do a spell to accomplish the same thing.

"True love is something most do not get the opportunity to experience." A sparkle appeared in the Trader's eye. "The Heartstring is imbued with this love, a strange and wonderful thing that cannot simply be conjured, leaving a bond that will last as long as true love does."

"Couldn't you just find it? Wouldn't that be faster?" Karim pointed out.

"How many fairies do you see wandering the desert, boy?" Karim had no response. "Unlike humans, our magic, and the magic of all the inhabitants of the Black Forest, is tied to the land we live on. If we left the Black Forest, our magic would die out and we would fade until we too were gone."

Both Karim and the Trader were silent. I could tell they waited on me. It was my decision. "Fine. How do we find this Heartstring?"

Glee filled the fairy's countenance. She pulled an empty hourglass from the fountain. "I have collected a great many artifacts over the years. This hourglass is powered by human desire, a strong source of magic overlooked by most." Handing it off to us, she told us to close our eyes as we each gripped either side. "Now think of the place you most want to be."

I thought of Pennah and Mama and our small house. The picture was so clear in my mind it was almost tangible, and my heart even ached when I opened my eyes. I'm not sure what Karim was thinking of, but together we had made a small pile of the whitest sand I'd ever seen at the bottom of the hourglass.

"Human emotions are powerful but never permanent, so this desire will last three days. That is how long you have to retrieve the Heartstring, at which time you will return here. You will also need this." She handed us a worn wooden cup. Confused, I took it. "Its twin will remain in the pond. When you put this one to your lips, water from this fountain will come out. As long as you are drinking water from the Black Forest, you will be able to recognize the magic within the Heartstring. Now—are you ready?"

"But where are we going?" I asked.

"Of course. How forgetful of me. Salim was once the heir to the Sukkadian throne, and by some miracle, it has stayed in his lands since his death. Grem has seen—with that special gift of his—that the Heartstring is located in the main bazaar in Dariz. But since neither of you have been to Dariz, you must think of where you have been before. Karim, think of your home." I barely registered the shock on Karim's face when the Trader flipped the hourglass, a knowing smile on her face.

Chapter 23

SABLE

I awoke on a bed of clouds with warm sunlight wrapped around me like a blanket. A vague memory of my last night of sleep included cold dirt and crunchy leaves, quite different from this experience. I could sleep like this forever.

Suddenly, I realized I had felt this way before, in the Bosk Snare. My eyes flashed open and I looked around. I was most definitely not in the Snare. I wasn't even in the Black Forest anymore. My sleepy mind caught up and I remembered the Trader telling Karim to think of home.

White silk caressed my cheek. I ran my fingertips along the smooth, goose-down quilt I lay on. I had never seen a material made with such a vibrant blue color or with such fine detailed stitching. It had to be extremely expensive.

Sheer fabric draped down the sides, creating a curtain around the gigantic four-poster bed. The window that was letting in the soft morning sunshine looked out at a very unfamiliar setting of dusty, dilapidated box buildings with shutterless windows, brown, arid shrubbery, and several people in worn clothes setting up shop for the day. The rising desert sun left a shimmering haze on the horizon in its wake. A glint on a vanity caught my attention. A jeweled armband was lying atop a blue sash.

Turning over, I inspected the entire room. It was larger than my whole house. Small trinkets lined shelves and pieces of furniture were scattered about. I could fit into the wardrobe alone three times over. I finally noticed

Karim sleeping heavily beside me. The bed was large enough that I hadn't even nudged his sprawling figure.

A gasp came from the doorway—a very intricately carved doorway with a decorated, brass-handled door hanging open. The onlooker appeared to be a maid, but I didn't get a good look since she darted away the moment I met her eyes. Panic finally overcame my sleepiness and awe of the room. Impatient, I swatted Karim's back, hard enough to wake him. He sat up, looked around the room and swore. My eyebrows shot up. Through everything we'd seen and done, I'd never heard him swear. Suddenly, it dawned on me.

"This is where you stole the sword from isn't it!" I swatted him again. "Why did you bring us here?" I rolled off the bed, nearly strangling myself in the decorative curtains surrounding the enormous thing. After pulling the curtains to one side, a thick, yellow cord fell on my shoulder. I brushed it off, but when I felt the smooth scales, I realized this was the tail end of an enormous snake that had been resting atop the bed frame. The yellow snake lazily decided to come down, showing me the entirety of its body. I thought I had seen every snake known to man, but here was a snake with sections thicker than my thighs and a length that was at least three times my own. It curled onto the bed and slithered onto the floor towards a patch of sun in the corner.

"Yes. And we need to get out of here as soon as possible." He scooted off the bed with considerably more ease than I had, ignoring the giant snake and snatching the wooden cup I had left in the center of the bed.

Thinking he should know just how little time he had, I told him about the maid who spotted us on the bed. He smacked his forehead, vigorously shaking his head in panic and frustration. Dragging me by my hand, he went out the door and down the hall to the right. It was a good thing he was in the lead, because every aspect of the beautiful hallway had me enraptured. Polished tables held crystal figurines and bowls with small, floating pink flowers that had a thick fan of pointed petals and a center with yellow tendrils curling up. Much of the wall space was taken up by intricate carvings into the sandy stone. There were trees and birds and suns, and each carving was so exotically beautiful that I wanted to examine each one for hours, just admiring the realistic detail and imagination.

Karim pulled me through hallways, whizzing past servants and around corners before they turned to see us. I briefly wondered if we were really here, or if we were just ghosts of our real selves sent here by magic. If we were executed for stealing a sword people would kill for, would we just reappear in the Winterwood? Or would we actually die? The Trader should have taken a little more time to explain.

My hope for survival was rekindled when I saw sunlight leaking underneath a door at the end of the hall. That same hope was crushed underfoot when a woman wearing gold bracelets and a silky orange dress with a beaded bodice stepped out in front of us. A curved dagger was in each of her hands, and they were directed at us. Her silver-streaked dark hair was pulled back with gold pins and covered with a light, sheer fabric.

"Karim." She eyed him while keeping me in her periphery. The woman was older, but she stood with confidence and kept her hands as steady as her gaze. If it weren't for the pock marks marring her face, she would have been beautiful. The scars did not, however, deter from her ability to intimidate.

Stepping in front of me, blocking the woman from my view, Karim began speaking in another language. I knew English was not his native language, but he spoke it so fluently that sometimes I forgot. Peering around my thieving companion, I attempted to read the expression on the woman's face. There was definitely hostility, though maybe that was the daggers.

When she spoke, I discovered the woman did not have the gentle whispering voice I imagined an aristocrat to have, but her strong, semi-rough tone was regal nonetheless. After a few more words were exchanged, the daggers were finally sheathed, but she did not step aside. The woman addressed Karim with a scolding tone, and that was when I finally recognized the dominating look in her face. It was concern. She said something more, but this time she was gesturing at me. Nervous, I scooted farther behind Karim. With a sigh, Karim stepped aside, exposing me to the dagger lady.

"This is Sable," he told the woman, apparently deciding I was now allowed in the conversation.

"Sable." The woman nodded, scrutinizing me.

"Sable, this is my mother." Suddenly I felt filthy and ragged in my kappa-shredded clothes.

The woman's eyes narrowed on me and her nose turned up in the slightest. "You may call me 'Your Majesty.'" Blood immediately drained from my face and I felt light-headed.

I came from a tiny village. The Black Castle was the castle nearest to me, and our actual ruler was nearly two weeks away. I had never had the occasion to address anyone as 'Your Majesty,' because that was a title bestowed only upon the highest royalty. This woman was telling me that she was the queen of whatever land we were in.

I brusquely snatched Karim by his sleeve and hauled him further into the hall, away from the queen. I ignored the crowd of servants that watched us from the other end, who all abruptly wandered off when we walked toward them.

"She is the queen." He nodded. "And you are her son." Nod. "So, you're telling me that *you* are not a thief. You did not steal the sword, you own it, by right of birth."

Karim nodded again and tried explaining, but I held up a hand to quiet him. Before speaking, I checked my language to minimize the number of serpents that emanated from me. We had so far escaped execution for thievery, so I wasn't about to be hung for witchcraft. Fortunately, the distance from the Black Forest seemed to dull the curse a bit. If we were there now, my thoughts alone would leave us swimming in spiders.

"Have you looked around this palace? What could you possibly need Pennah for? You have everything you could ever ask for."

"Alright, I fibbed a bit about the genie wish—"

"A bit?" I looked at him incredulously as he excused the web of lies he was trying to untangle himself out of.

"My father made the wish, and to pay the price, the genie said he would have to sacrifice his pride for his son to survive anything. My father didn't realize that the sacrifice would be the destruction of everything he was proud of. He had pride in his strength as a king, but he has been bedridden for years. He had pride in the beauty of his wife and daughters, and that was tarnished one way or another." I peered at the queen who watched on, still appearing to be on the fence between accepting the foreign girl who appeared with her son and executing her. "But he also had pride in the strength of his people, their thriving economy. I *was* searching for Pennah to help my family, but also to help my country."

I wanted to be angry, but I couldn't. Apparently it showed in my face, because Karim grabbed my arms and pulled me into a hug.

"Thank you for understanding, Sable."

"You're just lucky you have genie magic. I would have punched you by now if doing it wouldn't break my hand," I muttered, but didn't go unheard.

"You will do no such thing to my son." The queen had silently come up behind me.

"Mother, please," Karim pleaded, standing protectively close to me still.

"Roya!" She promptly ignored him. A maid scurried in and bowed to the queen, who gave her some orders in the foreign language. Roya told me something in the same language and beckoned me to follow her. Confused, I turned to Karim.

"Roya will help you wash up and give you some new clothes," he explained. "You'll be fine." He smiled to reassure me. Still uncertain, I followed Roya through winding hallways until she pulled me down some stairs and into a room with a shallow pool that smelled like sulfur. Naked woman lounged in the pool, talking, laughing and washing until they saw me walk in. I was well tanned from the time I spent outside working in the garden and walking into town this last summer, but I felt like an albino with the way they watched me follow Roya in. The skin tones of the women varied, but they were all some shade of brown and they were all much darker than I was.

The water wasn't steaming, and cold water felt impossible in weather like this, so it had to be lukewarm. The air was muggy, so I pulled off my winter jacket and draped it on my arm. Since Servans was outside of the jacket, I took that off as well and held it at my side.

With exaggerated motions, Roya pointed to the water and told me something. Obviously, I had no idea what she said, so I returned her remark with confusion. To resolve the problem, she somehow assumed speaking slower and louder would enable me to understand her. It didn't. Instead, she pointed to the water and mimed cupping it in her hand and drinking it followed by a sour face and shaking of the head. Assuming that meant don't drink the water, I nodded. It had a foul sulfuric smell anyway, so that was a given. Then she mimed washing her arms and nodded her head. Again, I had gathered this much, so I nodded. Confusion quickly returned when Roya attempted to undress me.

"Wait, what? Bathe here?" Roya had quick fingers and while I complained, she untied my pants and pulled them down. I dropped my hands, using my jacket to cover myself when Roya tugged my shirt up. I decided I wasn't going to get a better wash than this, so I dropped my jacket and sword, allowing Roya to finish undressing me. I removed my own breastband and before anyone could have enough time to stare, I climbed into the water, bringing my knees to my chest as I sat. The largest audience I had ever had while bathing was Pennah. Standing naked in front of so many strangers was mortifying, but sitting with my arms around my knees was less so. Once I was in, everyone else continued speaking, and I wouldn't be surprised if they were gossiping about me. I couldn't tell if it was my skin tone or the plethora of healing claw marks all over my body that instigated the gossip, and until I learned the entire language, I'd never know.

Roya handed me a cloth and bar of soap to wash myself with. The water was lukewarm, but it was still the warmest bath I had ever taken. Who knew they could be so relaxing? The cuts from my run-in with the kappa only stung a little as I washed up. A quick check assured me that none of the cuts had gotten infected.

During my wash, many women climbed in and out of the pool. At least I wasn't the only one whose ribs pushed out against my stomach's flesh. Karim had said something about a drought, hadn't he?

Once the grime and a layer of skin was scrubbed off and my hair was thoroughly cleaned, I began putting my spiderwebbed hair into its usual braid when my hand was swatted away by Roya. The next thing I knew, a comb was tearing through my matted hair, breaking through knots that had probably been there for years since my hair was unmanageable and I didn't own a comb. For being such a thin, older woman, Roya had strong hands. Even when my scalp was throbbing with pain, she continued tugging and twisting, doing who knows what to my poor head. Many times she paused and wiped spider silk on her apron, muttering something to herself, probably questioning if spiders lived in my hair. Several pins were stabbed into my hair before the pain finally ended.

I turned to face Roya when she began telling me something. Somehow—it must have been another servant roaming the bathhouse—she had gotten a towel and fresh clothes for me to wear. At the bench Roya led me to, I toweled off and slipped into the soft, pale green dress. It was similar in design to the dress I saw the queen wearing earlier, but it obviously lacked the same level of detail.

The pile of clothes I was handed included a dark blue sash. Copying the few other women I had seen walk in or out of the bathhouse wearing sashes similar to this, I looped it over my right shoulder and tied it at my opposite hip. With assistance from Roya, I was able to tie the strapped sandals to my feet. She nodded approvingly before returning my sword and dagger with my purse still tied to Servans's sheath. I asked Roya about my clothes, trying to mime to her by pinching at my new dress, but she just shook her head and continued out. I had no choice but to follow.

After a few corners and hallways, ensuring I was completely lost probably, Roya pushed me through a door. Waiting inside was a long dining table, more functional than the one I had seen in the Black Castle and yet more pleasingly to look at. At the head of the table sat the queen, who watched me enter with a little less disapproval than before. To the queen's right was a woman several years older than me. It was impossible not to notice the three thick, puckering scars that began at her left eye and cut through her cheek and the corner of her lips, skipped over her neck and continued on her collarbone. It may have gone farther but her dress concealed the rest. Her stare gave me goosebumps. The eye where the scar began was clouded over with white, contrasting her other dark eye. I now understood a little better what the price of the king's wish for Karim was.

"This is my sister Maram. Maram, this is Sable," Karim introduced us from the other side of his mother. He gestured to the seat beside him. "Take a seat." Nervously, I edged across the room and into the seat. Karim looked just as I felt—clean, well-groomed and more beautiful than I was used to. He wore a plain, silky, dark blue shirt. Judging from the amount of jewelry his sister and mother wore, I assumed he often wore jewelry as well, but he must have grown accustomed to going without it over the last month or two since he left here.

Servants brought plates with our breakfast on them. The pastries on my plate were flaky and the fruit preserves on top were delectable. I left the water on the table, knowing I should be drinking from the cup the Trader gave us so we would recognize the Heartstring.

Maram said something to Karim in their native language.

"Maram, please speak English." The princess rolled her good eye.

"I simply said the strawberry preserves were delicious." Maram's accent was even better than Karim's. How could I have never guessed he was more than a simple thief when he knew a second language so fluently? And seeing him now, fitting so perfectly in this setting surrounded by wealth and servants, I felt foolish for believing the lie.

"I agree. Breakfast was fantastic. Thank you, Your Majesty." I politely bowed my head to the queen, assuming that was the correct thing to do. I was utterly out of place here, and all who sat around this table knew it. Except maybe Karim, who beamed at me. I gave him a nervous smile in return.

"So, *Sable*." Maram said my name like she was testing the taste of it, unsure if she liked it or not. "How did you come to meet my brother?"

"Actually, I—" Karim tried intervening, but Maram silenced him with a finger.

"I was speaking to Sable, Karim." She looked back to me, seeming to enjoy my fidgeting.

"He asked me for directions," I answered truthfully. How much of his quest did Karim's family know?

"To where?"

I glanced at Karim for some sort of cue, but he stared at his empty plate. "To the Black Forest."

The queen slammed her fist on the table. "Magic is what got us in this mess in the first place. I told you not to go searching for fairytales," she scolded her son. Karim obviously did not inherit his mother's temper, because he stayed calm when he addressed her.

"Should I have sat by and waited for father to die so I could rule a dying kingdom? Doing nothing would have accomplished just that. Nothing." I was just beginning to wrap my head around Karim being a prince. Trying to imagine him actually ruling a country gave me a headache. Even stranger was the fact that I knew he would do well. He would be an amazing king.

"We can talk about this later," Maram interrupted sharply. "Karim has returned, so we have plenty of time." Karim didn't react. In the last two weeks I'd begun to think of him as easy to read. Apparently he was a better actor than I gave him credit for. If lying came so easy to him, now how could I know if he was being truthful?

"Since it is Sable's first day here, I wanted to show her around," Karim told the queen as servants gathered our plates.

"Of course," the queen said with a sweet smile, her temper completely gone. "I'm sure Harish and Savir would happily accompany you." Karim didn't argue, but he did look slightly put out with the offer.

Harish and Savir turned out to be royal guards. One was a young, gangly boy, probably even younger than Pennah, and the other was an old man whose dark wrinkled skin made his white hair even more conspicuous. I didn't know much about royal courts, but judging from these two, the royal guard had also been something the king was proud of that had to pay the price of the genie's wish.

"Would you like anything?" Karim asked as we passed a shop advertising metal bracelets with interesting designs. The vendor nodded his head enthusiastically as he leaned out from under his canopied cart, pointing to various pieces of jewelry. I shook my head. Out of habit, I didn't talk much in a crowd. A spider or scorpion wouldn't be too out of place in this particular market, but that wasn't the only thing keeping me silent. Every person we passed nodded respectfully to their prince, who stuck out like a sore thumb with his guards and now uncovered royal sword. As they bowed their heads, I could see their eyes landing on me. Not because they thought I was a witch, but because I was the mysterious foreign girl walking beside the prince that had gone missing for who knows how long. The whole situation felt wrong. Every inch of my skin itched with a desire to be anywhere but here.

"I'm sorry," he muttered, bending closer to me, though I doubted the common folk, or even the royal guard, understood English. "I was hoping we could slip away, but having the guards here makes it impossible." I glanced back at the guards. I wasn't sure which one was which, but neither seemed capable of catching us if we chose to run. Then it occurred to me that a prince fleeing his own guards might not be something Karim wanted his people to see. Though they wore ragged clothes and a thick layer of dust over their skin, they watched their prince with eager smiles and a hope in their eyes that comes with each new generation. Perhaps they would think he was abandoning them for good. They couldn't know that everything he had done was for their sakes.

After walking through the marketplace a bit longer, Karim took us back to the palace, where the guards returned to their original posts. He knew his way around, turning each corner with confidence. It shouldn't have been surprising since he grew up here. I couldn't even fathom growing up in a place like this, where you were never hungry, never cold.

"You can leave your sword in here for the time being. We can try to sneak out tonight." I glanced around the room, recognizing the giant bed, the yellow snake.

"This is your room?" What would it be like to sleep on a bed like that every night? Or to have a mirror? I caught a glance of myself. Roya had done a superb job with my hair. A braid coiled into a tight plaited bun. The silvery spiderwebs were still visible, but they actually added to the beauty of the hair style, in my opinion.

"Yes, it's mine. If the Trader had given me more than a moment's notice I might have thought of the marketplace or somewhere else in town." Karim sat on the bed beside the snake. It was lying in a patch of sun near the pillows, but coiled around his waist as he absent-mindedly stroked its muscled spine.

"What kind of snake is that?" I set my sword on the chest that sat at the foot of the bed.

He told me in the unfamiliar language. "I'm not sure what the breed is called in English. His name is Gilgamesh. He is not venomous, though. He actually squeezes his prey to kill them, but we keep him fed so he doesn't have to go around squeezing people." He laughed shortly. It was half-hearted. "I'm sorry I didn't tell you. Everything else I told you was the truth, though. About my family, my quest. And I really do want to help you rescue Pennah."

There was no logical reason for me to be upset. "It's alright. It was none of my business." And it wasn't. But why was I still bitter?

"We were travelling together. I should have told you. We should be able to trust each other." Standing across the bed from Karim, I reached out and ran my fingers along Gilgamesh's scales. "Actually, why have you trusted me so far? I let you believe I was a thief." A smug smile crept onto his face, like he was pleased with himself for earning my trust.

"Thieves don't scare me. I have nothing to steal." The only thing I had worth stealing was already gone, but I was working on getting her back.

"What about the sword?" he pointed out. I hadn't even known how valuable it was until the Trader informed me of the price my father had paid. A price I wish he had never paid. I would have preferred the ten years he had sacrificed.

"For one, it doesn't exactly *look* valuable. Plus, the Trader said only I could use it." I shrugged.

"Has anyone else tried?" I shook my head. The snake, annoyed, slithered off the bed when Karim unwrapped himself from Gilgamesh's tangled body. Karim stood and drew my sword from its sheath. It was strange to see the rusty weapon in his hands. I was used to seeing the curved, bejeweled blade there. Karim gave Servans an experimental swish in the air, but ended up throwing it across the floor. I knew from experience that Karim was a well-trained swordsman, so this had to be what the Trader meant.

"That's odd." Karim retrieved the sword and thrusted it into the air at an invisible opponent. The point dipped and pulled to the ground as if it suddenly gained twenty pounds. Apparently giving up, Karim put Servans back in its sheath.

"While we are waiting for night to fall, shall we take a turn around the gardens?"

The gardens turned out to be very beautiful. Apparently, this was not something the king cared much about before making the wish. There were so many flowers and plants that didn't look even remotely familiar. Many plants had sharp needles, and Karim said that in summer they would bloom with the most beautiful flowers. It was like a desert version of a rosebush—thorny but beautiful.

"Didn't you say you had four sisters? Where are the other three? So far, I've only seen Maram." I brushed my fingers against some strange sharp

131

leaves. Apparently everything in the desert was sharper. The plants, the people. Even the sun shined hotter.

"Aisha, Nawra and Laila were all married before the wish. Maram is the youngest daughter, but because of the scar many suitors from before have left." That sounded familiar. But Maram was such a strong, diplomatic woman. And underneath the scar she was beautiful. Could no one see that?

"Karim!" A young girl waved and glided toward us through the garden. She said something else I couldn't understand in a worried tone, probably about how he had finally returned. There were sparkling trinkets in her raven black hair and around her wrists and neck. I almost might have guessed this was one of the married sisters who somehow escaped the repercussions of the wish, but when the girl got to us, she threw her arms around Karim and kissed him. On the mouth. And it was not a sisterly kiss.

Karim pulled back and gestured to me. "This is Sable," he introduced, simultaneously signaling to this stranger that I only spoke English. The girl still clung to his side and gave me a wide grin.

"Hello!" Her accent was significantly thicker than Karim's and his family's and she had to speak slightly slower. "My name is Nadia. I am the wife of Karim."

Chapter 24

PENNAH

My conversations with Daria had produced many more gems. The more I got to know her, the less I felt like a captive. I hadn't thought much about *why* Marcus had put us in a room together, but he had probably figured that I wouldn't say nearly as many kind words if left alone in a bare room. Not only did my days feel less grim, but I was learning a lot about the magical world. For example, Daria taught me that each magical creature had different types of magic. Nymphs had what was called raw magic. Raw magic was part of the being's essence. This was where my particular gift stemmed from. Daria called it a reflection of raw magic, some of the most powerful she had seen or heard of in a human. Simple magic is the kind Marcus excelled at, which was why he could only create the illusion of a gem or a glamoured face. Witch's performed the same type of magic. It was only small things, and they couldn't infuse a person with it like raw magic or dark magic. Simple magic could only be used on inanimate objects. Daria didn't know much about dark magic, only that it drove humans mad and cost the user dearly.

I was even gradually learning more about the sprites. Now that I knew they understood me, that they had more brain capacity than a bug, I was able to use that to my advantage.

"If you want this ruby," I held up the jewel to the greedy bundle of sprites that had snuck in the window, "then you have to fuse these gold bits together." I had laid several gold strands from my hair on the ground. My plan was to collect enough gold to fuse, with sprite magic, into a rope

I could use to climb out the window. The little monsters tried stealing my gems over and over again and I had to repeat my request many times before they final gave in and melted the gold threads. I now had a foot-long cord about the thickness of yarn. I tossed the ruby to the sprites, letting them fight over it. It was going to cost a lot of pretty words to make a rope.

"I'm not sure why you bother. Do you think we haven't tried sneaking out of here? The goblins may be stupid, but they are everywhere. You'll never get out. Just wait for your sister to come again. If she doesn't get eaten alive by razor sharp goblin teeth, maybe she'll free us all." Daria braided her purple seaweed-looking hair. Now that she was finally comfortable around me, her skin was rarely transparent. Instead, she kept it pearlescent. If I didn't know any better, I'd think she was an interestingly-colored human girl with an affinity for water.

"I don't want Sable to risk her life again. Not if I can get out on my own." Twiddling the gold yarn in my hands I slid over to the empty fireplace and leaned back onto the mildewy cushion. "I can't blame her for coming alone, or at least mostly alone." I remembered the strange, dark-skinned boy who fought alongside my sister. "No one would help her, I'm sure. No one would even listen to her."

"Because of the snake curse?" After Sable's rescue attempt, I told Daria about the curse Sable had to live with. "I don't understand the fear humans have for those creatures. They aren't pretty, that's for sure, but they aren't anything special either."

"Snakes, spiders and scorpions as well as basically anything that is involved with Sable's curse are all bad omens, or so people think. Back home, everyone believes she is a witch, and they are all afraid of her." A jagged piece of black amber clattered to the stone floor, appearing out of thin air.

"There is nothing wrong with witches either," Daria scolded me, as if *I* was the one who believed the lies about Sable. "Human stories only show the worst of magical creatures. Not every water nymph is trying to drown every human, though it is entertaining to watch them flounder." I must have looked appalled, because Daria amended herself. "I don't let them *die*. Anyway, not all witches are evil hags. Many are healers. Humans are so judgmental."

Somehow, every conversation ended here. Humans are imperfect creatures, far inferior to the naiad race. I had discovered it was much easier if I didn't argue.

Gurgling from outside the door grew louder. Ever since Sable's rescue attempt, there were even more goblins stationed around the castle to prevent any more incidents. The guards currently outside my room were either excited or agitated by something. Finally, the door swung open and Marcus entered unannounced, flanked by the two ugly goblins that were posted at my door. As nonchalantly as I could, I dropped the gold string into my sleeve. If my plan worked, I'd have to figure out where to hide a golden rope.

Marcus's fingers touched a pendant of some sort that hung against his chest and his lips twitched up on one side in a half smile. "Gather up every jewel you can find," Marcus ordered the goblins, who obeyed without hesitation or emotion. When the goblins neared Daria's tub, she shrank into it, her skin and hair turning translucent and her eyes rippling with fear. I sat up, as always, allowing the goblins to search underneath the small cushion I used as a bed.

After every nook and cranny in the tiny room had been scoured, the three nasty creatures lingered in the doorway.

"There is just one last thing," Marcus said, pulling a small vial from his pocket. A whimper bubbled up from Daria's tub.

"What is that?" I asked, but Marcus didn't take his eyes off of Daria.

"Do you know what a bit of phoenix blood does?" A grin full of malice curled onto the warlock's face. "To a human, the blood is like acid. It can burn through bone, even." I cringed when he yanked out the cork with a loud pop. "For a water nymph, however, it is much, much worse."

Until that moment, I hadn't realized water nymphs could cry.

"You told my mother that if she did everything you wanted, you wouldn't—" Daria's voice hitched and broke into a sob. "Please, don't," she begged, her lips parting and quivering. I got to my feet.

"Stop! Why are you doing this?" I started walking to Marcus, but the two goblins stopped me, their sharp nails digging into my forearms, holding me back.

"You see, your lovely sister broke a gift I gave to my wife." What kind of demented woman married a man like Marcus? "And I need to replace it." Marcus tilted the tiny vial of phoenix blood into Daria's tub. The blood poured into the corner of the tub, red spreading like poison in the clear water. Daria had squeezed up against the edge, but she couldn't go anywhere. There was no escape.

"No!" A diamond tear, exactly what Marcus was looking for, fell to the stony floor. I pulled against the goblins, only deepening the cuts in my arms.

"Release her," Marcus told the goblins. They did, but there was nothing I could do now.

Tears rolled down Daria's face, mirroring my own. The water in the tub bubbled and steam rose from the water's surface and from every inch of Daria's skin. Her breathing became more and more labored until it sounded more like hoarse gasping. That was when she started screaming. As Daria writhed in her small tub in agony, gripping the edge of it with her child-sized hands, Marcus stood in the doorway watching, a satisfied smile on his face.

Chapter 25

SABLE

Wife? Just when I accept that Karim is a prince, I find out he is also married? No wonder the maid was so shocked to see Karim waking up in his bed beside some mysterious woman when he already had a wife!

"No!" Karim stepped away from Nadia in alarm. "She is *not* my wife. Nadia does not know English very well."

Confusion swept over the girl's features. "Did I speak incorrectly? We are betrothed."

"I think fiancé is the word you are looking for." I filled in, suddenly in a sour mood. My words were not malicious, but I could feel a spider crawling on the back of my hand nonetheless. Fiancé wasn't much better than wife. Deciding I would rather look at the plants than at the soon to be wed couple making eyes at each other, I continued along the slate path.

"Sable, wait." Nadia stayed back while Karim stopped me.

"Wait for what? Obviously, you've been away for a while. Go ahead and catch up with your fiancé. I'll just be looking around." I tried to keep my voice flippant, but I don't think it worked.

"No, it's not—" He sighed. "Technically, we're engaged, but I don't—"

"I don't care. You and I are travelling companions. We are acquaintances. Nothing more. You are a prince of a land very different from my own, and I couldn't care less about your personal life. I'll find my own way back. Good-bye." I turned on my heel and left him in the garden with his betrothed. How romantic.

Just before I went back inside, a small red, black and white snake slithered into the bushes.

It took a while, and I couldn't exactly ask for directions, but eventually I found my way back to Karim's room. It was an ironic place to go since he was the one I was avoiding, but there was literally nowhere else. And Gilgamesh was surprisingly good company. Yes, with the giant yellow snake I had finally found a man who wouldn't betray me. Until he got hungry, I supposed, but he was lethargic most of the time so I wasn't too concerned.

In fact, Gilgamesh's habit of taking naps in the sunshine seemed especially inspired at the moment, so I joined him on the cloudlike bed and relished in the silky material and warm sun, knowing it wouldn't last. I wished there was something I could do to help Pennah right now, but I was in a strange land where I didn't even speak the language. Without Karim's help, I'd never find the Heartstring, so until he figured out a way to get us out of this palace, I was stuck.

I hadn't napped since I was a child, so I hadn't imagined I would actually fall asleep in the middle of the day, but the comfortable plush quilt was impossible to stay awake on. I now knew where Karim's habit of sleeping so deeply came from.

When I awoke, I was still heavy with sleep, but I knew I shouldn't sleep the day away. I forced myself to sit up, thoroughly agitating Gilgamesh in the process.

"I brought you some supper." I turned to see Karim in the wooden chair near the other side of the bed. He gestured to a plate on the bed with a book he must have been reading before I woke up. I didn't understand the strange characters written on the pages, but they curled in the most unusual ways.

My eyes were drawn to the plate of food. Over the course of many years full of difficult winters, my body had adjusted to survive off of minimal food. I knew what it felt like to literally be starving, so if my stomach yearned for more food, I didn't notice. However, the meal on the bed looked delicious and I wasn't sure when I would ever eat this quality of food again, so I picked at the plate and tried a little of everything on it. As always, silence wasn't silence unless it was being interrupted by Karim.

"Nadia and I have been officially set to marry since she was born. We have grown up as friends," he attempted to explain.

"Yes, you two are obviously very close." I couldn't get the image of Nadia's arms around him as she planted a kiss on his lips out of my head. It was almost as bad as the wood nymphs. To banish the thought, I put a strip of some kind of very well-seasoned meat in my mouth. Using the wooden cup from the Trader for the first time was an interesting experience. When I lifted it, there was no sloshing, but when I put the edge to my lips, cool water soothed my throat. The distance from the Black Forest made it difficult for me to recognize the sparkles that were stronger in Karim and almost absent in the rest of the room, but the water from the Trader's cup made it so I could still see the magic when I wanted to. That alone distracted me plenty from the thought of Nadia, until Karim continued.

"She has never done that before." Karim's dark face reddened. "Nadia is actually part of the reason I left in the first place." I looked up, interested in the direction this story was going.

"I turned eighteen a few months ago, which means that once my father dies, I will become the king. And once I am crowned king, I am required to marry." He made inheriting a kingdom and marrying a beautiful girl sound miserable. "I grew up understanding that I would probably not marry for love, but there has always been a part of me that optimistically hoped that I could. I think that when I left I wasn't only trying to save my kingdom. I was also being selfish, indulging in my fear."

Unsure of how to respond to Karim's confession, I remained silent for a moment.

"Is there anything else you'd like me to know?" I asked him. "I'm beginning to tire of your endless surprises."

He grinned. "No, I think you know everything now."

At that moment, I wanted to tell him about my mother, but it was far too easy for me to envision a look of shock and disgust on his face. I couldn't tell him. He couldn't know what a monster I was, or I would really lose him.

The rest of the day was spent doing trivial things. Any time we approached a door exiting the building, the queen was somehow there, as if she knew we were going to leave tonight. Maram was also hovering quite a bit. The more I was around her, the less shocking her blind eye and scarred face were, and her personality was actually similar to my own. Unfortunately, that fact did not help us get along. And neither did the constant questions.

"So, Sable, how did my brother convince you to travel all this way with him? Where is your family? How long do you plan on staying?"

And the best of all was, "Why are there always snakes around? We have a pest controller. Perhaps he has started drinking again."

She never let Karim answer for me, so I struggled to keep my answers as ambiguous as possible while still somehow answering the questions.

Dinner was a small meal, which made me grateful I had slept through supper. However, Nadia had decided to reappear.

"Nadia, we are so pleased you could join us tonight. Isn't it wonderful, Karim?" the queen asked her son. I had been placed between Maram and the queen, across from Nadia. The young woman was leaning adoringly toward Karim, who made no effort against it. Fortunately, the chairs had armrests, preventing any physical contact.

"I, too, am pleased you were able to come, Nadia," Karim told her stiffly, glancing over at me every so often.

"And I am glad to be here." I felt mildly guilty for disliking the girl when she was so obviously head over heels for Karim. Or at least she was in love with his imminent kingship. "I only wish my English was better," she laughed. Actually, it was more of an awkward guffaw. Maram pursed her lips at Karim's fiancé. At least I wasn't the only one annoyed with her.

At the end of the meal, I was exhausted by all the idle chatter. The entire conversation was shallow and meaningless.

"Sable, was the meal not to your liking?" the queen asked, practically daring me to insult her hospitality.

"It was delicious, but I couldn't possibly eat any more." I barely managed to eat half of what was on my plate, but my stomach felt bloated already.

Finally, the servants retrieved the plates and I was sent with Roya to the guest room I would be sleeping in. Karim hadn't given me a solid plan for tonight, so I sat on the edge of my bed and waited. Roya had given me a nightgown, but I stayed in the pale green dress and midnight blue sash. After a half hour, I was beginning to doubt we would leave. Maybe he had decided to tell his mother that we were only here for three days and in that time we had to retrieve a magical artifact called the Heartstring of Salim. Though I didn't believe he would tell the queen what was actually going on, I still ended up curled up at the foot of the bed. It wasn't as large or comfortable as Karim's bed, but it was still far superior to anything else I had ever slept on.

I wasn't sure how long I had been asleep, but bright stars lit the sky through the small window when Karim shook my shoulder to wake me.

"I'm sorry it took so long. Here." Karim handed me white silky material.

"What's this?" I blinked away the sleepiness and unraveled the soft cloth, understanding when I held it up to see.

"Pants. You'll need them. I also restocked our supplies." He handed me a backpack that was much sturdier than the old pack I had left at the Black Castle. It also had more pockets and fresh supplies. There was a warm blanket, dried meat, dried fruits, first aid supplies, and my old boots, though I wasn't sure how he found those. He also handed me a thick winter jacket, far nicer than anything I had ever owned. It was tanned leather lined with a soft, thin layer of fur. It even had pockets. "The pants and jacket used to belong to my sister, Aisha, before she was married."

"Why do we even need jackets? I'm already hot just standing here." The cool breeze slipping in through the window almost made me doubt my words, but I knew even the chilly desert night couldn't possibly warrant such a thick jacket.

"I figured that if the Heartstring comes with us when we reappear in the Black Forest, then everything else will too, but we had no supplies there, and it was cold. We might as well use what we have while we're here."

"Alright." I slipped the pants on under my dress and buckled Servans to my back. "Lead the way."

Using many servant's corridors and empty rooms to hide from guards and servants roaming the halls late at night, Karim led me out of the palace. When I caught the scent of livestock, I suddenly feared Karim's plan to escape. I was proven correct when Karim pulled me into a stable full of horses.

Karim towed me to the back of the stable and stopped in front of a giant, brown speckled horse with ears higher than my hands could reach. A chill tweaked my spine in ripples when the enormous horse snorted hot air into my face.

"I can't ride that," I whispered, staring dumbfounded at the easy way Karim handled the huge animal. He grabbed a saddle and latched it in place on top of a blanket on the horse's back.

"This is Cyrus. I will ride him." He took the backpack from my hands and hooked it to one side of the saddle, opposite of his own backpack. "You will ride Tamina." He led me to another horse. This one was much smaller. Her coat was dappled white with a black snout and a yellowish mane.

"I can't ride any horse. I've never ridden one before."

"Tamina is a Khazar horse. Children can ride her easily," Karim explained as he saddled the mare. He was ready to help me up when we both realized the problem my dress presented. I couldn't straddle a horse wearing this. Before I could insist I just walk instead, Karim took my dagger and cut a slice at the bottom of the seam on either side of my dress. Pulling the seam apart, Karim ripped my dress almost all the way to the waistline of the pants underneath.

"There. That should work." He nodded at his handiwork.

"What a scandal." The newcomer's voice came from the front of the stable. Karim and I, both in a panic, looked to see Maram guarding the opening. "I leave you alone for a few hours, and here you are tearing her dress to bits in a dark stable. Karim, I thought you were a better man than that."

Karim didn't say a word, apparently unable to explain himself.

"I'm not sure why you came back home, Karim, when it was obvious you never planned to stay." His eyebrows shot up, shocked she had discovered as much in the single day we had been here. "Don't look so surprised. I grew up with you. Mother may be desperate to hold on to you, but I am not blind." She paused, giving a wry smile and dropping her eyes to the dirt floor. "Not all the way at least."

"Maram, I'm sorry. I have to do this. I will be back, though."

"I expect no less," she responded somberly. Her eyes drifted to where I stood. "Make sure my brother returns in one piece." I nodded, but I wasn't sure how she expected me to make a difference. It was already nearly impossible to harm him, which left any protection I could offer virtually useless. Then it occurred to me that his entire family may not know about the wish. But how else did the king and queen explain the stroke of bad luck that hit their family and lands?

"Ila-liqaa." Maram left us each with one last unnerving stare before turning on her heel and exiting the stables.

"Put your foot there." Karim pointed at the stirrup hanging from Tamina's saddle. Why didn't he tell his family that he was running away for them? Ignoring the urge to go to Maram and tell her that her brother loved her and was only trying to help, I obeyed Karim's instructions and clumsily pulled myself onto Tamina's back. Once settled, I looked over to Karim who had somehow mounted his horse in the moments it took me to adjust in the saddle. He sat upright with confidence, looking like he belonged there.

With a click of his tongue, Karim urged the two horses onward. He had confiscated my reigns so I gripped the saddle's edge to steady myself. Fortunately, the main road was dusty and not cobblestoned, so the horses moved stealthily. Once we were out of town, Karim gave me more instructions on how to direct Tamina. I learned to steer using the reigns, to stop, and to change speed. At one point we began to trot. It was uncomfortable, but I didn't say anything. Eventually we slowed to a walk.

"I'm assuming you know how to get to Dariz from here." Fortunately, even if we got lost we'd just reappear in the Black Forest. That possibility made me wonder what the Trader would do if we failed to return with the Heartstring. Obviously she wouldn't help us. But would we have to pay some other way? The stories Ulrich told in town said magic always had a price. Sometimes the cost was insignificant: a childhood memory or a first kiss. Other times it was a steeper cost: your firstborn child, or ten years of your life. I could never pay that. I just hoped the Trader didn't ask.

"Of course. Dariz is the largest seaport trading town in Sukkad. You just follow the scent of sea brine and cheap ale." Karim laughed heartily. He took a deep breath of the warm desert air. The farther we got, the bigger Karim's smile grew and the more relaxed he became. I couldn't help but wonder if part of the reason he left in the first place was to *leave*. To not be a prince for the first time in his life. Or perhaps he really was a posh prince down to his core, simply seeking out a never-ending source of wealth for his struggling kingdom.

Looking to the stars, I forced myself to stop wondering who Karim was and what he wanted. Once we got Pennah, he'd get his jewels and we'd part ways. I located Ursa Major and the North Star. It was comforting to know that despite my distance from home, at least something was the same.

"I think we've gone far enough." Karim pulled his horse to a stop and gracefully slipped off. "They are probably expecting us to go back to the Black Forest, so they shouldn't find us."

"Won't someone recognize you?" Clutching the saddle, I attempted to slide off just as Karim had. Theoretically, it should have been easier for me since my horse was shorter, but the ground was still farther than I had realized and my left foot was stubbornly caught in the stirrup. A pair of hands firmly gripped my waist, rebalancing me and easing me down.

"Would you recognize the prince of your land?" I turned to see Karim gazing down at me, the light from the full moon glinting in his eyes. His hands still rested on my waist, keeping my feet glued to the spot. Letting my fingers slip from the saddle until my palms gently landed on his forearms, I almost imperceptibly leaned toward him. My heart was full in my chest and it was hammering quickly. Anxiety tingled over every inch of my skin. I'm not sure where it came from, but Pennah's voice rang in my head. *There's a real prince out there for you.* My eager heart suddenly skipped a beat and went cold. What was I doing? I was a walking curse, and Karim had enough of his own curses to deal with. Also, Pennah was just a little girl who actually believed that someone like me could have a real prince.

Putting the slightest pressure against his arms, I stepped back, slipping out of Karim's grasp. The hurt was palpable in his eyes, but I knew it could have been so much worse. Nothing between us could ever last.

"No, I suppose not," I told him. Karim took the horses away from the road so we could set up camp away from bandits.

The area was relatively flat, but Karim found a large enough outcropping of rocks to camp against. We both set up the bedrolls Karim had packed. I asked if one of us should stay up to keep watch.

"The horses will hear anything long before we do. They will warn us." Without another word, he laid on his bedroll with his back toward me. Usually, Karim could fall asleep within five minutes. He laid still on his mat, but I could tell from his breathing that he wasn't asleep. I watched his back shift as his body rose and fell with each breath until the steadying rhythm put me to sleep.

Chapter 26

SABLE

I had expected the next day full of riding to be awkwardly silent, but Karim's talkativeness was difficult to deter. Most of the day was spent with him telling me about Dariz and the other major cities in Sukkad and he attempted to teach me his language: Arabic.

"Marhaban means hello," he told me. I attempted to repeat the word, but the accent was hard to copy. After multiple corrections, he nodded, satisfied with my pronunciation.

"Ana'asif means pardon me, or I'm sorry." Again, I tried the phrase. More often than not, Karim ended up laughing at my attempts to speak Arabic, but he did not give up. If learning the vocabulary and pronunciation for another language was always this hard, it made me wonder how Karim managed to learn English so well. I ran over the new words in my mind. Shukran is thank you, Na^am is Yes, La is No, Ma'as-salamah is good bye.

Somewhere along the way, there was a brief moment of silence and I made the mistake of asking him how to say *road*. Now that he knew I was genuinely interested in learning, Karim started handing me more and more vocabulary words. Sky, cloud, sun, hot, horse, man, woman. I forgot more words than I remembered, but by mid-afternoon my accent had greatly improved.

Just before the sun set, we arrived at the outskirts of the hot, dirty city of Dariz.

"What are you doing?" I asked as Karim hopped down from his saddle. Still unsure of his plan, I followed suit. This time, Karim did not help me down, but I managed to stay on my feet. I untied Servans from Tamina's saddle and strapped it to my back.

"The horses will be able to find their way back. We won't need them anymore since we'll return to the Black Forest tomorrow night." He unhooked the backpacks and handed one to me. Smacking the horses, he pushed them off back towards the palace. With long strides, Karim headed off to Dariz, the smell of which reached us already, and we were probably still a half mile away from the city. I thought Karim was joking before, but it truly did smell like sea brine and ale.

Taking a few steps after Karim, I realized that my legs needed the stretch—they were stiffer than a board—but they also had minimal range of motion as well as some very uncomfortable chafing, even though Aisha's old pants were clearly made for riding horses because they had thick padding right where my sore skin was. I couldn't imagine how torn up my legs could have been if not for the pants. Karim eventually realized that my pace was significantly slower than his and, without a word, he matched my steps. I just hoped tomorrow my legs were back to their normal functions.

Even though it was still too early to go to sleep, I was exhausted and grateful that all the stores in the market were closed, forcing us to wait until tomorrow to locate the Heartstring. Karim found a tavern near the market where we could eat and get a room.

"Marhaban," Karim greeted the tavern's host, a thick, gruff man with white streaking his otherwise dark and scraggly beard. My vocabulary wasn't good enough to understand the majority of the exchange, but I caught Karim's 'please.' When Karim began walking to a table, I asked him what the man had said.

"He'll get us a room after we've eaten." We sat at a table where a woman of questionable morality approached us and presumably asked us what we wanted to eat. For all I knew, though, she could have been asking Karim to take her upstairs. She certainly looked like an escort with all of the dark makeup around her eyes, the red paint on her lips, the dress that cut low against her breasts and stopped just past her knees, and the false jewel pendant made of glass hanging around her neck. Fortunately, Karim's response sounded more like 'we'll have bread and broth, please' than 'yes, I have a room, but I need to get rid of my friend first.' He followed her to the bar and returned with bread and broth.

"I hate how easy it is to readjust to three meals a day." Karim chewed on the strange tasting bread. He had nearly twice as much as me and seemed to be eating it twice as fast as I was. Watching him ravenously eat his meal was yet another reminder that he was a prince. As far as I could remember, there were four occasions in my life when I had three meals in one day: my mother's wedding with Matthew; Christmas day when I was five, though when my stepfather discovered I had stolen some of his supper, he beat me with his belt so I never did it again; on Pennah's fourth birthday when my stepfather had won a dice game; and yesterday at Karim's palace. Suffice it to say, I wasn't ever going to adjust to that much food in one day.

After we filled up on the stale bread soaked in broth, drinking water only from the Trader's wooden cup, Karim and I went off to find the tavern's host to get a room to sleep in. On the way across the stinky room that was so packed full of dirty men and promiscuous women, a rough hand wrapped around my waist and pulled me aside. The brown-skinned man grabbed my chin with his other hand and drunkenly spoke Arabic into my face, allowing me to smell the rancid alcohol on his breath. I caught the word 'sa'hera' before I reached for my dagger, having half a mind to nick his hand with my poisoned blade. Suddenly, the man jerked away when Karim snagged him by his collar. He told the man something in Arabic and shoved him away. Proceeding to lead me toward the tavern's host, Karim covered my hand with his own, easing my dagger back into place at my hip.

"I would have been fine." The man was long gone, but the lingering stench made my nose wrinkle.

"Ana'asif." *Sorry,* Karim said, his demeanor no longer pleasant. "But killing him might have created a bigger scene." He found the host and we were led upstairs to a tiny room. In the corner, a squalid mat slouched against the creaky floorboards.

"I don't think it would be chivalrous to offer you the bed in this case," Karim pointed out, revulsion painting his features. I couldn't blame his judgement on princely pettiness. The mattress was truly repugnant. In fact, as we stared at it, a large rat crawled out of it. Also, something in the farthest corner was squirming, and it was too dim to see for sure, but I was fairly certain there were maggots writhing in the rotting thing.

After closing the door, I laid out my bedroll on the wooden floor as far from the mattress as possible. Using what little room was left between my mat and the malodorous mattress, Karim laid his own bedroll out, overlapping it with mine by an inch or so. Neither of us needed a blanket for warmth, so we used them as pillows instead. The material was soft, but I could tell the blanket would keep me warm once we had returned to the snowy Winterwood in the Black Forest.

Laying on his makeshift pillow, Karim watched me. I, too, searched his dark eyes, not sure what I was looking for. It was not good how much I enjoyed being this close to him.

"What does 'sa'hera' mean?" I asked Karim, referring to what the drunken man had called me earlier. He frowned at the word.

"It means witch. It's because of your pale skin." He carefully watched for my reaction, but it was something I was used to being called, though not usually because of my skin. "You look different and people don't know what to think." A moment of silence passed, and Karim seemed to take this as a sign to close his eyes.

"Why did you agree to help me rescue Pennah when you knew how difficult it would be?" At first, Karim kept his eyes closed. Then, he took a deep breath and his eyes flashed open.

"I turned eighteen over three months ago. A day after my birthday I left, searching for something to help my people. After two months of wandering around with no luck, I heard about a town that traded multiple gems, all perfect and polished. The closer I got, the more rumors I started hearing about a girl that created these gems out of nothing." Apparently, people in town had connected Pennah and her jewels long before her kidnapper arrived. All it would have taken was a single person who noticed her dropping a jewel, and rumors would have started to fly. Karim continued, our eye contact remaining unbroken. "I followed the rumors to the edge of the Black Forest. Finding Pennah was the first real chance I had to save my kingdom."

Another beat of silence drifted over us like the arid draft that came in under the door. Karim looked away and then met my eyes again.

"What happened to your mother?" he asked me, his voice even. My eyes widened and my heart stuttered. He didn't ask it like someone who had no idea what was going on. He asked it like *he already knew*. Like he just wanted me to say it. Teeth clenched, I turned over so my back was to him. Tears stung at my eyes, so I closed them and forced myself to think of something else.

How did he know? Did he see the fresh grave while he swung upside down in my trap? Or did I talk in my sleep the nights I dreamt about my mother?

"I'm sorry, Sable. You don't have to say anything." I stayed frozen where I was until I heard Karim's deep breathing. Then, I turned back over and scrutinized his sleeping face. No, he couldn't possibly know. If he knew, he'd never fall asleep this close to me.

Again, the next morning, we pretended like nothing happened. Soon, the questions, emotions and secrets would pile up too high to stand and the dam would break. But for now, we could push it down until we couldn't see it anymore.

The chaos of Dariz in the daytime was even hotter and dirtier than it was at night. It was also significantly louder. Even if I spoke Arabic, I had the feeling that I wouldn't be able to understand a single word since everyone in the market was speaking over everyone else.

I saw young urchins sneaking off with a stolen prize. Some were caught and cuffed on the head. A few were beaten more severely. Vendors tried offering me fake jewelry. Some of it looked more realistic, but the salesmen couldn't possibly know the depth of my experience with gems. Fruits were being sold, much of which were halfway rotten with flies hovering over them. Karim teasingly pointed out some browning bananas. I indulged him with a sarcastic smile before pushing him past the fruit stand.

Searching for the Heartstring was easy. There weren't many things being sold that held the sparkle of magic that only our eyes could see. So far, we'd seen an unusual doll with a magical essence, but it gave both of us an uneasy feeling, so we quickly left that stall, and we'd seen a knife with a slight sparkle. I wondered if it was another blood blade like my own. Either the salesman didn't understand the value of the item, or the magic we saw was a curse put on the blade by a witch or warlock, because he displayed it among other bits of cheap jewelry and kitchenware.

Half the day passed and we still had nothing to show for our search. Many stores began packing up and the crowd thinned to the point that

I could walk without bumping into anyone. Soon, judging by the sun, there was only an hour left before our time was up. I tried not to look too nervous, but we *had* to find that Heartstring. My anxious perusal of a table full of magic-less trinkets was interrupted by a spindly old man calling us over to his stall. Karim's eyebrows came down in confusion at the man's words.

"What did he say?"

"He says he can see the magic in us. He says he has something for us," Karim translated. We approached the stall. The man's leathery skin sagged under his chin and his thin fingers pulled something from underneath his table. He nodded encouragingly as he showed us the gold bracelet. It indeed had magic, but it was not what we were looking for.

"Kalla, Kalla. Shukran." Karim waved the bracelet away and began leaving the stall, but the man called us back again. He pulled out a magic-infused feather with gold fringing its red core. Karim shook his head and we were about the leave again when the man, in desperation pulled out a worn, white ribbon, imbued with deep magic. Without even looking to Karim, I knew this was what we needed. I also knew that this man was aware of its value, and I had seen how much money Karim had brought. Short of pawning his royal sword, we didn't have enough to give. Except . . .

"I have something." I pulled out my small purse that I had filled with Pennah's jewels from the bottom of the pond. I dumped the contents into my hand, surprised by how few there were left. Honestly, they could have fallen out at any point in time over the last week. I had it with me when we fought at the castle and in the rain storm when we fled from the stormhawk. Regardless, the old man's eyes glinted with greed. I dumped the jewels into the man's hand and he tossed me the ribbon.

"We even have time to spare," Karim said jokingly, knowing full well that we might have had an extra hour in Dariz, and the shops were all beginning to close down already. With gentle fingers, Karim also inspected the ordinary ribbon that had yellowed and frayed with time. The magic must have kept it in one piece all these years.

"Ah!" the old man yelled out in the middle of counting his new jewels, making Karim drop the ribbon into my hands. The vendor pointed at me and yelled something in Arabic.

"He just called you a liar," Karim translated, though I had understood enough from his tone to get the point. We both watched the small pile of jewels. As the three of us stared, two rubies faded into nothing. The man screamed again and tried to snatch the Heartstring back, but I was faster and I pulled it out of his reach. The jewels were fading? Was the distance from the Black Forest affecting them?

The vendor yelled something again. I read between the lines and assumed he was shouting 'thief,' a taboo in markets as rough as this one. Before I could even react, Karim grabbed my free hand and we bolted through the market, weaving through clusters of people. I now desperately wished we still had the throngs of people teeming in the road like there were a few hours ago. Guards had appeared on our tail, and we pushed harder through the thinning crowd, headed for the shore.

Waves lapped against the docks and I took a brief moment to be awed. I had been to the ocean once, and I was just a toddler. Somehow, the memory of smelling the sticky, salty air and walking in the sand had been burned into my mind. Since I don't remember Pennah being there, I was fairly sure the trip was before my father died.

"In here." Karim's grip on my hand tightened and he pulled us into an alley just before we arrived at the piers, where I could see boats bobbing. The alley housed small piles of stinking garbage. Ducking behind a pile of crates that had the unpleasant aroma of rotting fish, Karim and I huddled as far into the corner as we could. The faded ribbon flapped in the wind as if it was alive. I pulled it to my chest protectively when the guards ran past the alley. Once they were gone, I rolled up the Heartstring and tucked it into my dress. I didn't want to chance tying it to anything. Would something happen if I tied it around my wrist? Surely not. This ribbon had survived this long without its magic being spent on someone foolish enough to waste it like that. Or maybe it reappeared when the person who used it died.

"I think we can hide here until our time is up." Karim slumped against the grimy wall, relaxing a bit but still keeping an eye on the alley's opening through a gap in the crate we hid behind. Carefully, I watched him. He hadn't said anything about the gems disappearing. Had he realized what that meant?

"If I had known about Pennah's gems, I never would have let you come. I wouldn't have lied to you," I promised, wrapping my arms around my knees. "I never knew that the curses grew weaker without the Black Forest." It also explained the fact that there weren't nearly as many snakes and spiders as normal. If I had known distance from the Black Forest would dull the curse, I would have left home long ago.

Karim said nothing. The alley was encased in shadows, so I couldn't see how disappointed he was. Frustrated at his silence, I continued. "The gems are useless to you." I paused and my voice grew quieter. "If we weren't already magically linked to the Black Forest right now, set to reappear there any moment, I'd tell you not to bother coming back. Pennah can't help your kingdom anyway. If the jewels get too far from the Black Forest, they'll just disappear." Perhaps when we returned to the Winterwood and I got help from the Trader, Karim could just go home. I had nothing left to offer him.

"I'd still come," Karim said softly as he slipped his hand in mine. His hand was warm, which was surprisingly comforting despite the desert heat. I looked up at him, trying to decipher the look in his eyes. "Sable—" He was interrupted by the stomping feet of the soldiers rounding the corner. They were saying something, but there was no alarm in their voices, so obviously they hadn't spotted us yet. "They're coming this way. Stay here."

"Wait, what? What are you doing?" His hand slipped out of mine and he leaped up, sprinting right at the guards. I watched through a crack in the crate as the guards reacted. Halfway there, he pulled his blade to deflect those of the guards as he ran past, his purse jingling slightly in hand as if it held the stolen treasure. Four guards chased after him. Karim was weighed down by his pack, but the guards had armor and weapons slowing them down. And from the look of it, the prince was far nimbler than the guards. Unfortunately, two armed men remained, still looking down the alley, unconvinced that Karim was alone. Sundown was nearly here. I only had to hold on to the Heartstring for a little longer.

Thinking quickly, I pulled a bandage from the medical supplies, tore off a strip and tied the fake Heartstring to my wrist. If they did grab me, I didn't want them searching me and finding the real Heartstring before I disappeared back to the Black Forest. This was of course assuming the vendor actually told them what was stolen. For all I knew, the vendor promised to pay them in Pennah's gems if they returned the ribbon. It would be ironic.

I gathered my skirt in one fist. Just before the guards got to the crates, I jumped out, sword in my other hand. They were too close for me to attempt sprinting past like Karim had done, and I stood no chance of fighting my way out when two guards who had trained in swordsmanship all their lives blocked my way. We stood frozen for a moment, but I needed more time than a moment. The second they realized I was a woman, despite the fact that I was an *armed* woman, they advanced, swords at the ready. Then I remembered what the Trader said. I might not have superior skill, but I definitely had the superior weapon. I knew from experience that it could cut through magic, like with Karim's genie-wrought shield, and it was sharp enough to cut clean through ogre armor. But could it really pierce anything?

Slashing out with as much strength as I could muster, I struck out at the guard on the left. He brought his sword up to block and followed up with a strike, aiming for my torso. However, the upper end of his sword was no longer there for his offensive move. I was as surprised as the guards were when the blade's top half clattered to the ground, sliced clean off.

The two men stepped away in momentary alarm, but did not back down. The one with half a sword muttered 'sa'hera.' Witch. I tried to remember the word for 'no' in Arabic, but before I could, the other guard attacked, clearly skilled enough to avoid my sword. I blocked a strike aimed for my chest, but it was just a feint. Instead, the guard sliced the back of my sword hand. In pain, I dropped my blood sword. Before I could retrieve Servans, which was only a foot away, the guard's blade was pointed at my throat. I should really learn how to actually use a sword.

The guard with a half sword, now precariously sheathed, approached me. Now holding his secondary weapon, some kind of club, he eyed the scrap tied around my wrist. Apparently, the vendor *had* told them what we had taken.

If they took the fake Heartstring now, the vendor would see it and make the guards find the real one. There was maybe a half hour before I would disappear. I needed more time.

"You want a witch? Fine." The guards, not understanding any English, paused in confusion. I proceeded to use the most foul language I knew, whether my description of the guards was accurate or not. The more personal my cruel words were, the larger and more venomous creatures I summoned, which was why the argument with my mother had gotten so out of hand. Since I didn't know these men or even speak the same language, it wouldn't have the same effect, but I could still scrounge up a few venomous things to scare the guards.

As I was insulting the mother of one guard and the sagging gut of the other, a shiny black scorpion the size of my foot crawled out from under my dress. The guards stopped in their tracks, only a foot away from me now. I remained still and the scorpion ignored me, heading straight for the guards. A thick, hairy spider snuck up from my chest to my neck. I carefully pulled it off and tossed it to the guards, who were familiar with these deadly creatures enough to fear them. While they were distracted, I snatched up my sword and sprinted back out of the alley, sheathing it as I ran.

I headed for the market, hoping I could lose my pursuers in the fray of people. When I got there, nearly everyone was gone. The only people left were the vendors cleaning up their wares and a few guards. They recognized me, an easy feat since I was as pale as a corpse amidst this group of citizens. The panic on my face undoubtedly helped them notice my guilt. The guards drew their weapons, both sword and club, and ran straight for me. Leaving a puff of sandy dust in my wake, I sprinted for the docks, getting a solid head start on the guards. Glancing around, I desperately looked for more places to hide. For a moment, I considered stealing a boat and drifting out on the sea until I disappeared, but living near a pond didn't exactly require extensive boatsmanship.

"Karim?" I called out as I ran. I spoke at a normal volume so the guards wouldn't hear. There was no response. "Karim?" Forgetting the idea of somehow finding Karim, I pulled in towards a shack. It was locked. The guards now had me in sight. I turned down a road at random so they couldn't see me. Frantically, I searched the area, trying to find somewhere I could hide for the next twenty minutes, because there was no way I could continue running. This road appeared to be residential. Blocky houses that blended into the sandy road lined the way. None of them appeared empty, and barging into someone's house would definitely attract too much attention. I bolted up stairs that wound around the outside of someone's stone house, running around the corner of the second story. Gasping to catch my breath, I slid down the wall and sat. The red sun still hovered above the horizon, not quite setting just yet. I forced myself quiet when I heard the guards turning down the street. They were sure to search up here. I had to move somewhere else.

The sway of a red curtain with a beaded fringe caught my eye. Careful to stay out of sight of the main road, I pushed the curtain aside and slipped into the window. The noises of people in their homes for the night had slid into a collective ambient sound. However, once inside the house, I could hear—and see—what was going on all too clearly. Smoke hovered densely throughout the room. Large, silky cushions that managed to look both extravagant and dingy at the same time were scattered around the room. Most of them were occupied by wealthy-looking, half-comatose men or women wearing very little clothing and too many cheap trinkets. The women were draped over the men, their dazed expressions matching. I had never seen the effects of opium myself, but I'd heard enough stories from traders that came through my town to guess that I had landed in some kind of opium den. Most of the occupants were too lethargic to even notice me, but somehow one man, coherent enough to stand, had snuck up behind me. His hands grabbed my shirt and he gave a weak attempt to pull me in. I looked into his empty eyes; he was just the shell of a man. If I were under the influence of whatever drug he was, it might have been hard to push him away. Under the circumstances, it only took a small nudge to get him to drift the other way. In a stupor, he moved towards the next woman he saw. On his way, he inhaled a deep drag from a thin hose connected to a glass bottle on a table.

To avoid further advances by the drugged men in the room, as well as hide from the guards who would certainly search the houses on this street, I squeezed into a wardrobe that stood against the wall. Thanks to the backpack I still wore, I barely fit. Fortunately, I'd only be there until sundown. Unfortunately, I was still in the wardrobe when I heard guards coming up the stairs. They attempted to speak with the men in the room when they entered—probably asking if they'd seen me—but a sober man, presumably in charge of this opium den, told them something. It was only a few moments of picking up cushions and searching the girls' faces before the guards opened the wardrobe. They didn't even have to pull me out since as soon as the wardrobe door opened, my body rolled out, limbs splaying out onto the floor. When a stupid smile spread on my lips, I realized that inhaling the ambient smoke in the room must affect people almost as much as using the actual hookahs. I must have been hiding here for longer than I thought.

I didn't struggle when the guards untied the ribbon from my wrist. In fact, I wasn't even worried. Everything was going to be fine. I grinned again. "That's not even the right Heartstring," I told them, but they didn't understand me.

Two guards dragged me out of the house, pulling my arms uncomfortably. At the pain in my arms, I finally resisted, but I had no strength left. Halfway down the street, the guards dropped me and yelled. I looked at my hands. They were fading; dissolving like sand in an hourglass. I waved my quickly disappearing hands at the guards.

"Time to go! Ma'as-salamah!" I butchered the Arabic word for 'good bye,' but it didn't matter. I laid down in the dust and closed my eyes, still smiling.

"Are you alright? Sable, wake up." Karim's voice was suddenly there.

"I'm not asleep." Though I *was* tired. I opened my eyes. Karim was hovering over me. His eyes were so dark, the pupils were almost impossible to distinguish. Thick, dark eyelashes any woman would be jealous of fluttered when he blinked. And his skin was so unusual. Most would call the brown shade olive-toned, but looking at it made me think of honey. I reached up to cup his face in one of my hands, tenderly stroking it with my thumb. It *was* as soft as honey. My eyes dropped to his lips. They were also a darker color than my own. And he had such full lips. And they were moving.

"Huh?" I kept my hand where it was, but this time focused on what he was saying.

"I said you are acting strange. What happened? Do you have the Heartstring?" My eyes lit up and I pulled Karim a bit closer, noticing how he didn't resist my grip.

"Yes. I have it," I told him with a coy smile. A beet-red color flushed over Karim's honey skin when I reached into the neckline of my dress with my free hand. I pulled the ribbon out and presented it to him.

"Good, you managed to hold on to it." He cleared his throat, not moving to take it from me. "Now, do you mind explaining what happened?"

"I hid in an obiun dem." I paused. That wasn't right. I hooked my elbow around Karim's neck, pulling him in closer as my eyebrows scrunched together, my brain trying to find the right words. "An o-pi-um den," I said slower, smiling at the success. My smile grew when I saw Karim's grin.

"That explains a lot." He sat up, pulling me with him. My head spun a bit when I was upright and my arm slipped from Karim's neck.

"I'm tired," I drawled. My gaze scanned the room. I finally realized we were back in the Winterwood. The sand in the hourglass must have run out. The Trader, in all her fairy glory, was standing in the corner, watching us with amusement in her eyes.

"You may stay here for the night. We will finish the deal tomorrow." The Trader gracefully drifted away, leaving a grumpy gnome behind to show us where to sleep.

"Follow me," the gnome said in a raspy voice. Karim pulled me to my feet. I balanced precariously and ended up linking my arm in Karim's, clinging to his bicep to stay on my feet as we followed the gnome. As we walked, I rubbed my eyes sleepily. The gnome glanced back at us, mostly at me and my stumbling walk, and shook his head. "Humans."

Chapter 27

PENNAH

The phoenix blood wasn't out of Daria's system for two full days, but the majority of the pain seemed to subside into a lingering burning that I equated to a bad sunburn after the first four hours or so. Our conversations grew fewer and shorter. Often, the only words exchanged were in a gurgling language, spoken between the two or three goblins outside my room.

Wings fluttered in through the window. The sprites had returned. They knew what I wanted now. Anxiously, they waited as I pulled out my gold rope. It was now as thick as my pinky and as long as my forearm. Picking gold strands from my hair had officially become a stress habit, and over the last two days I had collected quite a few. Setting the gold in a pile on the floor, I told the sprites to wait.

"I don't want a rope anymore," I said. I had realized that it would take far too long to construct a rope long enough and strong enough to accomplish anything. And that aside, I couldn't get the image of Sable walking away out of my mind. I knew she would have been doomed if she had stayed, but I couldn't help being bitter at the abandonment. Sable couldn't always come to my rescue. Perhaps it was time to take action; to start looking after myself. In that moment, I decided that I was not leaving this castle alone. Daria, her mother, and all the other creatures trapped here were coming with me.

The sprites waited expectantly, their glinting smiles full of greed. I looked into their vicious, glassy eyes. "I want you to build me a knife."

Chapter 28

SABLE

"I'm sorry I acted so strangely yesterday," I told Karim again. I wasn't so far under the opium's influence to have forgotten what happened. I could remember as clear as day when I caressed his face. I could also remember when he tried putting me on a cot the Trader had offered. Before laying down, I had pulled myself against him in a hug that had every inch of our bodies touching. Embarrassment heated my face just thinking about it.

Once Karim knew I had spent almost a half hour inhaling opiates, he was no longer embarrassed about anything I was doing. In fact, he seemed quite amused. Even now he just grinned.

"It was actually quite nice to see you relaxed for once."

"For once?" Karim had only known me during the most stressful time of my life, so I couldn't blame him for saying that. But still, I wasn't uptight *all* the time. "Also, I don't know about you, but when I am actually relaxed, I don't act like I'm drunk."

"Fine. When you actually are relaxed, maybe when we finally get Pennah back, let me know so I can see what you are actually like in such a state." It was good to know that when I smiled now, I wasn't grinning like a fool.

"I believe you wanted to make a trade?" The Trader appeared out of nowhere beside our cots. She was holding her hand out expectantly. I set the Heartstring of Salim in her hand. Putting that hand behind her back, she brought out her other hand, this one holding a purple flower with a pearl in its center. I'd seen many flowers through Pennah's curse, but this one was unfamiliar.

"This will help me get Pennah back?" I asked, skeptical.

"Have you heard the tale of Jorinda and Jorindel?" I nodded, but Karim shook his head. "Enlighten us Sable." The Trader waited for me to explain the story.

"Jorinda and Jorindel were two lovers wandering the forest when they came upon a small, white castle. As they approached the castle, a . . ." I paused, unsure what the Trader's version of the story was. ". . . a fairy hypnotized Jorindel, as she did with all men, sending him away. Jorinda was turned into a songbird and placed in a cage with hundreds of other songbirds in the castle. Jorindel was able to use a violet flower to prevent the fairy from hypnotizing him. He . . ." I paused again, positive the Trader would cut in, outraged. "He killed the fairy and used the flower to free all the songbirds and turn them back into women. He was reunited with Jorinda and they lived happily ever after."

"Very good, Sable," she praised, as if I were her student reciting a memorized poem. "Unfortunately, mankind has a way of sweetening the story. One blossom does not have that kind of power. Jorindel saw that his beloved had become a robin, and he only had four blossoms left. Taking a chance, he used the blossoms. He was reunited with his love and three other women returned home to their families, but thirty-two songbirds remained."

"Was it really a fairy who turned those women into songbirds?" I asked, giving the Trader a chance to defend her own kind.

"As you well know, Sable, not all fairies help humans as I do. So, here." She was about to hand me the flower, but she pulled back at the last second. "As you may have realized, this flower does have the ability to rid you of your curse." Actually, I hadn't even considered it. I had given up the idea of getting rid of the curse long ago. As she continued, I realized I was right to do so. "But I must warn you that because your curse has saved your life multiple times, using this flower to destroy the curse would surely kill you, allowing all the poison that the curse had absorbed to come into effect."

Disappointed by a crushed hope I hadn't even realized I still held onto somewhere in the depths of my heart, I paused when the Trader set the purple blossom in my hand. It was smaller than my open palm. "Be careful, though. It is fragile. You should use this on the man that stole your sister. At first I thought he was just a warlock, with access only to simple magic. But a half-breed warlock could not possibly have enough power to contain all those magical creatures you say you saw. Not without help at least. I suspect he is channeling power from dark spirits, as only a sorcerer can do.

"Since a sorcerer's power comes from dark spirits, blowing the crushed blossom in his eyes will counteract the dark magic he has performed. It will not dispel the spirit, but it will null its powers for a short time allowing you to escape."

She was quiet, as if she had finished. That still seemed like a long shot.

"That's it? You can't help us get into the castle? What about the goblins?"

"I said I could help. I never said I would retrieve your sister for you," the Trader said. "I will do one last thing. You may keep the cup I gave you, in return for one more favor." The Trader moved in close until her perfect, pale face was directly in front of my own. Suddenly, an icy blast of air hit my eye when the Trader blew in my face, forcing me to blink out a tear. The Trader pulled a vial and scooped the tear off of my cheek.

"You want my tear? Why?"

"My dear, this deadly drop is a powerful combination of fairy and human magic. This single, potent drop can kill any being, large or small. Even young Karim, on whom any other poison would have no effect." I was about to ask why we even needed the cup when she continued. "I have seen a glimpse of what is ahead for you. You are both going to need that cup if you wish to survive." I paused in thought, and nodded. If someone traded for that tear, then they would have to really wish someone dead. And if someone wanted it badly enough, they'd find another way to kill, even if my tear wasn't in the Trader's hands. And if it would save Karim's life? Not to mention my own . . . it was worth it.

Another request for more help was on the tip of my tongue when the Trader continued. "I have been more than generous, and I think you have overstayed your welcome in the Winterwood. Good bye." She finished with one last knowing smile. And then she was gone.

On the way out, more fairies stared. The fairy that had cursed me and Pennah had been moved, but everything else was basically the same, making it easy for us to find our way out of the Winterwood. We passed the guard, who still stood stoically at the Winterwood's border.

"I don't suppose you could point us in the direction of the Black Castle?" Karim ventured.

The soldier paused long enough for me to believe he might not even respond. Finally, he pointed south. "Go south until you reach the creek. Follow it downstream until you reach the fork at the Great Oak. Follow the western branch and it will take you to the bridge that is part of the Black Castle's road. Take the road west." During the entire explanation, he didn't once look us in the eye.

"How do we know we've found the right oak tree?" I pressed. The last thing we needed was to get confused by ambiguous directions. The fairy man's lips flattened in annoyance.

"You'll know it when you see it. Even humans aren't that blind."

"Well, thank you, kind sir, for your most generous assistance." Snarky as it was. The fairy didn't react to my sarcasm, but Karim grabbed my arm and pulled me down the hill, away from the fairy guard.

"Yes, thank you," Karim called back. Then to me, he muttered, "Are the opiates still in your system? You don't need to aggravate an armed fairy."

I scoffed. "No, there are no more drugs affecting me. I'm always like this. Uptight, remember?" I said it with a smile so he knew I was joking.

"That was not uptight. That was poking a sleeping bear."

"Sorry, apparently one day in a palace didn't teach me enough manners." My foot slipped a little on a patch of icy snow and I grabbed at an aspen tree, snapping of a thick branch as I regained my balance. Secretly, I hoped it was that nasty aspen nymph from a few days ago.

"You are welcome back anytime to learn a little more. Heaven knows you need it," he said, lightheartedly at first, before adding, "You and Pennah are both welcome if you'd like."

I hesitated. "I haven't even thought about what I'd do once I finally got Pennah back. I guess I always planned on going home." But now that he mentioned it, a fresh start somewhere else might be nice. And now that I knew how the distance from the Black Forest diminished my curse, perhaps leaving home would be for the best.

From there, the conversation slipped into normalcy. We talked about stories we knew, things we'd done, experiences with our siblings. Apparently, being the youngest in a family, as well as the only boy, was hard.

The trek back to the Black Castle went by quicker and easier than before. We were finally getting good at traversing the Black Forest. Plus, now that we actually had supplies, we didn't have to live off of bananas or curl up in a pile of cold leaves to sleep. We knew what plants to avoid eating or resting under, and few creatures attempted to eat us.

After following the river for a few days, I finally understood why the guard thought I was crazy for asking how I would know the 'Great Oak' when I saw it.

"Wow." That was all I had to say. The Great Oak was a gigantic oak tree with a trunk that must have been at least twenty feet in diameter. It hovered over the river, its roots planted in either bank keeping it suspended. Not only was it the largest tree I'd ever seen, but it had more glimmering stars than the night sky. I'm not sure if the magic infused in it was good or bad, but it was beautiful.

Keeping close to the water's edge, Karim and I ended up walking underneath the winding roots of the Great Oak. While under its shelter, we decided to wash up more thoroughly in the river. We made sure to keep our feet on dry ground this time since apparently physical depth of a river meant nothing to a kappa.

After my hair was cleaned with the small bar of soap Karim had included in my pack, I put it back in its simple braid. I should have had Roya teach me how she made my hair so elegant while I was in Karim's palace.

Karim had even been thoughtful enough to pack extra clothes so our washed clothes could dry while we walked. My secondary outfit was another pair of pants, these much thinner than the riding pants I had been wearing, and a brown shirt, both of which were both very much the Sukkadian style. As we continued downstream, following the western branch as instructed, with our damp clothes in hand or slung over our packs, I noticed Karim's fresh shirt was a dark green fabric. Both our pants were darker as well, and it made me wonder if he had intentionally chosen colors that would help us blend in with the forest.

"There's something odd about this tree. I just can't quite put my finger on it." At first, I thought he had to be joking, but I looked at his face and saw he was serious.

"You're right. Now that I think about it, I suppose it is slightly larger than most trees I've seen." The fact was, a troll could probably live in it with his wife and children. Of course, that was stacking them vertically, and trolls weren't known for living on top of one another.

"That is not what I mean." He stepped closer to a nearby root. "The air is pulsing with life. Can you feel it?"

Still not sure he wasn't hallucinating, I focused on the air around me. It *did* feel different. It felt heavy with magic.

"Sable." It was no more than a whisper, but I still jumped.

"Was that you?" I accused Karim. If he was playing a joke, I was prepared to push him in the river.

"Was what me?" He looked genuinely confused. I continued, less sure.

"I heard my name." I paused and listened for a moment, but there was only silence. "Or, I thought I did."

Karim wasn't really looking at me anymore. He was staring at a root large enough to encase his entire body. Suddenly, as if out of impulse, he reached out and flattened his palm against the rough bark. As if feeling for vibrations, he stood there, completely still, until he leaped backward like it had shocked him.

"Did you see that?" He looked incredulous.

"What? Does it bite?" I said, almost jokingly, but you never knew when it came to the Black Forest.

"No, I saw you in the castle. And Pennah. I'm not sure what it means." He scrutinized me, trying to decipher something. "You should touch the tree. Maybe you can see the rest."

"The rest of what? I don't want to touch the tree if it's going to—"

"Sable." I was watching Karim this time, so I knew it wasn't him. It was the tree. The tree was talking to me. But what was it trying to tell me?

Hesitantly, I reached my fingertips out to the root beside me. The moment my fingers made contact, it was like a magnet pulled my whole hand against the bark. Then, I was somewhere else. I was somewhere hot and dry, and someone's fingers were wrapped around my throat. The man, or rather boy, had desperation in his blue eyes. He wasn't killing me out of anger, but out of fear. Nonetheless, he was still draining the life from me. My fingers clawed at his arms, the need for air consuming my mind. Black filled my vision, beginning at the corners. The last thing I saw before everything went dark was a spattering of freckles on his nose.

Ripping my hand from the tree, I gasped for air. I felt no malice from the tree, but after nearly dying in a strange vision at the hand of a man I didn't even recognize, I was desperate to get away from it.

"Did you see the castle?" Karim asked, wanting his own answers.

"No," I choked out. I had gathered enough to understand that the vision took place in the desert, not the Black Castle. "Let's get out of here." Finally, Karim nodded and we followed the river.

Later, Karim mentioned the tree again. "I should tell you . . . what I saw, it was—"

"I don't want to talk about that tree." I cut him off. For all I knew, the tree gave you visions of your death that distracted you so a pack of gremlins living in its roots could eat you once you were incapacitated. Maybe Karim and I escaped unharmed only because we both had magic inside us. Regardless, I didn't want to dwell on it.

Four and a half days after leaving the Winterwood, we found the bridge. A few miles down the road, we ended up hiking just beside the road, in case we ran into goblin guards. We found the first goblins about two hours before sunset.

"There are more than before around the perimeter," Karim commented. Indeed there were. The Black Castle wasn't even in sight yet and there were already goblins marching around the forest.

"We are going to have to get inside if we want to find the sorcerer."

"Let's look and see how heavily guarded the sides are." He pulled me around to the north side of the castle, where many more goblins than before guarded the wall, preventing anyone from climbing up to a second story window.

"If we could draw him out, we could use the flower on him. Could we pretend we want to make a trade for Pennah and tell him we have something even better?" It was all I could think of.

"Even if we could convince him, how would we even tell him? Would we get the goblins to deliver a letter?"

Dropping into an exasperated heap on the ground, I buried my face in my hands. "I can't think of anything else." I wanted to scream in frustration, but I doubted that would help the situation. Instead, I directed my anger at the infernal backpack I had been carrying for days on end. I yanked my arms from the straps and threw the pack to the ground. Since I was already sitting, this only resulted in a small clang of materials inside and a puff of dust. My anger, though unvoiced, produced a rattlesnake that darted under a nearby bush. Being in the Black Forest again amplified the curse so that words weren't even necessary. Maybe if I got angry enough, a giant wyvern would appear and demolish the castle door for us.

"If the guards were human, I'd say we could convince them to take us inside as prisoners, but I think they are on orders to kill. I still have faint bruising from last time."

"I think part of the reason they tried to kill us was because we were swinging weapons at them. Pennah was roaming around and no goblins were trying to kill her." Remembering my sword, I momentarily considered just slashing through all the goblins. Unfortunately, not only would that be a lot of premeditated blood on my hands, even if it was goblin blood, but they would kill me first just with sheer numbers even if one swipe of my sword could cut them clean in half.

"The goblins were probably distracted by us."

I sat up, an epiphany forming. "Even so, they wouldn't be on orders to kill just anything. What if a prisoner escaped? They aren't just preventing people from getting in, but they are the reason Pennah can't just walk out." Assuming she isn't shackled now.

"How do they know which is which? We must all look the same to them, as humans I mean," he guessed. Karim was right. With other species, in my experience at least, it was difficult to tell the difference.

"They don't know the difference." I stood, a plan unfolding in my mind. Snatching up my pack, I snuck back to the front of the castle, Karim sticking close behind me.

"What are we doing?" he asked, his voice a hushed whisper.

"I'm going to escape," I whispered conspiratorially. Once I had found a decent hiding spot, I stashed my pack under a bush, keeping the strap looped out of the shrub so I could grab it easily if we left in a hurry again. This time, though, I found a dead branch covered in lichen. I stripped the entire branch save for one end and I stuck it in the ground, lichen bunch pointing up. It should be easy to spot this from the road. Then, I pulled Servans off my back. Even though my father had paid for it in blood, it was still the last thing I had of his. I desperately hoped I didn't have to leave it behind. Before I hid it on top of my pack, Karim grabbed the sheath, stopping me.

"What are you doing? You need that." I tugged the sword, but Karim wasn't letting go easily.

"I can't keep it with me or the goblins will know I'm not a prisoner."

"Fine." He released my sword and proceeded to unclasp Amani. I covered his hand with mine, stopping him.

"You can't come with me," I said softly.

"Why?" Anger flashed in him. It wasn't petulant anger or a bitter anger at being left out. It felt more . . . protective.

"The goblins might not recognize your face, but since you probably broke their teeth last time, they will remember the effects of your wish."

"You can't go in alone." He was like an indignant puppy. I just wanted to pull him into a hug and give in to whatever he asked of me.

But I had a different plan in mind.

Chapter 29

SABLE

With all the strength I could manage, I swung Servans at the tree again. A neat triangle was now severed from the trunk. It began creaking as the last few inches struggled to keep the tree standing. I sheathed my sword and tossed it to Karim who, after giving me one last nervous glance, sprinted off.

A marvelous crack sounded, echoing in the quiet twilight. As the tree tipped, the wedge was pinched out when the thick trunk closed the gap. Gaining speed quickly, the tree fell towards the castle until it made contact with the third floor. The tree was solid enough to break through the wall, but it didn't cut all the way through the castle façade. Catching on the third floor, the tree stopped falling, its branches reaching into the castle. Once it was secure, I climbed up the sloped trunk several feet until I heard goblins approaching.

Loud gurgling swarmed towards me from all directions. Ignoring the goblin-speak, I clambered back down the tree and headed for the woods, as if I were a prisoner attempting to escape. This plan hinged on the goblins not realizing the tree had been deliberately cut down or that I was not an escaping captive.

I only made it a few feet before hordes of rough goblins hands pushed me until I was disoriented and stumbling to the ground. When I fell, I took care to protect the valuable blossom I had hidden in the pocket of my winter jacket.

Showing more capability than I had realized, the goblins bound my hands in front of me tight enough to chafe as I walked with them back into the castle. Just before we reached the front of the castle, a hood was drawn over my head, though I'm not sure how the short creatures could reach that high. Apparently, the location of the main exit was not only a secret to us, but also to every captive in here.

Unsure where they were leading me, I followed the goblins blindly. We climbed up a staircase—I nearly tripped several times—and stopped on the second floor. Someone ripped the hood from my head unceremoniously. I blanched at the placid face that my eyes found. Then anger took over.

"Where's my sister?" There was no pretending with him. He knew I was no escaped prisoner.

"Sable." The sorcerer put on a cavalier smile. "You are nothing if not tenacious."

***

Something heavy shook the castle. This was not like Sable's rescue attempt when the goblins were swarming. This felt more like cannonfire. Were we under attack? Had someone finally come to help us?

"Daria, my knife." The gold knife with diamond teeth bubbled up and out of Daria's tub, clanking to the stone floor. Ever since Marcus put phoenix blood in her water, she'd been giving me the cold shoulder, as if that would prevent Marcus from doing it again. Fortunately, I did eventually convince her to hide the sprite-made dagger in her tub while Marcus and the goblins were checking in here for jewels. It had become too large to hide in my sleeve, and it would have created a bulge if I had tried to hide it in my dress.

I took the golden blade in hand. It was dainty—only so much gold fell from my hair each day—but fierce. The sprites did have an unnatural talent for creating beautiful things, but they also carried the skill for weaponry. The thin blade was melded to four of my tears that angled towards the hand grip, which had been perfectly formed to my small hand. The points of the tears were aligned like teeth so the dagger would cause more damage on the way out than on the way in. It was gruesome, but necessary.

If we truly were being attacked, then either the battle would die down and we would be safer staying in here, or Marcus would walk in with the goblin king at his side. I was probably the most valuable and most portable creature held in the Black Castle, so chances were that Marcus would come for me before any such battle was over. Not to mention the three goblins that permanently stood guard at my door now, preventing anyone but Marcus from entering. That meant, whatever came in the door next was going to die.

I stood beside the door, tensed and ready to attack anyone that entered, hopefully taking them by surprise. Gurgling voices came from the other side of the door. Slowly the gurgling quieted, just like the goblins did when Marcus neared, like a crowd silencing for a king. I felt smaller than a sprite and fear made my breaths come in short gasps. The golden blade quivered in my hand, giving me a little comfort, but I knew my courage had to come from the heart, not a knife. The door opened and I lunged at the tall figure that entered the room. It was too late to stop myself when I realized it wasn't Marcus at all. It was the dark-skinned man that had come with Sable last time.

Before my blade bit into his skin, causing irreparable damage, my wrist was diverted to the side by some miracle, as if I had struck a wall. He shouldn't have reacted quick enough to save himself, but just after my knife jutted out to the side, the man jumped aside and pushed my arm away in a belated effort to protect himself. I blamed the strange occurrence on my lack of skill with a knife. Hopefully I'd have better aim when it was the goblin king or even Marcus himself.

"Pennah!" He seemed more shocked to see me with a knife than to see me at all. Which meant he had been looking for me. The arm that held a curved sword covered in goblin's blood dropped, showing he didn't view me as a threat. I, too, dropped my arm, but my grip on the dagger didn't lessen.

"How did you find me?" I noticed Sable's sword at his back. Had he stolen it? Why? He obviously had his own, significantly better, weapon.

"The only goblins that didn't leave their post when the tree hit the castle were the ones guarding your door. It made you relatively easy to find." Tree? I'd figure that one out later.

"Who are you?" I scrutinized him, wondering what he expected to get from helping my sister. If he wanted jewels, I could tell him right now they wouldn't last away from the Black Forest. Daria, in our long exchanges, had informed me that no fairy magic remained potent when brought too far from the Black Forest, which was the source of raw fairy magic.

"Karim. I have been helping Sable look for you." The name sounded familiar and I remembered Sable calling it out the last time she was here. Karim, obviously foreign, had black eyes and dark hair that held a slight curl. He had a straight nose and smooth, sun-kissed skin. His gentle smile made me worry that he was going to break my sister's heart.

"And where exactly is Sable?" I still held the knife tightly, not trusting him yet.

Karim's dark eyes fell. Seeing him like this made me realize that he was still quite young, despite the confident way he carried himself. "She went to find the man that took you as a distraction. She wanted me to get you out of here."

Suddenly outraged at the traitorous idea I stepped towards the door, away from this foreign man my sister had trusted.

"I'm not going anywhere with you. And I'm certainly not leaving my sister here with Marcus. Nor am I about to leave any of the magical creatures he has trapped in here." I would have crossed my arms and stamped my foot for emphasis, except it would have made me look like a child. Instead, I set my jaw and didn't move.

A roguish smile played on his full lips. "I'm glad you feel that way, because I'm not going anywhere without Sable, either."

***

"I'm so glad you've come, dear. Pennah has been needing some fresh encouragement." Goblins dragged me behind the sorcerer. The man faced away from me as he talked, making it incredibly hard for throwing disenchanting dust at him. As it was, I held the blossom in my closed hand, careful not to crumble it just yet. "I haven't laid a finger on her yet for fear of breaking the fragile girl, but if we can't work out some arrangement I'm afraid I'll have no other choice."

"Stay away from my sister," I hissed. Two goblins snatched up the king snake that had slithered down my leg and onto the stone floor before it could strike. They swiftly ripped its head off with their razor nails. The man didn't even seem to notice.

"Tell the guards to bring Pennah to the dining room," the man ordered the slightly bulkier goblin he always kept at his side. The goblin paused before responding in his gurgling language. "What do you mean they aren't there?" He understood them?

The large goblin gurgled back and the sorcerer's gloating tone was gone. Now, he was satisfyingly agitated. I just hope that meant Karim had found Pennah and taken her out of here. The goblins yanked me onward, following their master as he ascended a large staircase. Why couldn't he just turn around?

After meandering through the halls, we stopped at a door. The man paused at the sight of blood on the ground, but ended up ignoring it and entered the room. My heart sank as the door swung inward and I saw Pennah sitting on the ground, leaning against the wall. Where was Karim? Had the goblins captured him?

Suddenly, as the sorcerer moved toward Pennah, Karim jumped from behind the door and swung his sosun pattah at the sorcerer, who brought up his forearm as if that would protect him. Much to my surprise, Karim's sword skidded off the man's arm harmlessly. The sorcerer smiled viciously and, taking advantage of Karim's shock, swung his fist into the prince's chest. The master of the house was not a large man, and nothing in his appearance warranted what actually happened. When his fist made contact, Karim was thrown across the room, skidding on the floor until his momentum was abruptly stopped by the far wall.

Terror gripped my heart for a brief moment before Karim began moving again. I wasn't completely consoled though. Karim didn't sit up and his breathing sounded pained. Amani had skittered too far for him to reach, and though he could reach my sword, I knew it wouldn't do him any good.

Still managing to act unimpressed, the man beside me rubbed his fists, which I now saw were covered with fingerless gloves that had bones on each of his knuckles.

"Even a thin layer of ogre's plating can stop a sword, and the knucklebones of a griffin bestow great strength. In fact, a blow like that should have killed you." His lip curled up in dissatisfaction.

"Just let them go, Marcus. I'll stay here, with you," Pennah bargained, but the sorcerer didn't seem fazed by her.

"I'm not sure you realize that it's not in your cards to negotiate here, my sweet." I pulled at the ropes, but the goblins had bound me well. I now wished I hadn't stashed my dagger in my pack.

"You're a sorcerer. You don't even need Pennah." I didn't so much care about whatever logic he had as I wanted him to turn around and face me.

"Sorcerer?" Marcus laughed sharply, still watching Pennah. "I'd have been consumed by dark spirits long ago if I were a sorcerer. On the up side, you'd be dust right now." He glanced at me, but I didn't have enough time to crush the flower and throw it at him. He had already turned back to Pennah, watching her like she was his next meal. "No, young Sable, I am but a humble warlock. Nothing but the power of illusion at my fingertips." Bitterness laced his words as he conjured an image of a rose in his hand. With a swish of his long, pale fingers, the rose vanished into smoke. "I have, however, managed to harness the power of the Black Forest." He reached under his tunic and pulled something out. It was small, white and round, attached to a string tied around his neck. As he fiddled with it, I saw what it was and bile crept up my throat. It was an *eye*.

"I have discovered many things over the years. One of which was the various magical properties given to the creatures of the Black Forest. One gift given to the gnomes was the gift of sight. Gnomes can see deep into a person. They can even catch glimpses of the future. When I have this around my neck, I have a similar gift. For example, I can see your weaknesses, Pennah. Why do you think I brought Daria in here? I knew you couldn't resist befriending a sweet, young water nymph. And right now, I can see exactly how to hurt you the most."

Marcus turned to face me. This was my chance, but before my mind registered the need to act, Marcus's hand was around my throat. I nearly dropped the purple flower in shock. Using my free hand I tried grasping Marcus's arm to pull him away, but as I got my fingers around his plated forearm, he lifted me up. Pressure was building in my head and I could feel my face turning red as bloodflow was completely halted. In the background I could hear Pennah begging him to stop. Just as black began inching in on my vision, Marcus tossed me into a corner, the impact jarring my whole body and bruising my shoulder blade.

***

"Stop!" Diamond tears rang against stone as they fell of their own accord. Normal color returned to Sable's face when Marcus finally tossed her aside. I ran to my sister, who now coughed and sputtered as she attempted to breathe again.

"I'm afraid none of you will be leaving this castle for some time." Marcus laughed maliciously.

"Sable, I'm so sorry. This is all my—" I froze, seeing what she held gently in her hand. It was a disenchanting violet. During our exchange of stories, Daria and I had talked about Jorinda and Jorindel. Sable had told me that story plenty of times, but she had always called the flower just a flower. Daria recognized the properties and described what a disenchanting violet looked like. She said they only grew where they could hear the singing of the water nymphs and that they could break any spell cast by fairy, nymph or witch. As gently as I could, I pulled the violet from Sable's limp hand. When she realized what I was doing, she protested weakly.

***

"Pennah, no!" I could only whisper, and even then a hoarse cough accompanied my protests. She didn't know what kind of power that tiny blossom held. Not that we could use it anymore. If Marcus was just a warlock, would it still undo his magic?

"I'll give you all the beautiful words you want. Just please don't hurt my sister," she said as she approached the warlock. Just before Marcus could respond, Pennah opened her clenched fist and blew the violet dust not at Marcus, but at the goblin beside him. The out-of-place pearl at the goblin's throat cracked and fell to the ground in a crumble.

"No!" Marcus backhanded Pennah, sending her spinning to the ground. Each goblin in the room scurried out. Marcus suddenly seemed very alone.

On the ground, Pennah remained unmoving. I wasn't sure if it was my imagination warping things, but I didn't think I saw her breathing. A warmth began building in my chest. I had only felt this kind of heat once before, and that time had ended in burying my mother. Instead of fearing the fire inside me, I embraced the hatred, eager to see the same end come to Marcus.

An eerie awareness settled on me, allowing me to stand and face the warlock.

"You are a monster. Can you not even see the lives you have destroyed? You couldn't be a sorcerer even if you tried. There is no soul for you to trade." A tingling sensation rippled across my skin. Marcus only half listened, not at all disconcerted by my rant. Until, that is, a burst of energy soared through my veins and the ropes that bound my wrists frayed and then snapped. With my now free hands, I snatched the eyeball around his neck and with sudden clarity, I could see every insecurity Marcus had. I could see his fears. I understood why he wanted this power, and why he had no regrets. If I weren't so consumed with anger, I might have been disgusted by what I saw. I threw the eye aside, ready to rip him to pieces. "I met your wife. She is as vain as you are. Do you think she stays because she loves you?"

My vision narrowed on the warlock and I could see the flicker of fear on his face. The gnome's eye had shown me what I looked like to him. I knew he was seeing the slitted yellow eyes of a snake instead of my normal mud brown human eyes.

"I'm sure you promised she would be a queen. Why else would she stay with a weak warlock that can only accomplish the smallest of parlor tricks?" As if suddenly remembering the other totems he possessed, Marcus swung out at me with his griffin-knuckled hands. He tried to mask his fear with anger, but I could still smell it. With the reaction of a viper, I dodged him and snatched his gloved hands and raked my nails down the his unplated forearms, pulling the gloves off. Marcus hissed in pain, as if my fingernails held a sting when they broke through his skin.

Power pulsed through me. I was stronger than ever before. If I'd known such power was possible, I would have stopped fighting the curse a long time ago.

***

I had grown used to my sister's curse over the years. But for the first time, what I saw in her terrified me. Scales had appeared on her arms and neck. Her eyes were slits of yellow. Her hair had been pulled from its normally meticulous braid and now hung in a scraggly mess on either side of her face.

What I saw . . . that was not my sister.

***

175

"Your father was never there and your mother abandoned you. Stop me, if I'm wrong," I growled. The gnome's eye had shown me that much, so I knew it was the truth. Marcus struggled a bit, but my grip on his wrists was unbreakable. The burning inside me almost hurt, but I let it stay. I urged it to grow into an inferno. "They left because you're a freak. A half-breed, parentless child no one wanted. They'd be so proud to see what you've become. A scared witless old man whose life's work is about to be torn apart by a teenage girl. Well you should be scared." I smiled venomously.

A searing cold replaced the fervid heat in my chest. I relished the iciness creeping into my heart, my blood colder than a snake's. This man deserved to die, and I was going to enjoy killing him. Quick as lightning, my hand snatched his throat with the unnatural strength I had gained in the last few minutes. Now, when he was dead he'd have bruises to match my own. When the warlock was about the pass out, someone moved in front of me, attempting to push me away from him but lacking the strength to do so.

"Move!" I snarled at him, barely recognizing my own voice. No one got between me and my prey.

"Sable, you need to stop." The voice was soft. Weak.

"You need to get out of my way." Warm hands laid on my shoulders.

"This is the moment I saw at the tree." My eyes found Karim's. "If you don't stop now, you will lose yourself." The heat from his hands penetrated through my clothes and I could feel it on my skin. It made the powerful cold inside me ache. "Please."

He was scared. Afraid of the power I now held. But when I inhaled, it wasn't his fear I tasted. It was Pennah's. She was alive. And terrified . . . of me.

My grip on Marcus's throat loosened and he slumped to the floor, his ragged breaths deafening in the silence. The moment I released Marcus, the heat from Karim's hands was unbearable. I attempted to pull away, but he refused to let go. The cold was no longer powerful and invigorating. It was sharp; unyielding. Like a monster had taken root and was clawing for control. Clutching at my chest, I fell to my knees, shivering. Still unable to stand on his own, Karim fell to the ground with me and we leaned against each other just to stay upright. My face was buried in his shoulder when I felt my muddy brown eyes return to normal. *Please*, I prayed, *just let it be over.*

Chapter 30

PENNAH

Marcus wasn't dead. I had half hoped my sister would kill him before changing back. Either way, everyone was alright. Assuming my jawbone was still in place from Marcus's blow. I laid back against the wall, closing my eyes and trying to figure out what to do next. Going home and back to normal life sounded like a refreshing change of pace.

"Pennah!"

I opened my eyes at the sound of Daria's panicked yelp. My mind was sluggish in processing the scene. Marcus had recovered far quicker than I thought he could, considering the damage caused by Sable. He had somehow gotten to his feet and retrieved the curved sword Karim had brought. With vengeance in his snarl, he was bringing up the sword, clearly aiming to behead both Karim and Sable.

Karim looked up at him, and faster than Marcus could readjust his swing, he pushed Sable to the floor, hunching over her protectively. The curved blade quivered and rang when impact was made, as if it had struck the face of a bell. It hadn't cut through Karim like Marcus or I expected, but instead left Karim crying out in pain, arching his back in an attempt to recoil from his own sword. Suddenly rejuvenated, by the pain it seemed, Karim sat back up, prepared to steal the weapon back. Before he even got to his feet, Marcus had pulled something from a pocket inside his coat. He blew a powder redder than a rose into Karim's face. In a sharp gasp, Karim breathed in the red powder.

With sleepy eyes, Karim sneezed. He looked lost for a moment before his head lolled to one side. There was one last, jerked attempt to stay awake, but Karim couldn't seem to help slumping to the floor at Sable's feet. Marcus, victorious, licked the gratified smile on his lips. He laid the blade on Karim's throat, but a magical barrier prevented him from breaking the skin.

"At least we know sleeping poppies work on him. Invulnerability can be so pesky." Though it had been proven that the sword would have no effect on Karim, that didn't stop Marcus from leaning on the sword a little harder.

"Get away from him," Sable croaked weakly. I hadn't noticed her sit up. Her skin was sickly pale, the scales almost completely gone now, and her purple lips pressed tightly over her chattering teeth. Whatever she'd done had sapped all the heat from her body.

"That was quite the show you put on." He frowned at her and she just sat there, helplessly shivering. "But I'm afraid I can't risk a repeat occurrence." His fist tightened on the leatherbound hilt of Karim's sword. Sable clutched her sides, trying to suppress her tremors. She was powerless. When Karim and I set the trap for Marcus, I had hidden my knife with Daria, so I was now unarmed. Regardless, I was up and running across the room before I even knew what I was doing. Marcus lifted the sword, but before he could bring it down, I had latched onto his arm, grappling with him for the sword.

Marcus roared in anger, eventually managing to fling me from his arm. I was scrambling up when he grabbed a fistful of my hair. Now vindictive, he slammed me into Daria's washbasin, its lip digging into the small of my back. I clutched at the rim, afraid he might try drowning me. Instead of forcing my head under the water, he set the smooth blade against my bare neck. Its edge bit my skin in the slightest, leaving my throat cold but unbroken. I could really use whatever magic protected Karim right about now.

Behind Marcus, Sable was attempting to stand on shaky legs with little luck.

"Obviously, I've been too soft on you," he breathed, the words hot against my face. I felt a thread of blood dribble down my neck as Marcus leaned in closer, smiling menacingly. "I told Sable I was afraid I might break you, but clearly our current method isn't working. After all, the best pets have to be broken first." A diamond tear slipped down my face, plopping into the washbasin and landing at the bottom with a hollow thunk. I had finally fought back, and I had ended up at the wrong end of a sword. Marcus grinned, satisfied. I hated how much he enjoyed terrifying me. And I hated myself for being so easily frightened.

My fingertips were in the cold water of Daria's tub, but I could still sense a change when something hard and even colder pressed against my fingers. The fear on my face melted away and I grabbed the smooth, golden handle Daria had placed in my hand. I could almost hear her urging me onward. Marcus had pushed me too far. Sable was still weakly trying to stand. She couldn't help me. The only one that could set me free was me. And there was only one way to end the nightmares, the fear. My teeth ground together and my fist tightened around the cool metal.

Marcus didn't even notice that there was a knife in my hand until I had thrust it into his heart.

He froze. The menacing grin I had become accustomed to slipped from his lips. His glazed eyes blinked. Somewhere in the enormous, crumbling castle, one of the captive creatures roared and the structure shook a little as it tore its way out of the prison. It must have been released when Marcus died.

Sable, leaning heavily against a wall, jolted when the sword Marcus was holding clattered against stone. Shock in her eyes, she just watched as Marcus's body fell.

Should I feel surprised like they were? Shocked at what I was capable of? Ashamed of what I'd done? All I felt was relief. Like I was waking up from a nightmare, happy to know it was all just a dream. Daria emerged from her hiding place within the washbasin, scowling at the corpse on the ground. The golden handle protruded from his still chest. It was an ordinary knife, nothing inherently magical about it. I supposed in the end, Marcus really was just a human.

I was slumped against the washbasin, not sure what else to do, when the poppy pollen wore off and Karim woke up. He joined Sable leaning against the wall, both of them now much surer on their feet.

"Pennah." Daria looked at me. She didn't say anything else, but I knew she wanted us to find her mother. After giving Sable and Karim a few more moments of rest, we investigated the rest of the castle. Several doors had been torn apart. With Marcus dead, most of the restraints must have been undone. I led the others into the nearest unbroken door, discovering a young fairy boy hiding in the corner, tears streaking his grimy face. The glow most fairies carried seemed faded on him.

Hastily, I approached him, ignoring his cringe, and fumbled with the lock, unable to figure out how to get it off.

"Pennah." Assuming Sable was going to try to convince me to leave him behind, I whipped around, ready to argue. But she didn't look resigned and prepared to leave all the magical creatures here to die. Instead, she pressed her blue lips together, straining to stand on her own as she reached to pull her sword from the sheath Karim had slung over his back.

The sword was as rusty as I remember, though it was infused with more magic than was visible before I was in the heart of the Black Forest. She wasn't going to kill him, was she? She couldn't possibly hate all fairies that much, just because of one curse.

"Please, don't hurt me!" the fairy boy whimpered.

"Hold out your hands." When the boy huddled in a tighter ball, I expected Sable to snap at him. But with shaking legs, she got down and crouched in front of him. "I'm not going to hurt you," she whispered. Reluctantly, the boy held out his shackled hands. A slow swipe of the sword across the metal bands that held his wrists resulted in the shackles falling to the floor. I had no idea how, but Sable had freed the boy.

The boy, overwhelmed with joy, grabbed Sable's face and kissed her square on the lips. Sable recoiled slightly, shocked. Daria told me once that a kiss from a magical creature was no small thing. Kisses were only given to someone they loved or as payment for a debt, an act of gratitude. Curious, I peered at Karim. He, too, was shocked, but he was leaning in as if to intervene, though the boy was my age or maybe even younger.

"Thank you." The boy released her face. "Please, do you know where my sister is?"

Recovering from her shock, Sable told him she was going to free everyone in the castle if she could. The boy nodded and decided to follow us until we found his sister.

The next room held a terrified little girl. I thought she was a human girl, but as we got closer, I could see in her round, amber eyes that she was most definitely *not* human. When Sable freed the girl, she too kissed Sable on the lips. This time, there was a noticeable increase in magic in Sable. The sparkles shined all over her skin. And her lips were no longer blue. By the time we found the fairy boy's sister, my eyes strained just to look at her from all the magical kisses the freed captives gave her.

Several of the captives were angry, baring vicious teeth and claws when we neared them. Fortunately, a freed nymph or fairy was usually around to calm the beast and communicate that Sable was going to help the creature, not harm it.

By the time we finished, the sun was up and we were all exhausted, but by mid-morning all the prisoners, including Daria and her mother, were freed. Sable, her eyes weary, sparkled like a diamond in firelight by the time we were done, the concentration of magic in her higher than anything I'd seen all day.

Karim, unusually peppy for such little sleep, found the exit and fetched his and Sable's backpacks full of supplies. None of us were fit to travel anywhere, and we were not about to sleep in the lush bed Marcus had slept in, so I retrieved the small cushion from my room, along with the knucklebone gloves—which would potentially retain their power even away from the Black Forest since the creature was dead already, coming in handy next time some warlock had the bright idea of kidnapping me— and we settled in a corner in the empty foyer.

As Sable tiredly unfolded her bedroll, most definitely not the same one from home, I watched, curious at the changes I saw in my sister in the few weeks we'd been apart. Or was it over a month? Judging from the chill leaching into the empty castle, winter was virtually here.

Before Sable sat on her mat, I pulled her into a tight hug. Every cruel smile, every awful act, and every doubt I'd endured since arriving at this castle came rushing back. And on top of all that, I had been awake for more than twenty-four hours. But now, it was all over. I had Sable back. I could go home.

"Thank you for coming. I'm so glad you are okay." I knew how dangerous the Black Forest was. I had grown up on its edges, hearing plenty of stories of people swallowed up by the forest and its creatures. Many of those stories were from Sable, her way of warning me to stay away. I may have snuck into town against her wishes, but I never wandered into the Black Forest alone. The fear in her eyes when she told me those stories was enough to keep me away. Despite all she knew of the dangers, she still came after me. Part of me wished she had never come, but most of me was just glad to see my sister again.

"I thought I'd never find you." Sable's fingers twined in my hair and she deepened the embrace.

I pulled away and looked into Sable's eyes. They were no longer slitted like a snake's, but they had become subtly more amber, containing flecks of magic that were not there before, though it also could have been because of the prisoners' gratitude. I'm still not sure what all those kisses did, but something was different about Sable now.

"I just can't wait to get home and see Mama. I want everything to go back to normal." Sable froze, fear and sadness plain as day on her face. "What?"

"Pennah," Sable stepped away from me and looked down at her feet before forcing her gaze back to me. "Mama is dead."

Chapter 31

SABLE

I had thought about what I would say over and over without actually coming to a decision. How did one confess matricide to one's sister? I contemplated lying and just telling her that Mama was so sick from hearing of Pennah's disappearance that her heart couldn't take it. But I couldn't look at Pennah every day knowing she believed that lie.

"When you were taken, I went straight home, already desperate to find you. I was in a panic, and when I told Mama, she—" She what? Gave up on Pennah, desperate to preserve her own well-being first? I had already murdered our mother. The last thing I needed to do was destroy the love she had given Pennah her whole life. "She was heartbroken. We argued, and the curse . . . I—it was more powerful than ever before. A snake appeared. It nearly killed me . . ." I didn't need to finish.

"So . . . what happened with Marcus—it's happened before?" She watched me carefully, as if my eyes were returning to the slitted, yellow snake eyes they were earlier.

"No! That has never—"

"She's gone . . ." Pennah stopped the rest of my explanation, her eyes glistening with unshed tears. I stepped towards her, but she lurched back. "You killed her."

I shook my head. Pennah was still panicked by everything that had happened, and I had just shattered her last bit of hope. I should have waited a while before telling her, but it was too late now. "Pennah, I—"

"No," she interrupted me, which was just as well since I had no idea of what to say; nothing more to explain. "I think you've done enough." Diamonds clinked to the stone floor as she fled up the stairs.

I scratched at the spot on my arm that had been covered with scales only hours ago. The marks had faded, but I could almost feel where there were when I nearly become a real monster.

A gentle hand laid on my shoulder. I had almost forgotten Karim's presence.

"What are you still doing here?" I didn't turn to face him, afraid of what I might find. "Now you know the truth."

"I already knew the truth. Or most of it. And that, just now, was not it." I turned to face him. There was no fear or disbelief on his face. There was a bit of curiosity, but his face mostly held understanding, which was the worst outcome I could imagine.

"Weren't you listening?" My strained voice was rising, echoing slightly in the empty castle. "I killed my own mother. Don't you understand? I'm a monster."

"What really happened?" he asked quietly. Is this what it felt like to be given the benefit of the doubt?

I pulled in a shaky breath and continued on with the story. "I told her Pennah was gone and she refused to let me go after her. She didn't want to be left alone. We argued. I was just so angry!" I turned away from Karim, unable to face him, but he sidestepped so he was looking at me once more. "She was willing to let Pennah go, just so she wouldn't be alone. I didn't . . . change . . . like I did with Marcus. That was different. I *wanted* to hurt him. But I never wanted to hurt Mama. I just couldn't keep my mouth shut, and now she's dead," I finished softly.

"Did you know she would die when you argued with her?" He was remaining infuriatingly calm.

"Of course not," I snapped back harshly.

"If anything, that fairy killed her. Reina." I thought back to the sleeping fairy we had seen in the Winterwood. I shook my head vigorously. It wasn't her fault. She was nowhere near us when I let that snake loose on Mama. "If a venomous creature appeared during every argument I ever had, I doubt I would have fared any better."

I pushed his hand away, refusing to be consoled. "I have had this curse for years. I've had plenty of practice in holding my tongue." I was practically yelling at him. Pennah had just walked away. Karim's temperate manner was not helping. I need someone to scream at me that what I did was wrong. Someone to cry and call me what I was: a murderer. Having Matthew reappear right about now would have been convenient. Yelling at me and calling me worthless were a few of his fortes.

"It's my fault." A tightness grew in my chest. I couldn't even get tears to come anymore.

"There's a difference between excusing and accepting. You need to figure out how to accept what happened and move on." I couldn't meet his eyes. I just stood there in front of him, frozen. After a moment, he pulled me into him. With my cheek against his chest, I had no other choice but to return the embrace. I found myself putting a significant amount of weight on him. "But for now, you should probably sleep."

He eased me down to the bedroll and within a few minutes I had succumbed to the heaviness in my heart.

Chapter 32

SABLE

I woke up numb. And extraordinarily hungry. Before resolving the hunger, and before Karim had woken up, I scoured the abandoned castle. Pennah was gone. Again. Unfortunately, this time it was my fault.

"What's wrong?" Karim asked around dusk when he woke up, surprisingly not long after I had. After the day I had had, sleeping deeply was the least of my problems.

"Pennah is gone," I told him sullenly.

"I'm sorry," he answered softly. "At least she's safe." Sometimes I wanted to curse him as much as I wanted to kiss him for being so optimistic. "You know, I'm not sure if it is something to be concerned about, but you are still very sparkly. From all the kisses from the prisoners."

"I do feel different, but not in a bad way." I couldn't quite put my finger on it, but I felt something. Well, at the moment I felt subdued, but that was likely due to my confrontation with Pennah yesterday and her disappearance this morning.

"You look different too." He watched me with a peculiar look.

"Different how?" My eyes weren't still snake eyes, were they? Did I still have scales on my arms?

He hesitated before speaking. "Your eyes are just a little more gold than before. And from what I can tell, your scratches are gone." My hand flew to the bite mark on my neck, but there was nothing there. The totem of my guilt had vanished.

"The bite—it's gone. From the snake that killed my mother." My hand moved from my neck down to my collarbone. The scratch from the ogre dragging my own dagger along my chest was gone as well. The kappa scratches, the blisters on my feet from walking for days on end, the residual chafing pains from horseback riding, the bruising on my throat from Marcus. Even old scars from my childhood were gone. I ran my fingers along my shoulder blade. When I was nine, just weeks before Matthew died, he threw a glass bottle at me in his drunken rage. Mama had had to pull out the large piece of glass that had imbedded itself in my back. It had left a thick roped scar, but that was gone now. In fact, physically, I felt amazing.

"The phoenix," I realized. Yesterday we had set the phoenix and its baby free. Instead of a kiss like all the other magical creatures—the humanoid ones at least—it had nuzzled its impossibly warm face up against my own. A tear in that warmth would have been imperceptible. Apparently the stories were true; a phoenix tear really *did* heal anything.

Since I knew Pennah was long gone, I had no troubles leaving this dismal castle behind me. The walk back to Payton was uneventful. I wondered if maybe some of the creatures we had rescued were making sure we got back through the Black Forest unharmed. Karim and I fell back into normalcy, which was interesting since in the entire time we had known each other we hadn't had a single normal moment. But somehow, we managed. Karim didn't mention my mother. I didn't even want to think about *his*. Between moments of conversation, when silence hung in the Black Forest, I had far too much time to think. One question weighed on me for most of the journey. Where was I going to go?

At first I had planned on going home. What else could I do? Would Pennah be there? If she was, she wouldn't be for long. Not if I came back. I doubted she ever wanted to see me again, and I couldn't blame her for it. She was probably safer without me in her life anyway. No. I couldn't go home. There was nothing for me at my old cottage besides a sad grave, a pond full of useless jewels, and a town full of hateful people.

But then where else could I go? Uncle Morrin hadn't spoken to me since he left after the curse. I wouldn't know where to find him even if he *would* let me stay with him. Mama had no living family that I knew of. Thinking about that just made me worry what Pennah would do. I shoved those thoughts away. I couldn't give Pennah help she didn't want. She would find a way. At least she was free now.

My mind kept returning to Karim. He had offered to take me in days ago. It was a strange idea—staying in a foreign land, in a castle no less. But I didn't belong in a castle.

Finally the day came that I had to make a decision. The change from Black Forest to open meadow was abrupt. Payton sat not far from where we walked now, its gray walls almost as uninviting as the Black Forest's dark treeline.

"I haven't asked yet," Karim slowly broached the subject as we headed around the walls to where the main road split. "But, do you know where you are going to go?" I stared down the south road that led back home. Then I looked east, where Karim's home was. There was no place for me in my old village. But if I didn't go home, I really only had one option, and making that choice didn't discourage me as much as it should have. In wordless response, I led Karim down to the east road. After walking down the road for a few yards, I noticed he was still standing at the crossroads.

"Are you coming?" He shook the stunned look from his face and replaced it with a silly grin.

"Of course." He jogged for a moment to catch up to me and we continued walking.

"You would not believe how long it takes to get from Sukkad to the Black Forest." Karim described his journey to the forest. The journey that led him to me. "Of course I had a horse for most of the trek, but I also stopped in nearly every town looking for answers. I saw more of my kingdom in those two months than I did the rest of my life put together. There are some amazing people. In fact, on the way back you should see this town. It is called Mosul. They were having the most interesting carnival when I was there."

I listened, fascinated by all the places he had been. Already, I was farther from home than I had ever been. For days we walked and talked. I learned much more Arabic than I thought I could, too. Some days Karim refused to speak English, except to teach me the occasional new vocabulary word, and I was finally beginning to pick it up. Understanding was easier than speaking, though.

"Could I have some water?" I asked Karim. He fished the wooden cup from his backpack and handed it to me. Our fire was small tonight since we only needed it to cook our dinner and not for warmth. The desert night provided enough of that. "Thanks." I returned the cup and he placed it back in his bag.

I leaned back on my bedroll, the sandy dirt underneath it forming to my back. Beside me, Karim followed suit, our faces only a few feet away from each other. "How did you know I lied to Pennah? About my mother."

"Because of what Grem said." I waited for more, not recalling anything specific that Grem had said. I only seemed to recollect a vague annoyance whenever I thought of him. Thankfully, our story was over so that odd gnome wouldn't be following us around and spying on us anymore. Karim went on. "He said something about your mother's response when you told her about Pennah. He said it was 'tragic' and 'traitorous.' I hadn't imagined that she tried to make you leave Pennah behind."

"Oh." I sat up. How did Karim always know what I needed to hear?

"Plus, I know you." Karim sat up as well and slid closer to my bedroll. "You don't start something unprovoked. And I know you love your mother and your sister enough to lie like you did." I was having trouble coming up with a response, distracted by his hand only inches from mine on the bedroll.

Before I could think of something to say in return, his lips were on mine. One of his hands held my face. His grip was soft, but unrelenting. Shock kept me in place for a full moment, but after that I didn't pull away. I even found myself leaning in for more. Finally, Karim pulled back and searched my eyes for a reaction.

Not knowing how to respond, I said, "Thanks." Realizing the word and the context, I immediately rushed to amend it, my face reddening. "For saying that, I mean. Not for—" I abruptly stopped talking.

"Right." He nodded, smiling. "You should probably get some sleep. I'll watch first."

"Good night, then." I laid down on the bedroll, determined not to look his way. What was happening? At first I my heart fluttered with giddiness and a stupid grin spread onto my face. But after lying on my mat for a few minutes, nowhere near sleep, I felt conflicted. Why? And then it dawned on me.

Make sure my brother returns in one piece.

That was what Maram had told me. Her one request. I'm not sure if she meant it the way I was interpreting it now, but after that kiss, I could only interpret it one way. I was not from the same world Karim was from. His family barely tolerated me for the day I had been there so far. They would never let me stay. Karim had to focus on saving his people. If I was there, he would only fight against his family, and I couldn't do that to him. To all of them. I would be a distraction.

While Karim watched, I let him think I had already fallen asleep, but my mind was wide awake, racing. How could I be so stupid? Did I really think there was a place for me in the palace? In his life? He would end up caught between a kingdom full of people who needed him, and a silly pauper girl who thought she could be a princess. But this wasn't some fairytale.

The rest of the time I attempted to fall asleep, there was one thought that would not leave my mind: I refused to be the one to tear his heart in two.

Eventually I fell asleep. When Karim woke me in the middle of the night, I kept watch until I could tell he had drifted into sleep. Once he was out, I gathered my things, careful to stay quiet, though I knew I'd have to make a lot of noise to bother Karim enough to wake him.

I watched him sleep for a few minutes before departing. Being around him made me feel like a better person. In fact, it *made* me a better person. But I couldn't do this to him. Did I think I could stay with him? Be a princess? I had already destroyed so many lives. Karim's was not going to be one of them. He deserved more than a girl with venomous words. I'm sure Nadia would be waiting for him when he returned. A dark tear escaped down my cheek until I wiped it away.

With one last glance at Karim's sleeping figure, I picked up my backpack and I left.

Printed in the United States
By Bookmasters